THE QUEEN OF HEL

THE NORSEWOMEN
BOOK FIVE

JOHANNA WITTENBERG

BOOKS BY JOHANNA WITTENBERG

The Norsewomen Series

The Norse Queen

The Falcon Queen

The Raider Bride

The Queen in the Mound

The Queen of Hel

The Queen of War

THE
QUEEN
OF HEL

THE NORSEWOMEN BOOK 5

JOHANNA WITTENBERG

Published by
SHELLBACK STUDIO

Cover design by Deranged Doctor Designs
Cover art by Bev Ulsrud Van Berkom

Author Website: JohannaWittenberg.com

PART I: THE QUEEN OF HEL

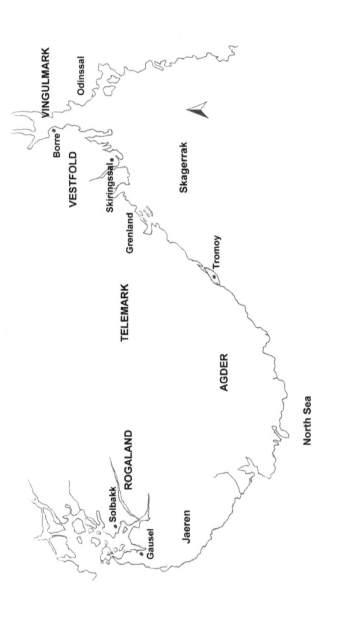

VINGULMARK

Odinssal

Borre

VESTFOLD

Skiringssal

Grenland

Skagerrak

Tromoy

TELEMARK

AGDER

North Sea

ROGALAND

Solbakk

Jaeren

Gausel

CHAPTER 1

Tromøy
April, AD 824

Åsa woke in the chamber off the main hall. It was dark, save for the faint glow of the embers still burning in the brazier, and impossible to tell what time it was. Stretching beneath the goose down comforter, she luxuriated in the heat of Eyvind's body beside her. She reached out and gently touched his hair, not wanting to wake him yet.

The door burst open, throwing morning light across the floor. Halfdan rushed in, trailed by Brenna and his wolf, Fylgja. Eyvind stirred, blinking in the sudden light.

"Apologies, Lady," said Brenna. "The scamp got away from me."

"It's fine," said Åsa. The fóstra was getting old. Keeping up with a four-year-old and a blind wolf was a bit much for her. "We were just about to rise anyway."

Brenna smiled her thanks and hurried back to the hall. The wolf settled himself on the floor while Halfdan threw himself on the bed. "It's time to get up!" he crowed. Åsa scooped him up, settling him between her and Eyvind.

The past winter with Eyvind had been idyllic. She had never realized how good life could be—to wake up next to him every day with the knowledge that they wouldn't have to part for months. Most of their waking hours were spent together, hunting, skiing, playing with Halfdan, telling stories by the fire, working side by side on the thousand projects that needed to be done over the winter. They were only apart when Åsa's presence was required to lead the magical rites which men were not allowed to attend.

Halfdan wriggled out of Åsa's grasp and capered about the feather bed, hampering their efforts to rise and dress. Eyvind proved adept at dodging the little boy and won his way to his clothes. He pulled on his linen tunic and wool breeks, then plucked Halfdan from the bed and swung him around. While her son shrieked in delight, Åsa grabbed a wool overdress and pulled it on over her linen shift. She opened the door to the great hall, where porridge was being served to the folk gathered on the benches. Eyvind set Halfdan on his shoulders and followed Åsa in.

She took her place on the high seat, gazing around at her people, thankful that they were safe and well.

As soon as breakfast had been demolished, everyone hurried outside. After the gloom of the hall the spring sunlight was nearly blinding, and they stood a moment, blinking. It was a glorious day to ask the gods' blessing before the crops were sown.

Åsa joined Heid to sacrifice a boar to the fertility god Frey for peace and plenty. Vigdis, Heid's principal apprentice, caught the animal's blood in a brass bowl. Åsa wielded a bundle of fir twigs, dipping it into the blood and sprinkling it over the folk. All the people of Tromøy crowded in to receive a drop of the holy blood and be blessed with prosperity in the coming year. The steward,

Hogni, and his staff butchered the boar and put it to simmer in a cauldron over an open fire in the yard.

Heid's apprentices hitched up their mistress's cart, then helped the aging völva into the driver's seat and tucked her wolf-skin lap robe around her against the April chill. Three men lugged a life-size wooden likeness of Frey and carefully set it beside her.

Heid, in her role as Frey's twin sister, the goddess Freyja, would drive the cart around the steading, bestowing fertility on the fields.

Åsa mounted her horse, Gullfaxi, and Vigdis handed her the fir sprinkler and brass bowl brimming with sacrificial blood. She shook the reins and the horse set off for the nearest barley field. Heid clucked to her horse and the cart followed. Her nine apprentices walked alongside the cart, singing the songs of blessing, while all the folk of Tromøy came behind.

Åsa led the entourage around each field, sprinkling blood on the soil. She called on the good will of the land spirits to descend over them. As queen, her personal luck ensured the land's fertility, and the responsibility weighed heavy on her. It was a critical time for the steading. The next day was the new moon, when they would sow the fields and watch the god's favor take root.

When the fields had been blessed, they returned to the hall to feast. Loath to sit inside the dim, rank hall where they had spent so much of the winter, they dragged benches and trestles out into the yard and sat glorying in the spring sun.

The meal consisted of a few cabbages and shriveled turnips that had survived in cold storage, augmented with seabird eggs, plentiful new-caught sea trout, and the sacrificed boar. Åsa had brewed the first ale of the season from barley remaining from their winter stores, and she brought out the last of her autumn-brewed mead.

Åsa raised her cup to Heid. "We made it through the winter," she said with relief.

"So it would seem," Heid said smugly, sipping her mead. "And you haven't had need of that cursed necklace either."

It was true, Tromøy had survived half a year while the Irish necklace lay deep in the burial mound, still clutched in the dead queen's hand. And so far, the haugbui's curse had failed to come to pass. But Åsa did not share Heid's confidence. "We haven't really been put to the test. The raiding season is about to commence."

Heid looked at her over her cup. "Surely you don't fear raiders now?"

Åsa shook her head. "I'm confident our warriors are ready for whatever comes." Jarl Borg had spent the winter honing the fighting skills of Tromøy's farmers-turned-warriors, making them into a formidable war band. Their agricultural expertise was put to good use with Tromøy's fields and flocks.

Still, Åsa worried about the summer, and not just raiders. Would the crops be proof against insects, blight, and weather? The livestock that survived the winter had birthed lambs and calves that gamboled about the steading. But would they fall prey to disease or predators? The summer's success was crucial to Tromøy's survival over the following winter. No matter how well prepared, there was so much that could go wrong. Was her good fortune strong enough to ensure Tromøy's welfare?

Åsa shook her head to clear it. For just one night, she let herself forget all that and enjoyed the celebration.

In the morning she rose before dawn. Eyvind got up with her and together they rode around the steading, overseeing the plowing and sowing of the barley. Her supervision was mostly for encouragement, since the young farmers of her hird were as knowledgeable as she. Åsa herself had learned much from her father, Harald Redbeard, a man who had loved the land as much as he did the sea.

"I've lingered as long as I dare. If I want to do some trading in the East and return before the snow flies, I must set sail soon," Eyvind said.

"I wish you didn't have to go," said Åsa, dismayed at the thought of the summer without him.

"And I wish you could come with me." *

They sighed in unison, knowing Åsa could not leave her people or her son, while Eyvind must respond to the call of far-off lands, where he could trade Tromøy's goods and bring back the profits. For now, the winters had to be enough for them both.

Åsa brightened. "I'll sail with you as far as Skiringssal. Ulf has made some new weapons for Olaf, and I can take Sonja some of our spring wool to trade with hers."

Eyvind smiled. "That would be wonderful."

"I know Halfdan would love the trip." Cheered by the prospect of a little more time together, they rode back to the hall. Halfdan and a dozen other children were chasing each other through the yard under Brenna's ever-watchful eye.

Åsa reached down and swung her son up into the saddle. "Would you like to sail to Skiringssal and visit your cousin Rognvald?"

The little boy's eyes brightened. "Yes! I want to sail!" he shrieked in delight.

"Halfdan loves the sea as much as I do," Eyvind said. "When he's older, I'll take him on my summer voyages."

Åsa's smile was tinged with wistfulness at the thought of them both leaving her behind for the summer. But that was still a few years off. For now she'd enjoy every moment she had with them.

When the day's plowing was done and everyone had gathered for the evening meal, Åsa called for quiet. "Make *Ran's Lover* ready to sail tomorrow. We're going to accompany Eyvind to Skiringssal." Her crew cheered, always happy to make the short trip up the coast at a moment's notice.

In the morning they set off down to the ships, Åsa riding Gullfaxi with Halfdan perched before her, the blind wolf, Fylgja, trotting alongside. Ulf and his assistant followed, driving a cart full of swords, axes, and shield bosses for Olaf, and loaded them onto *Ran's Lover*. Eyvind's ship, *Far Traveler*, was already loaded with farm implements, tools, and soapstone pots for long-distance trade. Bales of wool were loaded last.

Åsa and Halfdan boarded *Far Traveler* while Olvir piloted *Ran's Lover*. It was another rare warm, sunny April day and Åsa reveled in the freedom of the sea, treasuring this trip with her lover and her son.

The wind and tide favored them as the ships threaded their way between the skerries, arriving at Skiringssal's harbor before dark. Olaf waited on the shore, mounted on his horse. As always, Åsa's breath caught at the sight of his tall figure, blond hair glinting in the last of the sun.

Olaf welcomed them with a broad smile. He swung Halfdan up onto his horse and conducted the little party up the trail to the Shining Hall where Sonja waited at the door.

"Such a wonderful surprise," she said, scooping Halfdan up into her arms and kissing him. Her two-year-old son, Rognvald, emerged from her skirts and fell on the blind wolf with a cry of delight. Halfdan squirmed to get down and join the boy on the ground.

The two boys were half-brothers, though Sonja and nearly everyone else believed Halfdan to be Gudrød's son, a story Olaf and Åsa promoted. They had long since buried their secret love for each other, and the fact that Olaf was Halfdan's father.

Olaf clapped Eyvind on the back and took him to the guest-house, followed by the rest of the crew.

The fresh sea air had Halfdan yawning. "I think your boy is tired," said Sonja. "Come to the bower." They put both boys down for a nap in the big feather bed while Fylgja settled down on the floor close by. Rognvald's fóstra seated herself on a stool, gazing dotingly on her young charge.

"Please excuse me, I had better go see how preparations for

the evening meal are going," said Sonja, hurrying toward the hall. At loose ends, Åsa set off across the yard to find Eyvind.

"There you are," said Olaf, coming out of the guesthouse.

Åsa waited for him in the lee of the cow byre, empty now with the cattle gone to the summer pastures.

"Eyvind's good for you," said Olaf. "I'm glad to see you happy. You deserve it."

Åsa smiled at him, relieved that he'd gotten over his jealousy of her lover. "Thank you, Olaf. Sonja is such a good wife for you, and a wonderful mother. I'm so glad she wants to foster Halfdan."

"It will be good to have both my sons with me," said Olaf. "I'd hate to miss all of Halfdan's childhood." He gazed down at her. "I sometimes wonder how things would have been, if you had agreed to marry me."

Åsa squinted into the setting sun. "It's too late for that."

"You know I'll always love you."

"And I you. But Sonja makes you happy."

Olaf nodded. "She does. But she's not you."

A sharp cry sounded behind them. They turned to see Sonja standing at the corner of the byre, her face white. With a sob, she hurried away.

Shock jolted through Åsa. They had been too absorbed in their conversation to notice her arrival. She must have heard their entire conversation.

"Sonja!" cried Olaf. He started after her.

Åsa hurried in his wake, regret burning in her chest.

They came upon Sonja, lying in the grass, sobbing. "Get away!" she cried. Åsa froze.

"Sonja," said Olaf. "It happened long before I met you. Halfdan is almost five years old!"

"You still love her."

Olaf looked at Åsa, his face a mask of pain. "I will always love her. But I love you, too. You are my wife, my queen, and nothing can change that. I chose you."

Åsa wanted to flee from this scene. Anything she said now would make things worse, yet she couldn't bring herself to abandon them. So she stood, mute and miserable.

"Come," Olaf coaxed. "Come back up to the hall with us."

"No, leave me be." Sonja didn't look up at them.

Åsa and Olaf stared at each other in despair. Åsa shook her head. They couldn't leave Sonja there.

Sonja roused and pulled herself to her feet. Ignoring them, she stalked back to the hall. Åsa and Olaf followed at a cautious distance.

Sonja headed straight to the bower. Olaf stared after his wife miserably while Åsa hung back. "Best to leave her alone for now," she said to Olaf. "I will make preparations to depart at first light. Then the two of you can patch things up."

"Some things can't be undone," said Olaf.

"Give it time. You love each other, and you have your son." Despite her encouraging words, Åsa couldn't shake the feeling that something beautiful had been ruined, perhaps forever.

She turned sadly to the guesthouse to tell her crew there would be no feast tonight, and that they would depart in the morning. She sent Tova to the bower to fetch Halfdan.

Eyvind looked up from the rope he was plaiting. "What's wrong?"

Åsa shook her head. "Queen Sonja is not feeling well," she said.

Skiringssal's steward arrived with apologies and a makeshift meal. After they ate, Åsa led Eyvind down to the shore. As they walked along the beach in the starlight, she told him of her brief relationship with Olaf. "We loved each other, but Gudrød had great power over him when he was young. Olaf abandoned me to his father, and I don't think I've ever forgiven him. After I killed Gudrød, Olaf asked me to marry him. I couldn't bring myself to trust him after he'd betrayed me. At least, not enough to give him power over me or my people."

Eyvind was silent for a long time. Then he said, "Knowing that, I am honored that you decided to trust me at all."

"Learning to trust you was the best thing I've ever done," she said. "You have brought me great joy. I only hope that Sonja will come to forgive Olaf. They deserve happiness." She sighed. "That's one secret that should never have gotten out."

Eyvind nodded and pulled her close. Åsa was relieved that he didn't ask her if she still had feelings for Olaf. That was a question she was not prepared to answer.

The next day Eyvind departed on *Far Traveler*. Storm clouds hovered on the horizon and the world darkened. Åsa boarded *Ran's Lover* as fat drops spattered down. The rain kept up while they rowed out of the harbor, though it did nothing to dampen Halfdan's enthusiasm for being at sea. He romped about the decks, straining at the harness that kept him securely fastened to the gunnels, while Fylgja huddled miserably in the stern. The aging wolf did not enjoy being wet. Åsa covered him with a sheepskin, and he tucked his nose under his paw and shivered.

CHAPTER 2

Gausel

I n Gausel, the winter had passed with peace between
Ragnhild and her brother Harald. With the spring barley
safely planted, it was time to herd the cattle up to the high
meadows to graze. Ragnhild left her three trusted húskarlar,
Einar, Svein, and Thorgeir, with one hundred warriors to guard
the settlement, while she and Murchad joined the farmers of
Gausel on the trek to the mountains.

In the early morning, they packed their hudfat and saddled
their horses for the trip. The cows, sheep, and goats that survived
the winter had gained strength feeding on the lowland grass and
were able to travel the well-worn trail. The adult livestock
remembered the mountain pasture lands with tender grass and
led their offspring eagerly.

Several grazing sites were scattered throughout the mountains, each with a hut where the dairymaids lived in summer and
made cheese, skyr, and butter. A portion of the herd would be left
to graze around each saeter, tended by a boy.

At night they unrolled their hudfat beneath a star-filled sky.

Ragnhild loved sleeping outdoors with Murchad. She always woke refreshed from the cool spring air.

"You're a good herder," she told Murchad as they ate their breakfast of skyr.

"In Ireland, we spend our summers in the mountains with the herds. *Booleying*, we call it." His eyes had a distant look as if his soul was far away.

Worry nipped at Ragnhild. As the winter wore on, Murchad had become silent and morose. This was not unusual for anyone over the long, dark days, but Ragnhild had hoped the lengthening days of spring would lift his spirits.

She laid a hand on his shoulder. "What is herding like in Ireland?"

He sighed and shook himself, then smiled at her. "The climate in Ireland is much milder, and there is grazing outdoors year-round. We don't have to slaughter our livestock before winter as you do here. Our wealth is measured by the size of our herds."

Ragnhild lay back on the grass. "The farmers of Gausel have paid us ten cows and a dozen goats this spring in tribute. Tell me, would we be rich in Ireland?"

Murchad considered. "Middling well-off. We must divide the livestock between us, to be sure neither of us has a better herd than the other."

Ragnhild nodded, remembering the story of Queen Medbh, who started a war because her husband's herd was superior to hers. "We must make sure ours is a marriage of equals."

They drove the last of the cattle to the farthest saeter. After the milkmaids were settled in, Ragnhild and Murchad packed up and departed for the steading.

"When we arrive home, it will be time to make preparations to sail to Tromøy and claim the necklace," Ragnhild said to Murchad as they rode down from the mountains. "Then we'll set sail for Ireland."

The hopeful smile that bloomed on his face made her stomach churn.

"Are you sure you want to leave Gausel so soon?" he said.

Ragnhild willed her guts to settle. "I made you a promise to return the necklace to Ireland. It will be no easier next year than this."

"I do admit I long to see Ireland again," said Murchad with a sigh.

Ragnhild hoped the visit would satisfy his homesickness. What if he didn't want to return to Gausel with her?

It was a risk she must take. She couldn't keep him prisoner. Ragnhild firmly turned her mind to practicalities. "How will we handle returning the necklace?

Murchad stroked his moustache. "We can't tell Niall that you took the necklace. If he found out, he would never forgive me. It would destroy our relationship forever."

"I took it without your knowledge. He can't hold you responsible for that."

"He can and he will. You're my wife." Murchad raked his fingers through his glossy black hair. "We will have to replace it before he knows it's gone."

"Is it likely he doesn't know already?" said Ragnhild.

Murchad nodded slowly. "Niall won't look for the necklace until he marries, something I doubt he's done yet. For years he's been devoted to his mistress. But as king, he'll be pressured to marry a woman of noble blood to strengthen alliances. When he does, he'll go to the treasury to get the necklace for his queen. If we're going to return it, we'd better do it very soon."

"How will we accomplish that?"

"We'll have to sneak into the treasury and replace the necklace. There is a secret way into the treasury that only the king knows of." A look of melancholy crossed Murchad's handsome features.

Guilt uncoiled in Ragnhild's belly. "I am sorry, *a chroi*. You would still be king if not for me."

Murchad took her hand. "I would gladly give up a hundred kingships for you. But I regret the rift with Niall. We were once as close as brothers."

"He betrayed you," said Ragnhild.

"He didn't have a choice. The clan leaders and the brehons forced his hand."

Ragnhild made a face. "I don't know if I believe that. But if we are going to sail for Ireland and return before winter, we need to set out for Tromøy within the next few weeks."

"I thank you for doing this for me, *a mhuirin*. When we return, I hope you will keep your other promise," Murchad said wistfully. He nodded toward her flat belly.

Ragnhild stifled a wince. "Time enough for that."

The truth was, this voyage gave her an excuse to put off pregnancy. She knew Murchad yearned for a child. Much as she wanted to make him happy, Ragnhild dreaded the thought of being trapped in a body grown unwieldy, of the dangers of giving birth, and the responsibility of caring for an infant for years. Even after the child was seven or eight years old and sent to foster, one baby tended to lead to another. She could foresee being tied down by childbirth and child-rearing until she was too old to go to sea.

She had seen Åsa's wistful look as she watched Eyvind's ship depart from Tromøy while she had to stay behind. The idea of never being free to set sail on long voyages was unbearable.

She'd fought so hard for her freedom, yet it seemed her father had won. After all her effort, in the end she'd married the man he'd chosen for her. If she were bound to an infant, his victory over her would be complete.

Would she ever be ready? How long would Murchad wait? In returning the necklace to Ireland, she would keep at least one promise to her husband, even if she couldn't keep the other.

She hoped he'd be satisfied with that, at least for now.

～

THEY ARRIVED BACK at the steading late in the afternoon. When everyone gathered for the evening meal, Ragnhild rose and called for silence.

"We're sailing to Ireland on a trading voyage." An excited chatter rose from the benches. "We'll sail around the southern cape to Tromøy first to pick up more trade goods, then back west again to the Orkney Islands and south to Ireland. We'll take care of our business there, and make it back to Gausel before the winter storms set in. Who will join me and Lord Murchad on this voyage?"

Einar stepped forward. "Thorgeir, Svein, and I gave you our oaths long ago. We have no love of Ireland, but wherever you sail, we three will accompany you."

Unn rose. "My sisters and I will sail with you as well."

One by one, *Raider Bride*'s former crew came forward, eager to put to sea again. It was a chance for them to see friends and family they'd left behind when they had sailed with Ragnhild.

Ragnhild was pleased to fill her ship with experienced sailors. "I leave Gausel in Jofrid's capable hands." The headwoman had ruled the steading for many years and Ragnhild trusted her. She addressed the rest of the folk, farmers who'd lived in Gausel all their lives. "After the winter you spent training in combat, Gausel will be well defended in our absence. And now that Harald and I are at peace, you can rely on both of my brothers for support."

The following week was a frenzy as the crew prepared for the voyage, mending sails, caulking seams, braiding ropes. They packed up lengths of finely woven linen and wool for trade, along with combs and other items fashioned from antlers and bone.

The morning of departure dawned fair and calm. Ragnhild joined the crowd gathered in the shallows to launch the ship. Her boots in the water, she braced her shoulder against the wooden strakes and shouted, "Heave!" Everyone shoved but the heavy oak hull didn't move. "Heave!" she shouted again. After three more tries, the keel released its grip on the sand and slid into the water. As the ship floated free, Ragnhild vaulted aboard and took her place in the stern. The crew fitted their oars and began to row. Ragnhild released the lashing on the steering oar and lowered it into the water. The tiller quivered in her hand as *Raider Bride* came to life.

She looked back at the steading, shrinking in the distance. She'd fought hard to win her inheritance from her brother, but now she was glad to be sailing toward new adventures.

The wind stayed calm, and the favorable current hurried them along as they rowed north up the long, narrow Gandesfjord to Solbakk. The crew chattered at their oars, excited to set sail after the long winter.

"Are you looking forward to seeing your brothers?" Murchad asked.

Ragnhild searched her heart. A year ago, her elder brother Harald had been Ragnhild's enemy, denying her inheritance and tricking her into marriage to Murchad. The siblings had been at war until Harald's wife Signy had set things right between them. The Christian queen had proven to be a peace-weaver, something Ragnhild would never be. She smiled at Murchad. "Yes, I truly am. And I'm looking forward to seeing Signy and little Ragnhild."

Orlyg, Signy, and Harald waited for them on Solbakk's shore. Orlyg grinned with a promise of mischief. He'd been caught between Harald and Ragnhild in their feud, and he was clearly happy that his two siblings were at peace. Signy's open look of welcome and Harald's more restrained smile brought an unexpected surge of warmth over Ragnhild. This was a new feeling. She'd never cared much for family in the past.

"Welcome, sister," said Signy, embracing her. Ragnhild found herself returning the hug as unfamiliar emotions swept through her.

Harald clapped Murchad on the back. "Come, brother, let me show you our smith's latest efforts."

Signy smiled at Ragnhild. "I'm sure you are eager to see your little namesake. She's grown so much since you were last here."

Though she'd much rather go to the smithy, Ragnhild could not refuse her sweet sister-in-law. In resignation, she allowed herself to be led to the bower.

Inside, Signy hurried to the cradle. "Here's my little Ragnhild." Crooning, she picked up the nine-month-old baby girl and handed her to her aunt.

Ragnhild took the child gingerly, cradling her in her arms. The baby gurgled and stared up at her with a steady blue gaze. The little body seemed to radiate contentment, sending a peace over Ragnhild which she had never felt before. She looked down on the infant in surprise.

"Why, sister, you are a natural mother," exclaimed Signy. "When will you and Murchad be having a child of your own?"

Ragnhild frowned and handed the baby back to her mother. "Perhaps after this voyage."

"I can't wait to see the child you and Murchad produce. Sure to be brave and beautiful."

This remark got a faint smile from Ragnhild.

Courtesy required her to spend the afternoon with the women as they organized the evening meal. Unn and her sisters were already bustling about as if they were at home. Though Ragnhild left Gausel's household duties to Jofrid, she was impressed with Signy's well-kept stores. The storehouses were filled with dried fish and smoked meat as well as roots, dried berries, and grain. Flatbread was stacked on shelves next to a linen-covered crock of honey. Signy's kitchen staff proved more than competent, having already set haunches of venison and pork to cook in cauldrons over the outdoor fire.

That night, Harald and Signy feasted them in Solbakk's great hall. The food was ample and well prepared, the ale freshly brewed, and the mead potent. Stout warriors crowded the benches, their arms laden with silver rings, rewards from Harald. They welcomed Ragnhild's crew with good cheer.

"Perhaps Lord Murchad would grace us with a tale from Ireland," said Harald.

Ragnhild held her breath. Her husband had not been telling many stories recently.

Murchad bowed his head graciously. "That I shall. I will tell you of Ireland's greatest warrior, one who could challenge Thor himself."

"This I will have to hear to believe," said Thorgeir.

Murchad smiled and gazed into the fire, then began to speak in his lilting, resonant voice. Everyone fell silent, eager for the tale. "In ancient times, the Irish had shield-maidens just as the Norse do. The most famous of them was Scáthach, who had a school for warriors hidden among the isles of Alba. Scáthach trained many Irish heroes in the arts of war, including pole-vaulting over the walls of a fort, fighting underwater, and combat with a barbed spear.

"Scáthach's fortress, Dun Scaith, lay across a deep chasm. The only way across was an enchanted bridge that did everything it could to shake travelers off. It arched high in the middle and low at the ends, like the rainbow."

"That sounds like Bifrost, the bridge to Asgaard," said Thorgeir.

"Perhaps it is the same, for Scáthach's isle was a magical place," Murchad replied. "The hero Cu Chulainn, whom I've told you about before, was required to train with Scáthach for a year to win the hand of his true love, Emer.

"After overcoming many obstacles, Cu Chulainn finally reached the bridge. As he approached, the people of Scáthach's island gathered to watch the newcomer try to cross. They expected him to plummet to his death as most travelers did.

"Cu Chulainn ran onto the bridge, but it shrank to the width of a hair and froze, sending him skidding back to the start. He ran out again and the bridge bucked him off. He managed to cling to the bridge and crawl back to the start instead of falling to his death. The crowd laughed at him, and their laughter enraged Cu Chulainn. So great was his fury that hero-light shone around his head, and he gave his salmon leap, landing on the center where he hung on as the bridge bucked. He gathered his strength, and one more great leap took him to the end."

"Cu Chulainn was a berserker," said Thorgeir.

"He may have been," Murchad agreed. "After crossing the enchanted bridge, Cu Chulainn reached the fortress gate, guarded by Scáthach's daughter Uathach. She thought Cu Chulainn was the most beautiful man she had ever seen. His hair was dark and his gaze melancholy, lit by seven hero-lights in each eye. He wore a crimson cloak with seven pleats, fastened by a golden brooch. Though she was a fierce warrior herself, Uathach welcomed him with food and drink, and told him how to ensure that her mother accepted him as a trainee.

"She sent him to where Scáthach was training her own sons. Cu Chulainn ambushed the woman warrior and demanded that she teach him. Impressed by the young man's skill, Scáthach agreed to take him on as her pupil. She taught him things she taught no other.

"Scáthach's sister and rival, the warrior queen Aoife, declared war on Dun Scaith. Scáthach's three sons challenged Aoife's three greatest champions on the road. Scáthach was afraid her sons would be killed, and she sent Cu Chulainn to their aid. He ran out ahead of her sons and beheaded each of Aoife's champions, piling their heads on the ground.

"With her champions dead, Aoife decided to settle things with her sister once and for all. She challenged Scáthach to single combat. With no champions left alive, Aoife decided to fight herself. Cu Chulainn asked Scáthach for the honor of being her champion. She agreed. 'But,' she said, 'I do not want my sister dead.'

"Cu Chulainn said, 'I may know a way to avoid killing her. What does Aoife value the most in the world?'

"'My sister loves her chariot, her horses, and her charioteer above all else.'

"When Cu Chulainn met Aoife with swords drawn, he shouted, 'Aoife's chariot is going over the edge of the cliff!'

"Aoife turned to look, and Cu Chulainn grabbed her, threw her over his shoulder, and carried her back to Scáthach's fort where he held her at swordpoint. He demanded her surrender, and that she bear him a son. Aoife accepted his terms, and the sisters agreed to make war on each other no longer.

"Aoife and Cu Chulainn became lovers for the rest of his year with Scáthach. Before he left, Aoife told him she was with child. 'Our son will grow up to be as great a warrior as you.'

"Cu Chulainn was thrilled. When he took his leave to go back to Ireland, he told her, 'Name our son Connla, and raise him to be a warrior. When he grows big enough that my ring will fit on his thumb, send him to me in Ireland.'

"As a parting gift, Scáthach gave Cu Chulainn her enchanted spear, the Gae Bolga, the spear of mortal death.

"Upon his return to Ireland, Cu Chulainn went straight to find his true love, Emer, and made her his wife.

"When Aoife found out about the marriage, she fell into a jealous rage and vowed to take vengeance.

"Their son would become her revenge. She told no one of the boy's heritage, but educated him as a warrior's son, and sent him to Scáthach as soon as he was old enough. Under Scáthach's training, Connla became his father's equal in every way.

"When Connla was grown enough for Cu Chulainn's ring to fit his thumb, his mother gave it to him and made him swear three *geas*, sacred oaths that could never be broken: Connla could never give way to any man, he could never reveal his name first, and he could never back down from a fight, even if he knew it would mean his death.

"Having sworn these three oaths, Connla put on the ring, armed himself, and set sail for Ireland.

"He landed on a beach in Ulster, where the king Conchobar mac Neasa had gathered his court to hold a sacred rite. Conchobar sent a messenger to greet Connla and find out who he was, but the young man's oath prevented him from giving his name.

"The king took offense at this and sent one of his best warriors to force the newcomer to identify himself.

"The warrior was kind and gave Connla another chance to name himself. But again, Connla refused. And so the two did battle, and Connla overcame Conchobar's warrior.

"Conchobar sent for his greatest champion, Cu Chulainn. When Cu Chulainn saw Connla, he was impressed with the young man's bearing, as well as the fact that he had bested one of Conchobar's greatest warriors. Cu Chulainn did not want to harm such a promising young warrior and he begged the young man to tell his name.

"As soon as Connla saw Cu Chulainn, he longed to tell him his name more than anything. But he could not break his oath. Instead, he told Cu Chulainn of the three *geas* he had sworn.

"But Cu Chulainn was similarly bound by his oath to his king. He was obliged to challenge Connla. And so the two men fought. Cu Chulainn had not fought like this since the armies of Connaught. It seemed the boy had learned every skill and trick, and with the vigor of youth he pressed the hero hard. They fought each other to a draw and finally called for their spears.

"Cu Chulainn took up the mighty spear, the Gae Bolga, and the battle rage came over him. The hero-light shone out from his head and Connla knew his opponent was the great warrior Cu Chulainn.

"Connla was young and quick. He could have launched his spear first, but he deliberately held back. Cu Chulainn hurled the Gae Bolga and the blade pierced the young man's side. Connla lay dying, and he held up his hand to show Cu Chulainn the ring on his thumb.

"Cu Chulainn recognized his son, and cursed Aoife for taking her revenge in such a way. He had all the warriors pass by Connla and give the dying boy their names, and welcomed him into their company. When that was done, Cu Chulainn drew his sword and ended his son's suffering.

"So great was Cu Chulainn's grief that the battle rage overcame him. The king feared he would cause great slaughter. He had his druid put a spell on Cu Chulainn to make him fight the waves on the shore for three days and three nights, until he was exhausted and the battle rage left him."

"This is the same as Norse berserker and ulfhednar," said Thorgeir. "While they are enraged, no fire can burn them, no metal kill them. But when the frenzy leaves them, they are weak as babies."

Ragnhild nodded, remembering fighting Hrafn and his berserker.

"We have no such heroes in Ireland anymore," said Murchad. "That ancient art has been forbidden to Christians." There was a note of regret in his voice.

The crew was shown to Solbakk's spacious guesthouse. Signy conducted Ragnhild and Murchad to a private room off the main hall. "I would love to see a Christian land," Signy said wistfully. She had been converted in her youth by a captive priest, but she was a lone Christian among pagans.

"Perhaps one day you can sail with us to Ireland, sister," said Ragnhild.

"I would like that very much. But that will have to wait until little Ragnhild is old enough to foster."

Signy took her leave, and Ragnhild snuggled under the furs beside her husband. *How could I ever give up my freedom for years on end?* It was too much of a sacrifice, even for Murchad. She was glad she wouldn't have to worry about it for a while.

In the morning, Signy and Harald saw them off with gifts of food and ale for the voyage, along with a few parcels of trade goods. The folk of Solbakk escorted *Raider Bride's* crew to the beach, helping them load the longship and shove off.

Once they were on the water, Ragnhild gazed back at Orlyg, Signy, and Harald, all waving goodbye. To her chagrin, she realized she would miss them. She resolutely turned her back and focused on maneuvering the ship as the oarsmen rowed through the skerries and holms that littered the fjord.

Soon enough *Raider Bride* rounded the headland and came into the wind's full force. Everyone's attention was taken up with stowing oars and raising the sail. Ragnhild concentrated on keeping the sail full and drawing in the shifty winds between the islands as they sailed toward open waters.

The sea sparkled invitingly and the breeze freshened. Ragnhild exulted in being at sea and Murchad's cheeks shone with vigor. The crew spoke of seeing their friends and family on Tromøy.

A friendly breeze pushed them south along the Jaeren coastline. The first evening they put into a cove just north of Lindesnes, so that they could round the treacherous cape in daylight. It was a lovely, long May evening, and they sat late around the campfire while Thorgeir told one of his tales.

"Loki the trickster was a jotun," he began.

"I thought he was a god," said Murchad, who was still trying to get a grasp on the Norse pantheon.

Thorgeir nodded. "Loki was jotun-born. When he became Odin's blood brother, he was accepted as a member of the Aesir gods. He took a wife among them. But he already had another wife, his first wife, a jotun woman named Angrboda, mother of wolves. Angrboda and Loki produced three monstrous children. The first was a serpent named Jörmungandr. Their second son was the wolf, Fenrir. Their youngest was a daughter, named Hel, a girl who was half living and half dead. These children lived with their mother in Jotunheim."

Murchad frowned, trying to commit this lineage to memory.

Thorgeir continued. "Odin raised a dead völva from her grave and compelled her to tell him of the future. She prophesied that Loki and Angrboda's offspring would be the doom of the gods.

"The gods decided to eliminate the threat."

Murchad interrupted again. "I thought that no one could change their fate, not even the gods."

Thorgeir nodded again. "As you will see. But the gods still believed they had a chance. From his high seat in Asgaard, Odin watched Angrboda's hall, and one day when she was away, the gods invaded her home and took her children.

"Odin cast Jörmungandr into the deepest ocean, where the serpent grew and grew until he encircled Midgaard and could bite his own tail.

"As for Loki's daughter Hel, she was already a mighty sorceress like her mother. Odin sent her down beneath the third root of Yggdrasil, the World Tree, to rule over the dead. It falls to her to provide board and lodging to all not chosen for Odin or Freyja's armies. To each of the dead Hel ensures they receive what they deserve, for good or ill.

"Fenrir was prophesied to eat Odin at Ragnarok. The gods kept him in Asgaard until the wolf grew so huge that only Tyr, the god of war, dared to feed him. The gods knew they had to restrain him, but the giant wolf broke every chain they made. Finally they had the master smiths in Svartálfheim forge a magic fetter, called Gleipnir, made from the beard of a woman, the sound of a cat's footsteps, the roots of a mountain, a bird's spittle, a bear's sinews, and the breath of a fish. So cunning was the art of the Svartálfar that the bond appeared to be no more than a silk ribbon.

"Odin said, 'Mighty Fenrir, you have broken our strongest chains. Surely you can break this fragile ribbon. If you can't, of course we'll release you.'

"Fenrir was no fool. 'Delicate as it may appear, before I'll allow you to put that ribbon around my neck, one of you must place his hand in my mouth.'

"Tyr, the only one of the gods Fenrir had come to trust, volunteered. He knew what was about to happen to his friend and he felt bad about the betrayal. He placed his hand in the wolf's jaws while Thor draped Gleipnir around Fenrir's neck.

"Though the mighty wolf struggled and strove, he could not break free from Gleipnir. 'You must release me as you promised,' he demanded through gritted teeth still clamped on Tyr's hand.

"'Oh no, that we will never do,' said Odin.

"'Then the price will be paid.' Fenrir bit down with his powerful jaws, severing Tyr's hand at the wrist. That's why we call the wrist the wolf-joint.

"Fenrir snapped his jaws and tried to bite the gods. They propped his mouth open with a sword, then bound him to an enormous rock and sank it deep under the roots of the World Tree.

"But Loki took his revenge on the gods for what they had done to his children. The most beautiful of the gods is Baldr, son of Odin and Frigg. Baldr had nightmares that he would be killed, so Frigg demanded an oath from everything in the nine worlds not to harm her son.

"Loki thought, why should Odin's son be protected when his own children had been cast out? He decided to find out if there were any weaknesses to Baldr's indestructability. Loki knew that Frigg would never trust him, so he disguised himself as a woman and gained Frigg's trust. He asked her if there was anything in the nine worlds that had not sworn the oath. Frigg admitted that she had not made the mistletoe swear, for it was too young to take an oath.

"So Loki found a mistletoe. He carved it into the shape of a knife and took it to the feast where all the gods were having fun, shooting at Baldr with spears and arrows and watching their weapons bounce off him harmlessly.

"Loki saw that the blind god, Hod, was not participating in the sport. 'Why are you not honoring Baldr by throwing a weapon at him?' Loki asked.

"'Well,' said Hod, 'I am blind, so I have little chance of hitting him. And besides, I have no weapon.'

"'Here, you may use my weapon,' said Loki, putting the mistletoe into the blind god's hand, 'and I will guide you.'

"So Hod took the mistletoe knife and Loki guided his hand to fling it at Baldr. The weapon struck Baldr dead.

"The gods were devastated by Baldr's loss. Grief-stricken, Odin sent his son, Hermod, to Hel to offer the queen of the dead a great ransom if she would release Baldr back to Asgaard. Hermod rode Odin's eight-legged horse, Sleipnir, on the perilous journey. He rode nine nights through valleys so dark and deep he could see nothing. When he finally emerged, he came to the river of knives and swords. The only way to cross was a bridge with a golden roof, guarded by a shield-maiden named Modgud. When Hermod told her he was sent by the gods, she let him pass. He reached the flaming gates of Hel and mighty Sleipnir leaped over them.

"There in the hall Baldr sat in the guest seat beside Hel. Hermod offered her all the riches of Asgaard to let him take his brother home.

"'I care nothing for your ransom.' Hel swept her arm over her hall, festooned with gold and silver. 'I have riches in plenty.'

"Hermod hung his head. 'Is there nothing that will make you send my brother home? All the world weeps for him.'

"Hel smiled her grim smile. 'I will release Baldr if everything in the nine worlds, whether living or dead, animal or plant, rock or tree, all weep for him.'

"So the gods sent messengers throughout the nine worlds to ask all things to weep Baldr out of Hel. Rocks and trees and people and animals, everything, living or dead, all wept for the beautiful god.

"All but one old jotun woman who sat in her cave. She said, 'No good got I from the old one's son either dead or alive. Let Hel hold what she has.'

"And so Loki had his vengeance, and his daughter keeps the most beautiful of gods by her side. Some say the old jotun woman was really Loki in disguise. No one knows for sure."

Thorgeir sat back and swilled his ale while the others stared into the campfire.

"That is a sad story, brother," said Murchad. "As sad as any Irish tale."

Thorgeir sighed. "That it is."

CHAPTER 3

Tromøy
May, AD 824

Åsa set about brewing a fresh batch of mead, adding springwater and berries to the honey along with a little of the last batch as a starter. She covered the crock with a weighted linen towel, stirring it several times a day with the enchanted brew stick that had been hanging in the warm, dark brewhouse since before she was born, its magic passed down in the family for generations. If the mead turned out well, she would send some along to Skiringssal. Though she didn't expect Sonja to forgive her any time soon, she wanted to nurture goodwill between them in hopes of a future reconciliation.

In a few days, the brew began to froth and foam, and the bryggjemann—álfar of the mead—began to chatter among themselves.

Soon after the mead came to life, a longship was sighted off Tromøy. At the sound of the horn, Åsa ran out of the brewhouse, wiping her hands on her smock. She arrived at the shore just as the ship entered the harbor. Åsa recognized the new arrival as

Raider Bride. It had been almost a year since Ragnhild had set sail to wrest the steading of Gausel from her brother Harald. Since then, scant news had reached Tromøy from traders who came over the mountains or sailed down the North Way.

The longship nosed onto the beach and Ragnhild jumped down from the bow, grinning. Åsa threw her arms around her old friend. "I'm so glad to see you! Good to see you all. Come up to the hall and tell me all your adventures over a cup of ale."

Tromøy's shore watch helped *Raider Bride*'s crew haul the ship onto the shingle. When all was secure, they escorted the new arrivals up the trail where folk were gathering on the benches set out in the yard. Farmers came in from the fields for the day, and the crowd filled the yard and spilled out into the closest pasture. Voices rose as friends and family greeted the crew.

Over the welcome horn of ale, Åsa asked Ragnhild, "What brings you here, so far from your new home?"

Ragnhild cleared her throat and glanced at Murchad. "Lady, I made a vow to my husband that I would return the queen's necklace to Ireland. If his cousin discovers it's missing, it will cause a rift between them, one that may never be healed."

Åsa was silent for a moment. "I fear you have journeyed far for nothing. The queen in the mound has seized the necklace in exchange for Eyvind's freedom."

Murchad kept his face expressionless, though Åsa saw his shoulders slump.

Ragnhild hurried on. "Surely there's a way to recover the necklace? It means a great deal to Murchad."

Åsa shook her head. "I cut off the draugr's head and sent her to Hel. I tried to take the necklace, but her corpse holds it fast."

"It shouldn't be that hard to take it from a dead woman," said Ragnhild.

Heid spoke up. "I would be careful about rousing the fury of the draugr, girl."

Ragnhild snorted. "I have sent many to their deaths and I fear none of their ghosts."

"I think you've forgotten how the haugbui bested you, and Åsa had to come to your rescue," Heid huffed. "Even though the draugr no longer dwells in this world, she was once a mighty queen and her curse could yet cause harm. If the necklace is her price, you should let her keep it."

Murchad said nothing, but his face was a mask of disappointment.

Ragnhild patted his hand and said, "The necklace is our property. Don't worry, *a mhuirin*, I'll go into the mound and get it. No corpse will keep me from my vow."

Murchad shook his head. "It's too much of a risk for you to take. Remember how the queen held us both helpless." Worry creased his brow.

Ragnhild raised her chin. "I made you a promise. I'm not going back on it now. Åsa dispatched the draugr to Helheim. She can't hurt me."

Murchad fell silent, his arguments at an end.

Åsa sensed this meant more to Ragnhild than simply keeping a vow. There was a tension between her and Murchad. It was unlikely that Ragnhild could really retrieve the necklace, but it was their property. Åsa could not really forbid her from trying.

Åsa looked at Heid. "You said yourself the haugbui had no power to harm us. I say let Ragnhild try."

Heid shrugged. "You can't say I didn't warn you."

"Thank you, Lady." Ragnhild's gratitude sounded heartfelt. Murchad perked up and smiled. It was obvious that Ragnhild was doing it to make him happy, and Åsa was glad to help.

She smiled at the couple, ignoring the worry that niggled in her gut.

RAGNHILD DID NOT SLEEP well that night. Around her, *Raider Bride*'s crew snored. Åsa had assigned them Tromøy's newest guesthouse, bigger and more comfortable than the old one. Even so, Ragnhild tossed and turned, chiding herself. How could she be afraid of a corpse? It was Heid's fault. The old witch had planted a seed of fear in her mind. The draugr had bested her once, but never again. This time she would prove she was stronger.

She rolled over and closed her eyes resolutely, snuggling close to Murchad. His arm went around her and she tried to match his even breathing, hoping to lull herself into slumber. Scraps of sleep came in fits and starts, spasms of worry sending her jolting upright and staring into the dark.

In the morning, she dragged herself from the bed and pulled on her clothes.

Murchad didn't look like he'd slept much better than she had. "Are you sure you want to go through with this?"

She mustered a reassuring smile. "I'm sure."

They dressed and hurried to the hall, where her three húskarlar were already waiting, armed with shovels and grim expressions.

"I'm just robbing a corpse," Ragnhild joked as they sat down for breakfast. "We've done it many times."

Murchad looked a little sick, while the three húskarlar gave her faint smiles. Before their mood could completely overwhelm her, she jumped up from the bench and strode out the door, leaving the men to follow.

The day was overcast, gloomy for May and threatening a thunderstorm. Ragnhild marched down the trail to the beach, turned north and followed the shoreline until she came to the break in the trees. There she entered the forest, following the deer path that led to the mound. She plowed through the undergrowth, sweating in the muggy air, her linen tunic damp and sticky. Murchad and the húskarlar trudged in her wake.

The mound reared up amid the forest, dark and forbidding, so ancient and long neglected that mature trees sprouted from the top. They all halted and stared, catching their breath. Claustrophobia gripped Ragnhild with the memory of being imprisoned inside. She glanced at Murchad. His face was pale, but his jaw was set in a grim line.

Ragnhild wanted nothing more than to leave this place, but she shook off her misgivings. She wasn't going to give in to fear. "Well, let's get to it." She hefted her shovel.

They dug into the soft earth. The mound opened easily, like an old wound. Before Ragnhild was ready, the hole was large enough to fit through. She shivered, but dropped her shovel and climbed into the dark interior. Murchad sheltered a torch while Einar struck his flint and coaxed the flame to life.

Murchad handed the torch in to her. The flame faltered in the dank air and threatened to go out, then steadied and flared. Gooseflesh rose on Ragnhild's arms as she shone the light around the interior of the grave mound where the draugr had held her and Murchad captive. She'd never felt so helpless. Only Åsa's wit had won their freedom.

Ragnhild squared her shoulders. This time, she would prove herself stronger than the haugbui.

The torchlight picked up a glint of gold. Ragnhild sucked in a breath. The light revealed the corpse of the once mighty queen sprawled on the floor like a bundle of rags. On the far side of the grave chamber, her crushed skull lay in a tangle of silver hair.

Ragnhild's neck hairs prickled and she shone the light on the necklace, clutched in the corpse's skeletal hand. Pieces of rotting flesh still clung to the bones. Ragnhild took a deep breath, bent down, and grabbed the golden links. She gave a good yank, but the dead hand's grip held tight. Ragnhild tugged and worked it but could not pull the necklace free. Sweat broke out on her forehead and her breath came in gasps. Her hand began to shake and she fought a sense of doom.

The torch went out.

Ragnhild stopped dead and gasped.

"*A chroi.*" Murchad's voice was taut with worry.

"It won't budge," Ragnhild rasped.

"You've been in there long enough. Come, we will try again later."

Ragnhild jerked harder, but the hand gripped the golden links tight. Dread clenched her stomach. Determined, she set her jaw and drew her dagger. She hacked at the arm, but the bone turned her blade. Gritting her teeth, she sawed the wrist, pulling on the hand with all her strength.

The hand came off in a rush and Ragnhild tumbled backward, slamming against the timbers of the burial chamber. It knocked the breath out of her, and she lay gasping.

Thunder rumbled a warning in the distance.

"Come out!" The urgency in Murchad's voice ignited her terror. The rotting hand still held the necklace locked in its grip. Ragnhild's flesh crawled as she stuffed the necklace, hand and all, into her satchel. She slung the bag over her shoulder and clawed her way through the dark to the entrance.

Lightning flashed through the treetops, followed by a crack of thunder.

Murchad grabbed her and pulled her out through the hole. He wrapped his arms around her.

"I've got it, *a chroi*," she said, holding up the satchel.

"My heroic wife," he murmured. She glowed under his approval.

Hail pelted through the trees, lashing the tender spring leaf buds, stinging like needles.

"We should wait out the storm here," said Einar.

They huddled in the lee of the burial mound while the rain and hail pounded down and the wind howled in the treetops. Ragnhild shivered in Murchad's arms. They were all getting soaked, but nobody suggested they shelter inside the mound.

Eventually the storm eased to a steady rain. Stiff and drenched, the little party slogged through the sopping underbrush. They broke out of the forest onto the beach, where the wind sliced through Ragnhild's sodden wool cloak. The hall beckoned in the distance, smoke billowing out of the roof hole, promising a roaring fire within.

At last they reached the door. Ragnhild burst into the entry way. Glad to be out of the cutting wind, she doffed her soggy cloak and hung it on a peg with the others, then hurried into the main room where the folk of Tromøy crowded around the longfire.

"Were you successful?" asked Åsa.

"I was." Ragnhild opened her satchel and pulled out her grisly prize. The onlookers gasped.

"Now you've done it," said Heid, eyeing the half-rotted hand that still clutched the golden necklace.

Ragnhild glared at the sorceress defiantly. "The hand wouldn't let go, so I cut it off. She's dead. She can't hurt us."

"Foolish girl," said Heid. "There are some whose power reaches beyond the grave."

Ragnhild scowled and stowed the necklace and hand in the satchel. "I want a hot bath." She rose and stalked out of the hall to the bower, where a cauldron of water bubbled over the fire. Servants hurried to fill a bath for her. Relief flooded her as she sank into the warm water and scrubbed away the grave dirt. Why did Heid seem to disapprove of everything she did?

That evening she sat close to Murchad and drowned her fears in ale.

Åsa leaned forward and asked Murchad, "Tell me, why is it so important to return the necklace to Ireland?"

Murchad said, "No one knows the full story, but it has always been worn by the queens of our land."

Ragnhild looked at Åsa. "You wore it and used its powers."

Åsa nodded. "Yes, it gave me great strength. I believed it

enabled me to heal, and to win battles. Even without touching it, I can feel its presence in the room."

"I feel nothing when I touch it," said Ragnhild.

"Perhaps it is because you are not a powerful queen," Heid said acidly.

Ragnhild bristled. "I won Gausel from my brother. I rule there now, and I command a fleet of ships."

"Those things do not make you a queen," the sorceress said.

Ragnhild stifled a retort. She knew if she continued on this path, the old witch would find a way to make her feel worse than she already did. She turned to Åsa. "What makes you willing to part with the necklace?"

Åsa said, "Once, I relied on it to give me power and confidence. But it's not really mine. You were the one who was able to retrieve it from the haugbui, not me. I must find my own power."

Ragnhild heard the doubt in her friend's voice. Part of her wanted to give the necklace back to Åsa, but the happiness on Murchad's face made up her mind.

CHAPTER 4

Tromøy

The next morning dawned clear. *Far Traveler* rowed into Tromøy's harbor.

Word reached Åsa while she was dressing for the day. She had not expected Eyvind back for several months. Hoping nothing was wrong, she threw her shawl over her shoulders and hurried down to the beach, her red-gold hair streaming loose behind her.

The ship looked whole and fully manned. She could see no damage, nor any empty places at the oars.

Eyvind stood in *Far Traveler*'s prow. To Åsa's relief, he looked well. As the ship touched the beach, he leaped over the gunnel and sloshed ashore to sweep her into his arms.

"I wasn't expecting you back so soon," she murmured.

"We sailed as far as Gotland, where we made some good trades." He buried his face in her hair. "I began to miss my queen, and decided to stop and see you before I sail south."

Åsa let her body melt into his, inhaling his scent of sea brine and wool, feeling his arms strong around her. She tipped her head back and smiled up at him. "Come, rest yourself."

The ship secure, they hurried up to the hall where ale was served and Eyvind's crew crowded in with Tromøy's hird and Ragnhild's crew.

"I have precious gifts for you, my queen," said Eyvind, "and I'm very happy to see Lady Ragnhild and Lord Murchad. I hope you brought some goods from your homelands, for I have many exotic items to trade with you."

"We are excited to see your cargo," said Åsa, "but first, tell us of your travels."

To a rapt audience, Eyvind recounted his travels in the Eastern Sea, where he traded with voyagers from the distant reaches of the world. Åsa yearned to see those places. Maybe someday she would be free to sail with Eyvind, but for now she dared not leave her son or Tromøy for more than a few days, even with Jarl Borg in charge. Too many warlords coveted the island's strategic location, commanding the Skagerrak sea routes and the valuable soapstone quarries and farmland. Her presence kept those powerful men at bay, for now.

When the conversation wound down and the fire burned low, the ships' crews stumbled off to the guesthouses. Åsa led Eyvind to her private chamber. She shut the door and turned to him in anticipation. His eyes gleamed in the firelight as he took her in his arms. A sigh escaped her and she raised her arms, allowing him to pull her wool gown over her head. His touch through her thin linen shift made her shiver.

He unbuckled his leather belt and let it drop to the floor. She pulled his wool tunic off, then untied his breeches and let them fall too. Their bodies pressed together, the heat coming off their flesh as they edged toward the bed. Still entangled, they tumbled onto the soft down comforter.

∾

THE NEXT MORNING, Åsa woke in Eyvind's arms. His fingers lightly stroked her back. She kissed him and his eyes opened lazily. "I'm so glad you have returned to me."

"I couldn't stay away," he murmured.

After making love, they rousted themselves out of bed, dressed, and hurried to the hall for breakfast.

"Where's Oscar?" Eyvind asked, scanning his crew.

"He's sick," said a sailor. "He's throwing up."

"Too much mead," said another and the crew laughed.

The next morning, Oscar had a fever and five more of *Far Traveler's* crew members were sick.

Eyvind's brow furrowed. "We must isolate ourselves from the rest of you. I hope it's not too late." He turned to Åsa. "I'm sorry, love. It's been a week since we were in any port. I was sure we were free of disease."

Worry clenched her stomach as Åsa watched him go with his crew to the guesthouse. She called to Hogni and arranged for food and ale to be delivered to them, then issued orders.

"Everyone will stay away from the guesthouse. Halfdan and the other children will stay in the bower with the rest of the women. *Raider Bride's* crew will remain in their own guesthouse."

Heid gathered her nine apprentices. "I will move into the guesthouse to nurse the sick. Vigdis, you, Halla, Mor, and Liv will join me. The rest of you, stay in the bower."

"My sisters and I will come with you," said Unn. She was a skilled healer and her three younger sisters all had nursing experience.

Åsa reluctantly left Halfdan with the women in the bower and moved into the sickhouse. Though she trusted Brenna to take good care of the boy, Åsa dreaded being separated from her son. But the sick were her responsibility and as queen it was her duty to care for them.

She arrived to find Eyvind shivering, his forehead burning. "You shouldn't be here," he protested.

"I'm queen here, I say what goes." Åsa forced him to lay back. It worried her that he was too sick to argue.

For the next three days, Åsa fretted over Eyvind as his fever raged. He vomited and struggled to breathe, too weak to sit up. His back ached and he shivered. No matter how many blankets Åsa piled on him he couldn't get warm. She laid warm compresses on his chest and fed him willow bark tea to ease his fever.

Eight more of *Far Traveler*'s crew members fell sick. The guest hall echoed with their coughs and retching.

Red spots appeared on Oscar's tongue. They quickly spread to his face, then over his body. Then his fever abated. He sat up and took food for the first time.

The rash spread rapidly on the sick, and soon their bodies were covered as well as their eyes and mouths. At the same time, their fevers ebbed. The rash appeared on Eyvind, marching across his body. He rallied enough to swallow the broth Åsa spooned into his mouth.

"I think the worst is over," said Unn hopefully.

"We'll see," said Heid.

By morning, Oscar's rash had developed into blisters which quickly degenerated into sores and filled with thick, opaque pus.

"That looks like the cowpox we got on our hands from milking," said Åsa.

"This is not the same thing," said Heid.

The next day, Oscar's lesions became raised and hard. They swelled and burst, oozing pus and blood. The boy's fever spiked higher than ever and he began to rave, calling for his mother in a rasping voice.

Then his ravings stopped abruptly. An unearthly silence fell over the guesthouse, punctuated by the coughs and groans of the sick.

Heid bent over the boy. "He's dead."

An audible gasp went up. A chill shot through Åsa. Oscar had been a young, vigorous boy, bursting with life just a few days ago. She stared down at Eyvind. Would he be next? She stayed by his side, getting as much liquid into him as she could.

One by one, *Far Traveler*'s crew slipped into delirium. Their lesions blackened and peeled off, filling the guesthouse with a sweet, pungent smell. Four more of them died raving.

Eyvind's rash developed into pustules and his fever raged once again. He began to babble. In despair, Åsa kept a compress on his forehead and trickled willow bark tea into his mouth, mouthing prayers to Frigg, the mother goddess, to heal him.

Men and women began to arrive at the guesthouse door with fevers and a rash. Some of them were Tromøy's folk, others from *Raider Bride*'s crew. They joined the sick on the benches while those still standing did their best to keep them alive.

Unn and her sisters remained healthy, as did Åsa, Heid and her apprentices, and six of Eyvind's crew. Åsa prayed that none of the vital nursing team would get sick.

Ragnhild brought Murchad to the sick house with a raging fever. Åsa had never imagined Ragnhild as a nurse, but the shield-maiden refused to leave her husband's side, holding his hand as he retched and coughed, cooling his brow with cloths and spooning herbal brews.

Heid hobbled about the guest hall, barking orders at her apprentices. Suddenly she crumpled to the floor. Åsa and Vigdis rushed to her side.

"I'm fine, leave me be!" the sorceress grumbled, feebly pushing them away and struggling to rise. Between them they got Heid to her feet, but her legs buckled and her body shook with chills. Her skin burned with fever. They helped her to a bench where Åsa bundled her in furs while Vigdis brought her a concoction of willow bark and herbs. Heid swallowed the brew, but immediately vomited it up.

Vigdis and Åsa exchanged a desperate look.

They laid the sorceress close to Eyvind so Åsa could tend

them both. Eyvind thrashed and muttered, trapped in his delirium. Heid struggled to draw tortured breaths that rasped in her throat and rattled in her chest.

"I fear she will die, Lady," Vigdis whispered. "She is old and more frail than she lets on." An icy shard of fear struck Åsa's heart.

Åsa and Vigdis stayed with Heid over the next hours while the sorceress slid in and out of consciousness. As the völva's fever raged, she began to babble.

"Ragnhild, bring me the necklace." Fearing the shield-maiden might resist, Åsa put all the power of her galdr voice into her demand.

Ragnhild did not argue. She fetched the leather satchel.

Åsa took it from her with trembling hands, praying that it would heal the sorceress as it had once before. The necklace's power tingled through the leather. Just the solidity of it gave her strength. Åsa reached in and took hold of the golden links, shuddering when she contacted the shriveled hand that clung to it. The familiar vibration surged up her arm into her chest and she realized how much she had missed that power. She'd gotten along without it all winter but now desire set in. Even after months without contact, the gold had a strong hold over her. It scared her, but she had to try.

She laid her other hand on Heid's chest and let the vibrations flow through her into the sorceress's ravaged body.

Heid's eyes snapped open and she struggled to sit up. Her face was white and pasty. Sweat beaded her forehead and her words came out in gasps. "It's the haugbui," she croaked. "I was too complacent. The necklace was the only thing that held off her curse." She stared at Ragnhild. "You unleashed her rage by doing violence to her corpse and taking the necklace." Heid fell back, panting. "It has no power to heal us."

Åsa sagged in dismay. All these misfortunes were her fault. When she had cut off the queen's head and sent the draugr to

Helheim, the haugbui cursed her. All winter, it had seemed as if the curse had not touched them, but it had only been held at bay by the necklace's power. Now Ragnhild's actions brought that evil down on them.

"What can I do?" Åsa asked.

Heid drew a grating breath. "You must journey to Hel and convince the queen in the mound to lift the curse."

A chill passed over Åsa. The dangers of the journey into the Otherworld were well known from tales and songs. Time passed differently there, in a place inhabited by fearsome creatures. Heid herself had been trapped there, unable to return without the help of a master sorcerer. Åsa could never hope to survive such a journey. "Even if I make it to Helheim, how can I persuade the queen to lift the curse once I get there?" Her voice came out as a quaver. "I have no power in the land of the dead."

"You have the one thing she wants," the sorceress rasped. "You must take the necklace to her." Heid's eyes closed and she sank back into her stupor.

Vigdis leaned over her mentor, a worried frown on her face. "You can't go," she said to Åsa. "You might never come back. How would Tromøy survive without you? We'd fall prey to every warlord in the land. The Danes would come roaring across the Skagerrak in an instant if they heard you were absent."

Åsa shuddered. Even Heid only undertook this journey in times of the greatest need, and no one else on Tromøy had any experience with the Otherworld. The odds of coming back from Hel were slim. Åsa might never see her son again, or Eyvind, or any of those she held dear. Panic flared in her at the thought of being trapped, alone, in Helheim forever.

She stared down at Eyvind. He burned with fever, struggling feebly, imprisoned in a troubled nightmare. What if he died while she was away?

If she didn't go, she might lose them all.

Åsa cleared her throat and forced strength into her voice.

"Heid said I must take the necklace to the queen in Hel. I have no choice but to try. If I don't, many people will die."

From his bed, Murchad spoke in a whisper. "I give you the necklace, Åsa."

Ragnhild caught her breath. "What about our vow to return it to Ireland?"

"What good is a vow if we are all dead? Take it, Lady, with my blessing."

Ragnhild had enough grace to look abashed.

Åsa blinked back tears of gratitude. "I know how much this means to you, Lord Murchad. I thank you, and all the people of Tromøy thank you too." Fear welled up inside her again. She turned to Vigdis. "Will you help me?"

Vigdis looked up from Heid's unconscious form and nodded. "Though I have never ventured to the Otherworld, I have assisted the völva in her spirit journeys. I will do my best to guide you through. But, Lady, all the tales of the journey to Hel speak of the need for a horse, one who can leap the flaming gates of Hel itself."

Åsa stared at her, aghast. "To enter the land of the dead, the horse must be…" she whispered.

Vigdis nodded. "Dead. Choose your swiftest mount and I will perform the sacrifice."

Åsa thought of the beloved horses in Tromøy's herd. She could not part with any of them. "We've lost so much already."

"You can't walk the Hel road," said Vigdis. "By the time you get there on foot we'll all be dead."

Åsa frowned but was silent. She knew Vigdis had the right of it. "Maybe I could ride a goat, like Thor, or a boar, like Freyja?"

Vigdis snorted. "You're not a god. You need a horse, and a champion horse at that."

Murchad cleared his throat. "As a Christian, I know little of your afterlife. If such a place exists, my brave Svartfaxi will be there." His voice caught, and Ragnhild squeezed his hand. "I trained him well for battle. He should be able to carry you through any dangers. He would have no fear of flaming gates."

Åsa knew how great the bond Murchad had with his horse, and how he'd grieved Svartfaxi's death in battle. She turned to Vigdis. "Is there a way to call upon a horse in the land of the dead?"

Vigdis chewed her lip. "Perhaps. I've never heard of it being done, but it would be like contacting any spirit of the dead and asking for assistance."

"I have faith in you," said Åsa. "You have learned well from Heid. And my bond with Svartfaxi is strong. I raised him from a colt, trained him, and spent many hours on his back before I gave him to Murchad."

"I will do what I can to reach him," said Murchad.

Vigdis looked at him. "Doesn't that go against your Christian beliefs?"

Murchad smiled faintly. "My people have never completely severed their contact with the Otherworld. And the end justifies the means." He closed his eyes. His lips moved in silent conference as he sought his former mount. Eventually, he stilled and slept.

Åsa did not sleep. She longed to go up to the bower and see Halfdan before she left, but she dared not expose him to the disease, nor did she want to upset the boy. It was easier for them both simply to continue the separation. He was safe with Brenna.

In the morning, Murchad's fever spiked and he began to rave, writhing in his sweat-soaked covers. Ragnhild was wild-eyed. "You must go, Åsa," she said. "I promise I will nurse Eyvind while you are gone. Please. You must save Murchad. Save them both."

"I will," said Åsa. She reached out and touched Eyvind as he moaned softly in his sleep. "I will see you soon, my love, in this world or the next." She turned to Vigdis. "Are you ready?"

"Yes," said Vigdis. "This whole enterprise is risky, but we have little choice and less time." She motioned another apprentice over. "You're in charge of our mistress until I return. If any harm befalls her, I'll lay such a curse on you…" The apprentice's eyes widened. Vigdis didn't need to continue.

Åsa went to the hall. She stood outside the door and addressed the warriors. "I must journey to the Otherworld to see what can be done about this sickness. It's possible that I won't return. While I am gone, I task you, Jarl Borg, my old friend and mentor, to take charge of Tromøy as you have before. If I do not return, hold Tromøy for my son."

The old jarl bent his head. "I will be honored to watch over your kingdom and your son until you return. And return you will. I have faith in you, my queen." He looked up at her. His eyes were red and watery.

"Thank you, old friend." Åsa turned to Olvir. "You have been my right hand ever since we came here. I charge you to support Jarl Borg, to watch over my son and ensure his safety until he is old enough to rule. I command you all to keep Tromøy safe, and defend it and my son."

Olvir nodded, his face rigid. "Yes, my queen. It shall be as you say."

The warriors beat their weapons on their shields and swore their oaths.

Åsa called upon Einar, Thorgeir, and Svein to come with her. They saddled their horses while Vigdis hitched up Heid's cart, loaded shovels and an extra saddle and bridle. Åsa climbed in beside her, the leather satchel containing the necklace over her shoulder.

The little party set off for the mound, two of Heid's apprentices following on foot.

As they approached the haugr, dread flooded Åsa's stomach. Terrifying memories clamored in her head, of being trapped inside the dank earth where she had battled the haugbui for the lives of those she loved. She shuddered at how close she'd come to losing them. When Åsa struck off the draugr's head, she'd thought she'd won. But the haugbui's curse had been waiting, held back only by the corpse's grip on the necklace. And now Åsa must seek the wily queen in the land of the dead, and pit her wits against her once more.

Inevitably, they reached the mound, hidden deep in the forest, far from the living. The hole Ragnhild had used to break in still gaped like a maw ready to swallow her.

Åsa got down from the cart. Vigdis pulled out Heid's skin drum, painted with scenes and figures from the Otherworld. It was a Saami drum, created by the powerful sorcerers of the north, and Åsa had not seen it in a long time, not since Heid had first taught her to leave her body. It was a powerful thing, meant for the soul journey. Åsa shivered, realizing this would not be as simple as entering Stormrider's familiar body and soaring across lands she knew well.

She squared her shoulders and set her jaw, then hefted the saddle and shoved it through the opening into the mound, followed by the bridle and the leather satchel containing the necklace. She took the torch Vigdis offered her and climbed in.

Scanty light filtered in through the opening. Åsa shone the torch around the interior until she spotted the bundle of rags that had been the haugbui. Sadness filled her for what she had done to the once mighty queen, but she shook it off. It was a false glamour cast by the queen's shade. The draugr had to be dispatched to save the living.

And now Åsa must face her enemy again, in a place where she held no power.

She set the saddle upright on the floor, then jammed the butt of the torch in the dirt. From her belt pouch she drew a seed of henbane and cast it on the flames. Powerful fumes billowed up from the fire. Åsa inhaled deeply as she seated herself astride the saddle and took up the bridle.

Holding the reins in one hand, she reached into the leather satchel with the other and rummaged for the necklace. The flesh and bone of the dead hand sent a shudder through her. Her fingers found the cold metal links. The vibration started in her hand and surged up her arm to her chest.

A violent urge came over her to drop the golden links and flee from the mound. She gritted her teeth and inhaled the smoke deeply. It must be done.

"I'm ready," she said to Vigdis.

With the leg bone of a reindeer, Vigdis beat on the skin drum and chanted in a sing-song voice. Åsa closed her eyes and let her mind follow the apprentice's words as Vigdis murmured spells of protection. The other apprentices joined their voices with hers, and Åsa chanted along with them, trying to memorize the spells to protect her from the evil things that could befall her in the Otherworld: wandering deprived of will, overwhelmed by powerful rivers, encounters with malignant ghosts. With every word, Åsa's foreboding grew.

Vigdis spoke. "The first part of the journey will be in utter darkness. Nine nights will you ride through valleys that have never seen the light. Beyond that lies the land of the dead."

Åsa's inner vision turned black, blacker than the night, black as a deep well to which there was no bottom. She was falling, into the dark. Far down in the depths voices called. Her skin crawled, her stomach churned, and she bit back the vomit that rose in her throat.

She took a breath to calm herself, then called Svartfaxi. She invoked the black stallion's image in her mind and set it adrift in the clouds of the drug. The world spun around her and images flashed before her eyes. She struggled to keep her balance while another wave of nausea passed through her. The voices called to her.

CHAPTER 5

The Road to Helheim

A velvety muzzle nudged Åsa's cheek. She blinked and looked into Svartfaxi's soft brown eyes. The black horse snorted in her ear and a wave of relief swept over her. She would not be alone on the road to Hel.

She had fallen off the saddle and now lay in soft grass, still clutching the bridle in one hand and the necklace in the other. She sat up, stowed the necklace and the hand in the satchel, then scrambled to her feet.

The horse stood patiently while she stroked his neck and murmured in his ear. "Greetings, brave Svartfaxi. I'm so glad to see you." He nuzzled her hair. "Your help is needed. Lord Murchad is very ill. I go on a quest to save him and many others. I must surmount great obstacles and I can only do it with your great strength and courage. This is a journey of many perils from which we may never return. And so I ask, will you take me on the Hel road?"

The horse tossed his head, snorting and pawing the ground.

"You have always been the bravest of horses," Åsa said.

She lifted the bridle. Svartfaxi bowed his head and let her slide the strap over his ears. He took the bit politely and stood while she picked up the saddle and heaved it over his back. She tightened the cinch and mounted, then looked around to get her bearings.

In the distance rose a huge ash tree, the tallest tree she'd ever seen. Its branches disappeared into the clouds, and the three roots stretched for miles before they plunged underground. Åsa stared in awe. This was Yggdrasil, the world tree, whose branches and roots reached all the nine worlds.

At the base of the tree stood a hall, its roof glinting in the sunlight as if it were made of silver. It was there she knew she must go.

Åsa clucked her tongue and Svartfaxi moved toward the tree. Three tall women strode out of the hall. Each of them filled a bucket of water from a spring, and each poured water on one of the tree's great roots. They shooed away the deer that came to nibble on the leaf buds, then turned to their loom against the wall. One picked up the shuttle that dangled from the crossbar and began to run the weft thread through the warp strands across the broad loom. Another woman received the shuttle at the center and guided it through the warp to the far end while the third woman picked up a weaving sword and beat the weft into place.

As Åsa drew near, she saw that the warp threads of their weaving were weighted with human skulls. Looking closer, she saw the threads were entrails, slick with blood.

The hair on the back of her neck stirred. She had come to the right place. These were the Nornir, who wove the threads of mortals' lives and cut them short with their shears.

Svartfaxi whinnied and tossed his head at the scent of blood, but he kept walking toward the bloody loom. At Åsa's approach, the three women laid down their weaving tools and looked at her.

One of them spoke. "Greetings, Åsa, Queen of Agder." A linen veil obscured her features, but her voice held the sweetness of youth. "I am Skuld, she who is becoming. What do you seek with the Nornir?"

"I seek the road to Hel," said Åsa.

"No mortal travels that road by choice," said a middle-aged woman, whose face was plump and plain. She did not introduce herself, but Åsa knew she must be Verdandi, the Norn who embodied the present.

"Yet I must go, for my people are dying," Åsa replied.

"All people die," said Verdandi.

"But not before their time."

The woman who had not yet spoken stepped forward. Her face was lost in the depths of her hood, and from her belt dangled a pair of bloodstained shears. This was Urdr, the eldest of the Nornir, she who determined the fate of all.

Her voice rasped as if with a dying breath. "What makes you think you can change what we weave, child?"

"Lady Urdr, I have to try. Will you let me pass through to the Otherworld?"

Urdr nodded toward the bloody tapestry on their loom. "You must know, sometimes when you avert one thing, something much worse takes its place."

Åsa bowed her head. "This I know from experience. But I must try. Those I hold dear are in mortal danger, and the fault is mine."

The three women exchanged glances as if holding silent counsel, then nodded.

From the depths of her hood, Urdr's voice emanated. "We do not understand a human's heart, but since you had the skill and courage to find your way to us, we will grant you passage."

"Thank you," said Åsa.

"Don't say we didn't warn you."

Skuld led the way to one of the world tree's three huge roots.

The Norn gestured toward a dark cavern that yawned beneath the root. "To reach Hel's realm, you must pass through Niflheim."

The land of freezing mist. Its very name struck a chill in Åsa's heart, yet it was there she must go.

She clucked to Svartfaxi, and he stepped bravely down into the dark. The footing was solid and his hooves echoed on the trail. The path wound around, going deeper beneath the world tree. Somewhere far below came a gnashing of teeth Åsa knew must be the serpent Nidhogg who gnawed on the root, trying to reach his enemy, the eagle who roosted in the top of Yggdrasil.

A shadowy light gleamed ahead. Svartfaxi passed beneath the root and emerged into a landscape hidden in a chill fog, and Åsa knew she was in Niflheim. Beside the root flowed an icy spring which legend named Hvergelmir. From it rose all the rivers in the nine worlds.

From the saddle Åsa surveyed the impenetrable fog with dismay. Here were the most fearsome legends come to life. When the frigid winds of Niflheim clashed with the fire of Muspelheim, the nine worlds were created: the worlds of men and gods, the light and dark álfar, the jotnar, and the primordial worlds where nothing lived.

Though her heart shrank at the thought, Åsa knew she had to ride through the mist to reach the realm of Hel. She urged Svartfaxi forward. He snorted and stepped out into the dense, freezing fog, picking his way carefully across the icy ground.

As they fared through the gloom, the air gradually warmed and the mist began to thin. They emerged onto a gray plain stretching far beneath lowering thunderclouds. At the plain's end rose a tall bluff of obsidian that gleamed dully in the gray light. The cliff was riven by a deep ravine blacker than the rock, yawning back into darkness.

Åsa swallowed and patted Svartfaxi's neck, as much for her own comfort as his. The horse strode boldly toward the black maw.

When Svartfaxi ventured into the ravine, utter darkness swallowed all light. The air stank of stagnant water. Åsa shrank from the cold, slick walls that seemed to close in on them.

Shivering, she urged Svartfaxi on through endless darkness. All was eerily silent except the sound of the horse's hooves on hard rock and the echo of water dripping in the distance.

Her damp hair clung to her face like tentacles. Her nose ran and her skin was clammy. Clop went Svartfaxi's hooves. Drip went the distant water. Åsa sagged in the saddle, half sleeping, half in a trance. Time was meaningless as Svartfaxi plodded through the dank, cold black valleys. Vigdis said the journey took nine nights. In that amount of time, everyone on Tromøy could be dead. But she had to try.

After what seemed an eternity, the din of rushing water sounded. Faint gray light glimmered in the distance. Åsa roused and straightened in the saddle. Svartfaxi quickened his pace.

A jagged hole of brightness cleft the dark. Åsa craved the light, but this cold glow filled her with dread. Svartfaxi's pace slowed as the opening widened. The rushing water sounded like a battle, with deafening clashes of metal.

Svartfaxi stepped from the dark valley into a wintry light that seemed colder than the darkness had been. Below them rushed a swift and tumbling river the color of steel. The water steamed and reeked of sulphur. Men struggled through the water, screaming and falling. Åsa stared at the angular waves and realized the water was full of blades—knives, swords, axes, all clashing together as if a battle raged beneath the surface, cutting men down as they fought their way to shore. On the far bank, a giant wolf ripped at corpses.

Among the men in the water, she saw the outlaw Onar, henchman of the evil wizard Hrafn. Slick black coils surged in the waves and a dragon's head reared, snapping Onar up. The outlaw screamed and writhed in the slavering jaws, but the dragon gulped him down.

The river was so broad Svartfaxi could never jump it, and trying to swim through the churning blades was impossible. Åsa scanned the riverbanks for a way across.

Gold glinted in the distance and she urged Svartfaxi toward it. As they neared, the glint resolved into the roof of a covered bridge. The din of battle emanated from within.

The bridge was blocked by a tall jotun woman in chain mail, armed with a sword and shield. She eyed Åsa with suspicion. "I am Modgud, guardian of the Gjoll Bridge, over which only the dead may pass. You are not silent as are the dead, nor pale. Who are you and what business has a living woman here?"

"Hail, Modgud," said Åsa, mustering all of her command into her voice. "I am Åsa, Queen of Agder, daughter of Harald Redbeard and Gunnhild. I seek a kinswoman of mine in Hel's realm. Let me through."

Modgud stared at her. "Why do you seek dead kin? If she has passed here, she wants no dealings with the living."

"I am sure she is expecting me. She's cast a curse upon my kingdom and I must compel her to undo the harm she has done. Stand aside, Modgud, for my business is pressing."

The jotun woman lowered her sword. "If you can get through the battle, you may pass."

Beneath the golden roof a battle raged. The melee was so thick all Åsa could see were slashing blades of swords and axes. The screams and clashes of metal were deafening.

Åsa hesitated. She had neither weapon nor shield. How could she fight through this bloodthirsty crowd?

She must.

Gazing up at the golden roof, she thought Svartfaxi might be able to jump onto it—she hoped.

She turned the horse back as if to leave and Modgud stood down.

When they had put some distance between them and the bridge, she turned Svartfaxi around and halted. They gazed back at the roof. Åsa leaned forward and whispered in his ear, "Can you jump it?"

The black horse whinnied and tossed his head.

He set out at a gallop straight at the bridge. Modgud's eyes widened and she leaped out of the way of the charging horse.

Åsa closed her eyes and reached out to touch his mind. She felt Svartfaxi's stride shorten. He shifted back, concentrating his power in his hindquarters. Åsa lay flat, hanging on to his neck as he lowered his head and gathered his legs beneath him, preparing for the jump. Svartfaxi's back flexed as he pushed off his legs to make the leap. Åsa clung like a burr, muttering Vigdis's spell of protection.

Svartfaxi's hooves left the ground. As they soared into the air, Åsa's spirit merged with the horse and became one with him. The wind rushed by her ears, her hair flowing out behind, and her stomach did a flip. It was like being in Stormrider when she stooped on prey, exhilarating and terrifying all at the same time.

Svartfaxi gathered his legs beneath him in preparation for landing on the roof. Åsa braced herself and hung on tight.

His hooves touched down and he thundered across the golden roof. He stretched out his forelegs and leaped off the other side, landing on the soft earth at a run, leaving the bridge and battle behind. His elation bubbled up inside Åsa, filling them both with triumph.

Svartfaxi slowed from a canter to a walk, sides heaving. Åsa exhaled and sat upright, stretching her back, shaking out her cramped hands.

But what confronted them made her suck her breath in again.

Before them rose a forest of iron trees, their leaves sharp blades that whipped in the Hel wind, clashing together and singing a deadly tune.

~

Tromøy

THE GUEST HALL stank like rotting flesh and echoed with the sound of breath rasping as the sick struggled to breathe. Ragnhild wiped the sweat from Murchad's brow as he flailed in delirium, his breath wheezing in his chest. She slid her hand under his head and raised a bowl to his lips, coaxing a dribble of willow bark tea down his throat to ease the fever. He swallowed convulsively and she set the bowl aside, staring at her husband in despair.

Heid was in worse shape than Murchad. Her skin was pale and waxen. She hadn't spoken or opened her eyes since the previous day. Unn held a piece of down over the völva's nose, its motion the only sign that the sorceress still lived.

Those who had escaped illness scurried among the sick, bathing foreheads, helping them sip herbal brews to bring down their fever or bone broth in hopes of building their strength.

Worry chewed at Ragnhild like a monstrous wolf. Eyvind still breathed, but he was mired in delirium. Three more of his crew had died. Some had survived their crisis but were still too weak to rise from their beds. Their scabs crusted over and fell off, leaving them scarred. One boy whose eyes had been ravaged by the lesions was blind, and Unn did not know if he would recover his sight. And there were so many others in the early stages of the disease.

Ragnhild's three húskarlar had returned from the mound, leaving Vigdis and two fellow apprentices standing watch over Åsa. The warriors busied themselves outside, thus far untouched by sickness. They slept in the great hall, and helped Hogni take care of the chores and cooking, but kept their distance from the sick. Brenna and the older women had stayed in the bower with the children, who had all remained healthy so far.

Burrowing into her hudfat, Ragnhild gave in to exhaustion and she fell asleep immediately. She slept like a stone but woke to a heavy weight of dread. Who would be among the dead today? Murchad's chest still rose and fell, she saw with gratitude and relief. She whispered a prayer to the gods, promising to make a sacrifice to them if Murchad pulled through this. She even prayed to his Christ god, though she knew sacrifices would get her nowhere with that one.

She stumbled out of bed to join the survivors in their grim rounds, checking to see who yet lived and who had died during the night. She helped one of Eyvind's sailors load a dead shipmate onto a stretcher, and together they carried the corpse to the storehouse. When they opened the door, the stench was overwhelming. Ragnhild managed to help lay the corpse gently among the dead before she vomited up the contents of her stomach.

She wiped her mouth, hoping she wasn't falling sick. She shut the door on the dead and turned wearily back to the sick house.

There was a commotion down on the shore. Someone was shouting. Ragnhild hurried down the trail to see that a merchant ship had entered Tromøy's harbor. As the knarr neared the beach, the shore watch waved them away. "We have sickness here," he cried.

"What kind of sickness?" the captain called.

"A pox. Many are dying. Stay away."

Without a word, the rowers backed their oars and pulled away from the beach, making a hasty exit from the harbor.

Ragnhild's spirits plummeted. Would the world ever return to normal? Could Åsa truly get the curse lifted? Ragnhild wished she'd never taken the necklace. If only she could put it back, but it seemed impossible that she and Murchad would set sail for Ireland.

She turned away from the harbor and trudged up the hill, back to the dead and dying.

~

Skiringssal

OLAF WELCOMED the trading ship landing on the dock. Birger was a gnarled old sea dog who should retire from sailing. But what else would he do? He was too old to start farming. He usually had a supply of local trade goods, from wool to reindeer horn to soapstone pots. Birger didn't venture far anymore, but he always brought a cargo of local gossip.

"Greetings, Birger," said Olaf as the old trader climbed over the gunnels. "Come on up to the hall. Sonja will be happy to hear your news."

Olaf escorted Birger and his crew up the hill to the hall, where Sonja welcomed them with fresh-brewed ale. Olaf brightened at her smile. She had been silent and grim for a week after the discovery of his relationship with Åsa and Halfdan's parentage. He'd left her alone, respecting her need to come to terms with the information.

Recently, she'd started speaking to him again, but he dared not bring up the subject for fear of shattering their fragile truce. Sonja was still reserved with him. In time, he hoped they could discuss the situation, but for now it was too raw.

Tonight, she laughed and chatted with their guests while serving them ale and seeing to their comfort. The perfect hostess, but Olaf was not fooled. He knew she was still wounded.

Olaf raised his cup toward Birger, ensconced in the guest seat. "What's the news?"

"It's not the best news," said Birger, obviously relishing his gossip. "I've just come from Tromøy. They have sickness. It's so bad they wouldn't let us come ashore. Folk are dying there."

Olaf and Sonja both gasped. "Those poor people," said Sonja. Olaf was relieved to hear the sympathy in her voice. That was his Sonja, caring for all.

Birger spat. "That's what happens when a little girl rules a kingdom."

Olaf bit back the retort that rose to his lips. He didn't know how Sonja would take him defending Åsa.

"She's not a little girl," Sonja said. "She's a queen who's fought off men more than a match for the likes of you, Birger. She rules her kingdom fairly and with great skill."

Birger's mouth opened, then closed.

A light flared in Olaf. Perhaps there was hope for reconciliation between the women he loved most in the world.

After making a sizeable dent in Skiringssal's food and ale, Birger and his crew stumbled off to the guesthouse.

When Olaf and Sonja retired to their chamber, Sonja announced, "I'm going to Tromøy."

Olaf was caught off guard. "What? No. You can't expose yourself to that disease." He was glad Sonja wanted to help Åsa, but not at risk to herself.

"Åsa will need my help. She can't handle this all by herself. I can help nurse the sick and take care of Halfdan. After all, he's your son."

"What about Rognvald?" Olaf's worry escalated. He could lose both Åsa and Sonja to this disease.

"It's my duty. Erna can look after Rognvald perfectly well for a few days. I'll leave in the morning." Sonja turned her back on him and finished undressing.

Olaf wanted to forbid her to go, but he knew his wife could not be dissuaded once she set her mind on a course of action. He had never dictated to her in their marriage, and it would not do for him to try to start now.

He got into bed and waited hopefully while Sonja climbed under the covers, but she turned her back to him.

Telemark

THE HALL OF ORM, Jarl of Telemark, stood tall on its manmade hill, though not so tall as Skiringssal. Orm had always wanted to take the Shining Hall, but Gudrød's pup Olaf had grown too strong. Orm had waited too long. He should have struck at the same time Alfgeir of Vingulmark had grabbed Oppland from his grandson, right after that girl-queen had killed Gudrød, while Olaf was still weak. Then Orm would be king, with hinterlands paying tribute to him.

But that horse had escaped the byre. No sense running after it.

From his high seat, Orm presided over the visiting trader while his housekeeper served ale. The trading ship had just come from the south, stopping first at Tromøy, then Skiringssal. Orm had done business with the ship's captain, Birger, for many years. Birger was a great one for news. He could always be relied upon to ferret out the best information.

"What's the news?" Orm asked.

The old trader leaned forward, eyes gleaming. "Tromøy's got sickness."

Orm sat up on his high seat. "What kind of sickness?"

"Pox," Birger spat. "They warned us off. It must be serious."

"That's too bad." Orm smiled to himself. Harald's girl, Åsa, had fought off the raiding parties he'd sent against Tromøy to test her. Telemark commanded a narrow strip of coastline, sandwiched between his neighbors, Vestfold to the north and Agder to the south. Åsa and Olaf stood united against all attacks. It was just a matter of time before the two youngsters squeezed him out. If he lost access to the sea, Telemark was as good as dead. He wouldn't be able to ship his reindeer hides and antlers, his silver and iron to foreign ports, or launch profitable raids. He needed to drive at least one of them out, but he couldn't stand against them both at once. He needed an opportunity to pick off one without the other coming to its aid.

If Tromøy had been struck with sickness, now was the time to attack.

The girl-queen had inherited an impressive fleet from her father, and she'd added more ships to it since. She was too strong for Orm's fleet, especially if Olaf came to her aid. But if her warriors were dead or dying, she wouldn't be able to mount a strong defense.

But Olaf could. Orm had to find a way to distract Olaf while he swept in and took Tromøy. If he could get the young pup to sail off to the north while Orm attacked Tromøy in the south...

Once he'd taken Tromøy, married the girl and made himself king, he could go after Skiringssal.

"Well, that's some news." Orm raised his cup in a toast to Birger.

CHAPTER 6

The Road to Helheim

Åsa gulped, eyeing the swinging blades of the iron forest. Svartfaxi snorted and blew out a steamy mist as he recovered from the jump.

She whispered in his ear, "Can you get through them?"

He stamped a hoof and whinnied. Tossing his head, he dashed into the forest.

Åsa laid herself low along Svartfaxi's neck, her cheek pressed to his mane as he galloped into the trees, swerving through the chopping blades that lashed by her face. Muttering Vigdis's warding charms, she wrapped her arms around the horse's neck and let herself touch his mind. She could feel the strength of his leg muscles, the sureness of his stride as he wove and dodged through the slashing leaves. An axe-shaped leaf flashed into her vision, bearing down on her head. She ducked to the side just before it struck. The blade caught her braid, hacking it off and sending it flying into the treetops, where the steel leaves chopped it to pieces.

She clung to Svartfaxi, not daring to look up. Sweat lathered his withers as his chest rose and fell. Åsa chanted furiously, lending her mind to his to help maintain the arduous legwork through the wood without going lame. She sneaked a glance ahead but this forest of steel seemed to have no end. She was sweating so hard she nearly slid off the saddle. Åsa kept her head down and hung on while the swinging blades whipped around them.

Ahead the trees parted to form a clearing. Svartfaxi halted and let out a whinny of alarm. Åsa peered above the horse's ears to see a jotun woman seated on an iron log in the center of the clearing. The woman was middle-aged, her hair as gray as the metal she sat upon. Her face sagged, as if she might begin to sob at any moment. Around her lounged a pack of wolves. Their ears perked up and they eyed Åsa and Svartfaxi with interest, noses raised to scent the air.

"I am Angrboda." The woman's voice was a low grumble, like the threat of a thunderstorm. Her nostrils quivered. "You are yet among the living. Who are you?"

A chill passed down Åsa's spine. This woman was the mother of Hel, queen of the underworld. She stilled the quaver in her voice. "Hail, Angrboda. I am Åsa Haraldsdottir, Queen of Agder."

"What brings a living woman to my forest, little queen?" the jotun woman demanded.

Åsa sat up tall in the saddle. "I seek my foremother who has passed on to Helheim."

Angrboda scowled. "What business have you with one of my daughter's subjects?"

"My kinswoman has laid a curse on my kingdom. My people are dying of disease."

The jotun shrugged. "They will pass through here and become my daughter's subjects."

"Yes, but long before their time."

Angrboda gave her a hard look. "And why did your foremother curse you, her own kin?"

Åsa swallowed hard. "I sent her here," she whispered.

Angrboda cackled, her laugh cutting like steel. "So you brought her curse on yourself. What hope have you of gaining her favor?"

Åsa hung her head. "Little or none. But for my son, I must try. He has only seen four summers, and he deserves many more years to dance in the sun."

At Åsa's words, the woman started as if struck. "Dance in the sun," she repeated. She gazed wistfully into the distance. Åsa wondered how long it had been since Angrboda had seen real sunshine, not just the chill gray light of this world.

"Go, then, for your child," said the jotun woman.

Relieved, Åsa clucked to Svartfaxi.

Angrboda gave Åsa an evil grin. "If your horse can outrun my children. They have not scented living prey for a long time."

The wolves rose, shaking their fur and licking their chops.

"Go, Svartfaxi!" Åsa shouted, digging her heels into the horse's flanks.

Svartfaxi lunged into the swinging blades. Glancing back, Åsa saw the wolves loping along behind. Their backs were low enough to clear the sharp edges. Svartfaxi's serpentine course helped him evade them, but, unhampered by the need to avoid the iron blades, the wolves fanned out, flanking the horse as he ran.

Clinging to Svartfaxi's neck, Åsa wished for a weapon more than ever.

She realized she was surrounded by weapons. Keeping low to the horse's neck, she watched the iron knives, timing their movement. When a long blade swung near, she reached out and grabbed the lashing stem as it whizzed by her face. She jerked hard and snapped it off. Now she had a weapon the length of a sword, the tree branch stub forming a pommel.

As the wolves surrounded them, she lashed the blade low,

slashing a nose, cutting off an ear. The wolves yelped in pain but kept coming.

The leader leaped at her, jaws snapping at her boots, trying to drag her from the saddle. She drove her sword into his neck, piercing the artery. The wolf dropped away, spraying blood.

Their leader down, the pack halted in confusion and set up a wailing howl.

"You're just a bunch of puppies," said Åsa scornfully.

Svartfaxi kept running, dodging his way through the swinging blades.

The trees thinned and they reached the edge of the wood. Once in the open, Svartfaxi slowed. Åsa patted the horse's lathered neck. "Good boy. You always were the bravest, the most skillful of horses." Svartfaxi gave a faint whinny and plodded ahead.

When he'd walked himself out of his sweat, the horse stopped and Åsa slid gratefully from his back. "We should rest a bit," she said. He snorted his agreement.

She examined the blade she had snatched. It was dull gray, but it had a sharp edge. The woody stem she'd broken off fit her hand as if made for it. It was a well-balanced weapon.

She gazed into the distance. Far off a mountain range hulked, dark and forbidding like everything else in this land. Åsa knew that was where they must go, though her heart quailed at the sight.

After they had rested, she set off walking, leading Svartfaxi. Her feet were leaden, every step a heavy weight, and the horse's head hung low.

As they neared the mountains, Åsa discerned a gaping hole in the mountainside, darker than the gray of the rock around it.

The Gnipa cave.

The entrance to Helheim.

A black dog howled outside the cave, straining at his chains to get at them. His jaws dripped with foam, his chest ran with gore as if he'd been savaged, but the wound did not seem to weaken his fury. He was the Helhound, Gorm. They had to get by him and into the cave to reach the gates of Hel.

"Are you ready, Svartfaxi?" asked Åsa. The horse neighed and tossed his head. Åsa climbed onto his back and hung on tight, weapon in hand. The black stallion charged the cave entrance, setting Gorm to barking furiously. Svartfaxi gathered his legs and leaped. As the horse flew over the lunging hound, the Helhound sprang into the air, jaws open, to bite the horse's hoof. Åsa slashed down with her sword and caught the dog in the mouth. He chomped down on the blade, gripping it firmly in his teeth. Åsa felt herself begin to slide in the saddle. She gripped hard with her legs but the hound's weight dragged her down. She jerked the sword, trying to yank it out of the dog's jaws, but the Helhound held firm. There was no choice but to let go or fall off Svartfaxi's back. She released her hold on the pommel. Gorm dropped away as Svartfaxi soared.

The horse landed hard, jarring Åsa's spine. His hooves skidded on the slick rock floor, then he got his legs under him and set off at a gallop.

Glancing back, Åsa saw the dog chewing up the iron blade as if it were a bone.

Before them stretched a sullen gray plain. In the distance, flames shot high into the lowering sky. Svartfaxi slowed to a walk. He seemed no more eager than Åsa to reach the gates of Hel. She tried to send hopeful thoughts his way, but the world around her dragged on her spirits. The best she could do was endure the long, gloomy journey, wishing it would end but fearing what lay beyond.

Gradually Hel's walls materialized, dark and threatening against the dismal horizon. All along the perimeter walls flames shimmered, feeding a gate of fire. Flames shot up and lashed the sky, setting the clouds alight.

Beside the fiery entrance loomed a grave mound. A jotun sat

on top of the haugr, playing war songs on his harp. Behind him, a tree reached dead branches into the sky and in it perched a sooty red rooster whose comb shimmered with the colors of the Northern Lights.

Svartfaxi halted before the mound. The jotun put aside his harp and looked them over with interest. "Greetings, woman. I am Fjolsvith, wisest of the jotnar, guardian of the gates of Hel. The rooster here is one of the three cocks who will herald Ragnarok. Gullinkambi dwells in Valhöll, and he will wake the Einherjar. Fjalar will call all of Jotunheim. This one will summon the dead to march from Hel."

"And what is his name?" asked Åsa, hoping to gain his cooperation with a friendly tone.

"He has no name, at least none that I have heard. And I have heard most everything." Fjolsvith sniffed the air and leaned forward, peering at Åsa. "Lady, you don't smell of death to me, though you ride a corpse horse. It is rare for the living to reach these gates. There are many formidable obstacles. Tell me, how did you get past the Helhound, Gorm?"

"My horse is swift, and I had a weapon," said Åsa.

Fjolsvith's eyes widened. "Impressive. Who are you, and what do you seek?"

"I am Åsa, Queen of Agder, daughter of King Harald Redbeard and Queen Gunnhild. I have business with my kinswoman within. Will you let us pass?"

"Ah. Family matters. I am sure they are important. I will gladly let you pass."

Åsa smiled and nudged Svartfaxi forward.

"But first, you must solve some riddles," said Fjolsvith. "I love riddles."

Åsa froze, smelling a trap, but she had little choice. "Very well, riddle me."

The jotun grinned hugely and rubbed his hands together in delight. "Oh, what fun! Here's the first one, are you ready?"

Åsa nodded.

The jotun cleared his throat. "What has eight feet and four eyes and bears knees above its belly?"

Åsa was relieved. It was an old riddle, one that she had heard many times since childhood. Perhaps they didn't hear new riddles down in Hel. "A spider."

Fjolsvith's smile fell. "Right." Then his face split in a grin. "Ah, try this one, then. No mother or father has Eager-to-shine, who stems from stone and lurks in the hearth, where he will spend his life."

"Flint!" cried Åsa. This was going to be easy.

The jotun furrowed his brow, lost in thought. Then he brightened. "Who clings to the earth, swallowing wood and water? He fears no man, but only the wind, and picks a fight with the sun?"

"Every sailor dreads him! It's fog!"

The jotun scowled and pounded the mound with his fist. "Well then, Lady All-wise, what creature cradles men, bears a bloody back, shelters fighters from shaft and point, gives life to some, and lays itself inside a soldier's grasp?"

"I've wielded enough shields to know when I hear of one," said Åsa.

"Four hang, four sprang, two point the way, two ward off dogs, one dangles after, always rather dirty." The jotun was yelling now.

"A cow!" shouted Åsa.

Fjolsvith looked so upset, for a moment Åsa felt sorry for him. But she seized the opportunity. "Brother, will you let us pass?"

He hung his head. "You may pass." Then he grinned smugly from under bushy brows. "If you can get me a feather from the rooster's tail."

Åsa stared up at the sooty red cock. He gave a raucous crow and shook his iridescent tail at her.

She urged Svartfaxi up to the tree. The lowest branches were within her reach and she swung up on a sturdy one. The tree was easy to climb, but as soon as she reached the cock's branch, the rooster squawked and hopped to a higher limb.

"Come, Nameless," Åsa commanded, but he swooped by, just out of reach. She tried chanting a drawing spell, but the rooster lit higher in the tree, crowing. As she climbed up, still chanting, he hopped to another limb.

The branches were thinning, and she could see the next ones would not hold her weight. She would have to lure the rooster to her, but what could she use to entice him? She needed something that would attract his attention. Something shiny.

The necklace.

She reached inside her bag and drew out the gleaming chain, the queen's dead hand still gripping it. The cock peered at it with interest. Åsa dangled the necklace, its gold links glinting in the light.

The rooster swooped by and grabbed the necklace in his beak. Åsa reached out and yanked a feather from his tail. The red cock gave an indignant squawk and flapped his wings, lofting into the air, the necklace still clenched in his beak. Åsa held on tight to the golden links and the tree branch, but the bird was strong. She needed both hands to keep her grip—she had to choose between the necklace and the tree. Reluctantly she released her hold on the limb. The next thing she knew she was flying through the air, holding on to the necklace for dear life.

Glancing down, she saw the gates of Helheim flaring far below. If those links broke, she was dead. But at least she didn't have far to travel if she died.

How could she get back to the ground?

She began to swing, trying to drag the rooster lower. The red cock swooped in a zigzag course to shake her off. Åsa held on, but her head spun and her hands began to sweat. Her grip slipped on the smooth links. She lost her hold on the necklace and plunged toward the ground. Crowing in triumph, the rooster flew on with his prize as she fell.

A black shape leaped up to meet her—Svartfaxi! The horse soared toward her. She grabbed his flying mane and scrambled onto his back.

They hurtled toward the ground with all the speed of Stormrider stooping on her prey. Åsa laid her head on the horse's mane and closed her eyes, hugging his neck, pressing her legs tight around him, bracing for impact.

Svartfaxi met the ground at a run, light as a feather, and raced across the plain. He ran so fast the wind snatched Åsa's breath away.

As the horse slowed, Åsa sat up in the saddle. The jotun grinned at them. "Well done!" he cried.

"Where has that rooster taken my necklace?" she demanded, holding out the glimmering tail feather.

Fjolsvith snatched the feather. "Why, I would assume he's taken it to our mistress." He smiled even wider. "Queen Hel herself."

Åsa's heart lurched and a chill passed over her. "I have to get it back!"

"I wish you luck, Lady. I know your horse can jump, but how high?" said Fjolsvith, and began to play his harp.

CHAPTER 7

Tromøy

Vigdis ceased her chanting as two apprentices approached through the trees. They bore steaming bowls of porridge and a pitcher of ale. The smell of food made Vigdis's stomach growl. She and the apprentices who had been chanting with her rose and hurried to receive the food and drink.

"How are things at the steading?" asked Vigdis.

Liv handed her a bowl of porridge and shook her head. "Not good. Many have fallen ill, and more are dying every day."

"How is our mistress?"

Liv grimaced. "The völva is very sick. I fear for her. Unn and her sisters are good nurses, but I don't know if they can get her through this. She's so frail."

"She's tougher than you think," said Vigdis, trying to believe her own words. It was true the völva was tough, but she was old and ill. Both Heid and Åsa were at risk. If the two of them were lost, Tromøy would be left in a dire predicament. "Let's hope our lady succeeds in the Otherworld, and quickly."

The two apprentices who had been with her rose to return to the steading while Liv and Mor took their places beside Vigdis.

"Why don't you come back with us, Vigdis?" said Halla. "You need rest."

Vigdis shook her head. "I can't," she said, though she was sorely tempted to return to the bower and rest on her fur-padded bench, instead of the hudfat on the cold, wet ground. Her throat was hoarse from chanting and she longed for a hot bath. But she couldn't leave Åsa. None of the other apprentices had as much experience in guiding a sojourner through the Otherworld as Vigdis did. If anything went wrong for Åsa, Vigdis must be on hand to help her.

She picked up a bowl full of broth and climbed into the mound. For a day and a night Åsa had lain on the floor where she had fallen from the saddle, deep in a trance. She clutched the reins in one hand while the other was buried in the satchel, touching the necklace. Her chest rose and fell in regular breath, but she had not twitched a muscle as far as Vigdis could tell. The apprentice dared not move the queen, but she'd covered her with a cloak and put a pillow under her head.

She sat beside Åsa. Holding the bowl of broth in one hand, she slipped the other hand beneath Åsa's head and lifted. As the queen's head came up, her hair fell away. Vigdis caught her breath. Åsa's red-gold tresses lay on the pillow, her hair shorn short as a stubble field.

Vigdis shivered. What had befallen Åsa in the Otherworld?

She tipped the bowl and trickled a little broth into Åsa's mouth, careful not to let her choke. So far it had kept her alive, but for how much longer? If Heid died, Vigdis would be left to lead the other apprentices, a thing she did not feel ready to do. But if Åsa died, who would rule Tromøy until Halfdan came of age? The thought filled Vigdis with dread. Jarl Borg was an old man. He was not likely to live until Halfdan was old enough to take his mother's place. Olvir was a good leader, but he did not have the noble blood required to act as regent in Åsa's stead. He would face strong opposition from the other jarls. Tromøy would become a bone the warlords fought over. Devastation would fall on the ordinary folk. They would all pay the price, as they had when Gudrød murdered Åsa's father and brother and carried her off to Borre. Homes destroyed, fields burned, livestock slaughtered. Those who survived would starve in the cold.

It couldn't happen again.

Vigdis tucked Åsa's cloak around her. Sure that the queen was well covered and warm, Vigdis climbed back out of the mound. She settled down with the two replacement apprentices. With a deep intake of breath, the three women resumed chanting the vardlokkur, calling the spirits to protect their mistress in the Otherworld and help her in her quest.

RAGNHILD JERKED AWAKE, lifting her head from Murchad's chest as he convulsed. Panic tightened her chest. He gnashed his teeth and she felt around the bench for a strip of leather to slide into his mouth. Then she just held on tight and tried to keep him from crashing to the floor.

Unn hurried over and took hold of the Irishman's legs as he flailed, arching his back and writhing. The two women's eyes met as they struggled to restrain him.

As suddenly as it had begun, the fit was over. Murchad lay limp, barely breathing, face waxen beneath the pustules that covered it.

She stared at her husband in despair. If Murchad died...she drove the thought out of her head. The stink of the sick house was suddenly unbearable. Nausea swept over Ragnhild and she retched into the bucket that sat beside Murchad's bed. Fear gripped her. Was she getting sick too?

Three more of Eyvind's sailors had died during the night.

Their shipmates carried them away to the old storehouse, which was filling up with bodies. Its evil reek filled the air. They would have to burn it soon, but nursing the sick had left the able-bodied no time to tend to it.

The bell rang in the yard, signaling that the cooks had left breakfast outside the door. Three women hurried out and lugged in a cauldron of steaming porridge and one of hot broth. Ragnhild swallowed the warm porridge, feeling a little of her strength return. Then she filled a bowl with broth and tried to feed Murchad. She was able to trickle a little down his throat, enough to moisten it, no more. Not enough to keep him from wasting away.

She remembered him balancing on the ship's gunnels, laughing while he fought off pirates. It was impossible to reconcile those memories with the pale, wasted body that lay before her.

What if he died? Her heart clenched like a fist.

She had done everything she could to avoid marrying him. But now they were bonded for life as far as she was concerned. If she lost him now, all her plans for the future would be ashes.

Åsa had been gone a day and a night. It was clear that things were not going well, but there was nothing Ragnhild could do about it. For once in her life she couldn't solve her problems with a sword. The helplessness and confinement filled her with despair. They should have stayed home and none of this would have happened. She should have given Murchad the child he longed for. She'd believed she had all the time in the world to fulfill that wish. Now it might never come to pass.

As usual, this was all her fault. It seemed like everything she did brought disaster. If she got another chance, if Murchad survived, she'd do things differently.

She shook off those thoughts. They weren't helping. She needed to focus on what she could do—nursing Murchad and the others. It was little enough but it kept her occupied.

He was sleeping peacefully now, so she rose to tend some of the others. Heid was one of the worst off, her breath rumbling in her chest. The sorceress would stop breathing altogether for a time and then gasp for air. She'd taken almost no nourishment in two days. Ragnhild soaked a rag in a bowl of broth and wiped the völva's dry, cracked lips. Heid's eyes flickered open as she roused long enough to swallow some of the broth. Then, exhausted, she slipped back into unconsciousness.

Late in the afternoon a horn sounded, proclaiming the arrival of a ship. Ragnhild hurried out into the sunshine and down the trail. The lookout would warn them away, but she wanted to see who it was. It was a relief to escape the guesthouse, to have a distraction from sickness and death. She felt fine, no trace of fever or disease. Perhaps it was only the stench of the sick house that had made her vomit.

The ship entered the harbor and she recognized it as one of Olaf's fleet. She sloshed into the water to help bring it in.

Olaf's queen, Sonja, stood in the prow. She was dressed in an immaculate linen gown, a light cloak pinned at her throat with a jeweled brooch. Her blonde hair was braided and wound round her lovely head like a crown.

"Lady, you must leave," Ragnhild called. "We have sickness here."

Sonja smiled. "So I have heard. I am here to help."

"But the sickness passes from one to another, and some have died already."

Sonja said, "I have brought you some medicines. Let me help." She nodded at a sailor, who set out the boarding plank. She stepped onto it with agile grace and walked down it to the beach. "My crew will stay aboard the ship, anchored in the harbor."

A sailor handed down a linen-covered basket. Sonja took it and started up the trail. Ragnhild hurried after her.

Sonja looked her up and down, making Ragnhild feel like a cowherd in her soiled tunic and breeks. "You don't look sick."

"Some of us seem to be proof against it," said Ragnhild.

Sonja scanned the shoreline. "Where is Åsa?"

"She has gone on a spirit journey, to try to lift the ill magic that is causing this disease."

Sonja inhaled sharply. "She is very brave. I hope she will succeed. Where is Halfdan?"

"He's in the bower with his nurse, away from the sickness."

"Very wise. I will go and see to him." She handed her basket to Ragnhild. "Take these medicines to Heid."

Ragnhild took the basket, though she did not care for Sonja's dismissive tone. Who was this queen, to come sailing in and lord it over everyone? She was likely to be more burden than help, with her royal demands. "Heid has fallen ill."

Sonja stared at her. "If Åsa is on a spirit journey and Heid is sick, then who is in charge of Tromøy?"

Ragnhild said, "Before she departed, Åsa appointed Jarl Borg."

"That old man?" Sonja gave her a disparaging look.

Ragnhild bristled. "Jarl Borg may be old, but he is a great battle commander and more than capable of defending Tromøy." She turned on her heel and marched back into the guesthouse, leaving Sonja to find her way to the bower.

Unn took Sonja's basket from her, exclaiming over the medicines. "These will help us greatly. Queen Sonja is a skilled herbalist." This gave Ragnhild a little hope. Perhaps Olaf's queen was more than the pretty ornament she seemed.

An hour later, Sonja appeared at the guesthouse door. She stayed outside, speaking to Ragnhild through the open door. "I'll be leaving in the morning. I'm taking Halfdan with me to Vestfold until the plague is over. This is no place for Åsa's only son and heir. I will stay in the bower tonight and we'll sail in the morning."

Ragnhild's guts churned. She didn't like the way Sonja was taking over. "Does Jarl Borg know about this?"

"I did not consult him. He's an old man. He doesn't know what's best for a child."

Ragnhild was not at all sure that Åsa would want this woman to take her son away, but she couldn't think of a good reason to stop Sonja. She was right that Halfdan, the only heir to Tromøy, must be kept safe from the sickness at all costs.

Sonja departed for the bower, and Ragnhild returned to Murchad, still feeling unsettled. She was immediately swept up in the work of tending the sick and thought no more about the matter. But that night she slept uneasily, waking often, worried about Sonja taking Halfdan. It didn't seem right.

In the morning, it seemed she'd barely slept. She dragged herself up, feeling wretched. Her head ached and her stomach roiled. The guesthouse was stifling and evil smelling. She gave up the contents of her stomach again into the slops bucket and was grateful when Tova came to lug it away.

Murchad moaned and stirred restlessly. Ragnhild dipped a cloth in the fresh water bucket and mopped his brow. Unn brought her a steaming cup. "Here, see if you can get him to sip a little of this. It's a mixture of the herbs Queen Sonja brought us yesterday."

Ragnhild held the cup to her husband's lips. "Here, *a chroí*, take a little swallow for me." Still in his fevered trance, Murchad gulped down some of the warm liquid. It seemed to calm him. Ragnhild took a sip herself and her stomach settled a bit.

The door burst open and Brenna rushed in. "Is Halfdan here?" She scanned the room anxiously.

"No, we haven't seen him," said Ursa, looking up from the man she tended.

"The boy is missing!"

Ragnhild joined the others in a collective gasp. They all stared at the distraught fóstra. "Yesterday Queen Sonja said she would take him to Skiringssal for safety. The child threw a tantrum. He

75

refused to leave Tromøy. This morning, he's disappeared. We must find him."

Several women hurried after Brenna to join the search. Ragnhild gazed at Murchad, afraid to leave him. He could die while she was away. Her throat thickened and she swallowed back tears.

CHAPTER 8

Helheim

Åsa patted Svartfaxi's neck while staring up at the flames shooting from Hel's gate. Eruptions blasted tongues of fire high in the air. The horse had done the impossible and jumped onto the golden roof of the bridge, and leaped high to save her from falling, but the gate of Hel was much higher, and far more lethal.

"I can't ask this of you," she said. "You've been braver than any horse already."

Åsa gave Svartfaxi his head. He turned and walked away from the flaming gate while the jotun sneered.

Svartfaxi halted. He wheeled to face the wall of fire, tossed his head and neighed. He broke into a gallop, straight at the gates of Hel.

Åsa closed her eyes, mouthing chants. Without the necklace, she felt powerless.

The great horse shortened his stride, gathering energy with every step. Åsa clung on, chanting louder. His back rounded and she felt his hind legs push off. Her eyes flew open as he sprang into the air. Before them the Helgate blazed, flames licking high. Svartfaxi's forelegs reached out and they soared. Åsa's face heated and her breath seared her lungs. She smelled burnt hair as ends of her shorn tresses sizzled. Embers sparked and died in Svartfaxi's mane.

They soared through the fire, Svartfaxi's tail flaming behind him, filling the air with the stench of burning horsehair. The ground rushed up to meet them. Åsa held tight and squeezed her eyes closed, trying to merge her mind with her horse.

His hooves hit the ground. They landed hard and Åsa's eyes flew open as Svartfaxi stumbled, but he found his legs and raced away from the fire.

When he slowed to a walk, Åsa jumped off his back and beat out the fire on his tail with her cloak.

"Well," she said, surveying the damage, "your tail's a little shorter, but the fire's out."

Svartfaxi snorted and nuzzled the burnt stubble of her hair.

Åsa stared around her. The plains of Hel stretched as far as she could see. There were no landmarks of any kind. How would she find the Queen of Hel? And if she did, how would she get the necklace back?

She saw a figure striding toward them across the plain. For an instant she thought it was Hel, but then her heart leaped as she recognized the person.

"Heid!" she cried in relief. "Thank the gods you're here."

The völva looked at her sourly. "You look a fright. What happened to your hair? Never mind. Let's find that wretched queen."

HEID LED the way across the parched plain. Svartfaxi plodded beside them. It seemed the leap over the Helgate had drained his spirit. Åsa worried about him. Could a dead horse die again? Or was there something worse than death?

Heid was grimly silent.

"How are things back on Tromøy?" Åsa ventured.

"Dire. We must hurry." The sorceress kept up a fast pace. Åsa realized that Heid wasn't hobbling. She was striding. Her injuries must not have followed her to Helheim.

"There's one problem. A rooster stole the necklace," Åsa said. "He's taken it to Hel."

"We'll have to get it back," said Heid.

"How will we find Hel's hall?" Åsa asked.

"We're heading there now." The völva's reply was clipped.

Åsa tried to get her to say more. "Have you been to Helheim before?"

"A völva travels many paths," Heid said shortly.

Åsa gave up trying to get more information from the sorceress. They had covered a lot of ground quickly, and now in the distance a storm cloud hovered low over the roof of a great hall, sending sleet down upon the thatched roof.

"Eljudnir, Hel's hall," said Heid.

As they drew near, Åsa could see that the cloud sat stationary over the hall. They walked into the storm, blinded by sleet that stung like needles, struggling against a headwind that seemed determined to blow them away from their goal. By the time they fought their way to the door they were soaking wet and shivering.

Åsa brushed the sleet from her eyes. The door was twice as tall as she, made of oak intricately carved with twining beasts whose eyes were red jewels. The creatures seemed to writhe and flick their tongues at her.

Heid raised her iron staff and pounded on the door, sending the beasts scattering through the cracks.

Nothing happened.

Heid pounded again, uttering spells that demanded entrance.

They seemed to do the trick, for the door creaked open to reveal a dim interior. In the gloomy recesses, something moved.

A voice came, faint as the groan of a dying man. "Who knocks on my lady's door?"

"I am the völva Heid, and with me is Åsa, Queen of Agder." Åsa shivered at the compelling galdr tones in the sorceress's voice. "Do not hinder us. We have urgent business with your lady."

"My lady sees no one," moaned the voice.

The wind shrieked at their backs, as if trying to tear them from the doorway. "Let us pass or I will curse you," said Heid.

A laugh like a rusty hinge emanated from the shadows. "I fear no curses. Nothing worse can be done to me than to be doomed to stay here until Ragnarok."

Heid seemed to grow, her shadow looming into the darkness. "I have powers of which you do not know. I can curse you in ways you have never imagined." Her voice resonated into the room. "You will let us pass."

After a long pause, a sigh escaped the shadows. "Very well, witch, enter if you dare."

Åsa stepped forward, but Heid flung out her staff and blocked her way. Åsa looked down and gasped. Beneath her feet yawned a vast pit, nearly invisible in the gloom. It stretched the width of the entry, so deep she could not see the bottom.

Beyond the pit came a chuckle. "Mind the gap."

"Follow me," said Heid. Gathering her robes in one hand, she sprang across the pit. Åsa looked into the depths and quailed, but if the sorceress could make the jump, so could she. She took a deep breath and launched herself into the air. She fairly flew across the chasm, landing beside the völva.

She turned back to Svartfaxi. "Come on, boy," she said. After jumping the Hel gate, this should be easy for him. But the horse balked, tossing his head.

Åsa was filled with foreboding. What did Svartfaxi sense that would make him refuse to enter? Well, she would find out soon enough. There was no turning back. She bowed her head to the black horse. "You have brought me far enough. I release you, Svartfaxi, and I thank you for your service."

He whinnied and tossed his head, then turned back the way they had come. A great sense of loss overwhelmed Åsa as the black horse trotted away. Svartfaxi halted in the shadows and looked back at her.

"Come," Heid said.

With dread in her heart, Åsa turned away from the horse and followed the sorceress into the dim interior. The air was thin and smelled of rotting things.

The servant who had greeted them materialized from the gloom, a look of disappointment on his face. He was thin as a skeleton and gray as the walls. His hair hung in stringy hanks, his jowls sagged, and he wore a robe of faded rags. He carried an iron staff. "I am called Ganglati. Follow me."

Ganglati led them through the entryway to another oaken door, bound with brass and swarming with carved serpents. He struck the door as Heid had done, and the beasts scattered, then he pushed the door open and stood aside.

Within, a longfire blazed, casting a dull light, but the room was frigid. Icy water dripped from the thatch, and snow covered the rushes on the floor. If anything, it was colder inside than out.

The ceiling seemed to writhe, and as she stared upwards, Åsa saw the roof was thatched with living serpents, woven together. It was their venom that dripped, hitting the frozen floor with a sizzle.

The benches lining the walls were empty, but at the far end of the hall, the high seat was occupied. A tall woman, richly dressed, sat there. At her feet lay an enormous wolf, twice the size of those who had chased them through the iron forest. He was bound by what appeared to be a silk ribbon to a boulder sunk into the floor, as if it had been hurled there by a mighty force. Åsa sucked in her breath.

The wolf eyed them, slavering.

Beside the woman sat the most beautiful man Åsa had ever seen. His golden hair shone and his smile lit the gloom. From his arms hung golden chains. The woman gazed at him in adoration.

In profile, the woman's face was hidden by her long dark hair. She turned her head toward them as they entered, and Åsa gasped. One side of her face was young and beautiful, the other a rotting corpse, a shade of blue so dark it was almost black.

On the woman's breast gleamed the Irish necklace, the dead hand nowhere to be seen. On the back of her chair, the sooty red cock preened.

Heid stopped before the longfire and inclined her head. "Greetings, Hel, queen of the dead."

"Greetings, sorceress. Tell me, what brings so powerful a völva to my hall while you yet live?" Hel demanded.

Heid dragged Åsa forward. "This woman is Åsa Haraldsdottir, Queen of Agder. She seeks your help."

"What does a living woman want from me? Speak, girl," said Hel.

Åsa's throat was so dry she could barely get the words out. "Lady, I seek my kinswoman here. She has laid a curse upon my kingdom. I must convince her to lift that curse before all my people perish."

"And why has your kinswoman cursed your kingdom?" Hel's living eye sparkled with malice.

"Because I cut off her head," whispered Åsa.

The queen of the dead laughed in delight. "So, you sent her to my kingdom, but now you regret the consequences. That's rich." She leaned forward in her high seat. "And how will you persuade her to lift her curse?"

Åsa clenched her jaw. "I had planned to give her the necklace you are wearing."

"This is too good!" Hel guffawed. Then she sat up and fixed Åsa with her good eye. "Why this necklace in particular?"

"She values it above all else. It is the only thing that might persuade her to help me."

Hel fingered the golden chain. "I can understand that. I'm rather fond of it myself. How do you propose to get it from me?"

Åsa gulped. "I do not know, Lady."

Hel laughed again and turned to her companion. "Well, Baldr, what should I ask her for in exchange?"

When the man beside Hel smiled, he glowed brighter, so beautiful that Åsa could scarcely breathe. When Baldr turned his smile on Åsa, she could understand why the queen of the dead refused to part with him. Åsa noticed that Hel sat with the beautiful half of her face toward him. Chained as he was, the god may never have seen her bad side.

"I think you should just give her the necklace," he said. "That would be nice."

Åsa's heart leaped in hope, but Hel chortled. "Oh, you're as funny as you are beautiful, my love. No, there would be no sport in that at all."

Heid glowered at the Queen of Hel. "Stop toying with the girl. Tell us what you require for the necklace."

Hel stopped laughing and glared back at Heid. Åsa held her breath, fearing the consequences of the völva's insolence. "Very well, witch," said Hel. She stroked the Irish gold. "This is a beautiful, ancient charm, with strong magic. Giving it up would be quite a loss to me. Freyja has always thought she was better than me, but this necklace gives me the same power and status she has. The only way I'd give it up is if I had something she does not. And that could only be one thing." Hel smiled at Åsa. "Bring me Brisingamen, and this necklace is yours."

Åsa gasped. "How could I get Freyja to give me her necklace?"

Hel grinned at her. "Why don't you ask her? I'd like to see her reaction." The wolf drooled and strained at his bonds. "Now go. My brother, Fenrir, grows hungry."

Heid took Åsa's arm and guided her away from the high seat. She muttered, "The wolf can't get loose from those bonds. They were made by the Svartálfar and they will hold until Ragnarok. But there is no time to lose."

CHAPTER 9

Svartálfheim

A s they departed Hel's great hall, Åsa said, "How can I get Brisingamen from Freyja?"

"You can't," Heid murmured. "Only Loki has succeeded in taking the goddess's treasure, and you know how that turned out. But the dark álfar made Brisingamen. You may have better luck persuading them to make you another like Freyja's necklace."

Åsa shuddered, thinking of the price Freyja had paid the dark álfar to make Brisingamen—sleeping with four of them. "How will we find Svartálfheim?"

"Their realm is near, under an adjacent root of Yggdrasil. Come, I know the way." Heid set off across the gray plain toward a distant mountain.

Åsa wondered how much more of the Otherworld the sorceress was familiar with. "How can we persuade them to make us a necklace like Brisingamen?"

"The dark álfar are vain and proud of their art, none more so than their king, Dvalin. His vanity is his weakness. It has been used to trick him before."

The idea of trying to trick the king of Svartálfheim filled Åsa with doubt. She was glad Heid would be there to use her wiles.

Without Svartfaxi, they had to cross the barren plain on foot. Heid moved faster than Åsa had ever seen, and they reached the mountain all too soon. A cavern yawned on the rock face, dark as anything Åsa had been through since she arrived in the Other-world. She hesitated at the entrance.

"Come." Heid gestured impatiently, taking Åsa's arm and propelling her into the cave. The völva shook her iron staff and the end glowed, casting a faint light, just enough to reveal the cavern floor.

Somewhere in the darkness, there was the beating of wings that could be bats—or worse. Åsa stayed close to the sorceress as they traversed the cavern floor, deeper into the dark.

Eventually a faint radiance appeared in the distance. The quality of light was different than anything Åsa had seen before, like the glow of a thousand stars. As they approached, the light enlarged until it revealed itself to be an opening in the rock.

Heid halted at the entrance and Åsa gazed inside with awe. It opened onto a vast cavern, its ceiling vanishing out of sight. Thousands of gems set into the granite walls glittered like multi-colored stars. They reflected off the smooth rock floor and cast a glow bright and warm as daylight.

"Remember, the dark álfar are very clever. Don't underesti-mate them," said Heid. She let go of Åsa's arm and turned back toward Hel's hall.

Åsa whirled on her. "You're not coming with me?"

"I wore my welcome out with Dvalin long ago. I would not be an asset to you here."

Åsa couldn't believe Heid was leaving her to deal with the Svartálfar alone. "I have no weapon, nothing to bargain with."

"I'm sorry. My presence would only make things worse. You're a clever woman. Remember, the Svartálfar are vain about their work. And there are no female dark álfar. You should be able to use that to your advantage."

Åsa stared after the sorceress. Heid strode on toward Hel's hall without looking back. Soon the faint glimmer of the völva's staff vanished into the darkness.

Åsa turned toward the vast, shimmering cavern. The sound of marching feet echoed in the distance, signaling the approach of a troop of warriors. She straightened her back and faced them.

The Svartálfar were short and stocky, just as they were said to be. Their chain mail gleamed silver in the cavern's light, helmets flashing, speartips pointed toward the ceiling. When they reached her, their leader held up his hand and the war band stopped, marching in place for three beats. Åsa's courage drained away.

"What brings you here, human?" demanded the leader. His beard was gray, and he was a little shorter than Åsa, but he kept enough distance between them that his steely gaze met hers directly.

Åsa gritted her teeth and squared her shoulders. "I would speak with your king."

He gave her an appraising look. "King Dvalin does not receive your kind."

Åsa realized that she must not look very queenly, with her shorn, burnt hair and ragged, filthy clothes. She took a deep breath and summoned all her galdr into her voice, casting it like a spear at the dark álf. "He will speak with me. I am Åsa, Queen of Agder."

"Oh, a queen of men, are you?" said the leader, obviously not impressed by her galdr voice. "Well, by all means, let me take you to him. He might find you amusing."

The sneer in the Svartálf's tone unsettled Åsa, but she followed him. She had little choice.

He led her through the cavern into a room even more vast and glowing than the one they had just left. Like the other, the rock walls were set with glittering gems of all colors, but the ceiling, walls, and floor shone golden. Åsa stifled her awe and kept pace with the Svartálf leader.

At the far end of the hall rose the high seat. Nine steps led up to a broad platform. On each step an álf stood at attention, armor gleaming, spear clutched at his side. The high seat itself was carved with entwined beasts, gilded and set with more precious gems.

On it sat a dark álf resplendent in a gilded chain-mail brynja. His dark beard bristled and his black hair curled from under his golden helm to his burly shoulders. His beefy hands were bejeweled with rings. Beside him rested an axe with a silver head, inlaid with glowing runes.

"Well, Fundinn, who have you brought me?" The Svartálf king's voice boomed in the chamber, echoing off the high ceilings.

"A human woman, Lord. She claims to be a queen of men."

The king leaned forward and peered at Åsa. "She doesn't look like much. Come closer, human, let me see you."

Åsa took one step forward and drew herself up as tall as possible, lifting her chin to return the Svartálf lord's stare. She stopped her hand from going to her cropped and singed hair. Once more she summoned her galdr voice. "I am Åsa, queen of Agder."

"Are you, then?" said the king. "I am Dvalin, king of Svartálfheim, lord of the underworld and all its riches. What brings you to my realm?"

Åsa bristled at his sneering tone. "I hear that you are passable smiths," she replied, loading her voice with scorn.

It was Dvalin's turn to bristle. "The metalwork of the Svartálfar is the finest in all the nine realms. Odin himself prizes the famous ring Draupnir, that sheds eight more rings of pure gold every ninth night, and Gungnir, his mighty spear."

Åsa took heart at the defensiveness in the dark álf's tone.

Heid's advice had been sound. "I have heard that you claim to be the greatest smiths, but I find it hard to believe that your work is finer than the smiths of Ireland."

"There are no finer smiths anywhere!" Dvalin thundered. "We created golden tresses for the goddess Sif, making her more beautiful than she was before Loki cut off her hair." He sneered down at Åsa's shorn hair. "That's something you could do with. For Frey, we built a ship that he can fold so small he can stow it in his pocket. And, of course, we made Freyja's golden necklace, Brisingamen."

"Yet Hel wears a golden necklace crafted by the Irish, and it is said to be finer and more powerful than Brisingamen," said Åsa.

"That is not true!"

"Well, naturally you would say so. But that's what I've been told."

"Who dared say that?"

Åsa tried not to wince at his thunderous voice. She kept her tone casual. "Oh, I've heard it from a number of sources. It's common knowledge. Hel herself has said so."

By now King Dvalin's face was red and his eyes were nearly popping out of his head. "Lies!"

Encouraged, Åsa kept up her attack. "I'd like to believe you, Lord Dvalin, but how can you prove it?"

"Bring the necklace here, we will examine it."

"That I cannot do, for Hel is loath to part with her treasure. Besides, you are not an impartial judge. It should be judged by Queen Hel herself. Perhaps the goddess Freyja would loan you Brisingamen so they can be compared?"

"The goddess Freyja will not part with her treasure any more than Hel will."

Åsa frowned in feigned worry. "Well, I don't know how we can resolve this. If your work is as fine as you say, it certainly isn't right for the people in Helheim to call you second rate."

"Second rate!" screamed Dvalin. "We crafted Thor's hammer,

Mjölnir, in our workshop—I am sure you have heard of the greatest weapon in the nine worlds."

Unruffled, Åsa continued. "I have heard that your smiths made the handle of Thor's mighty hammer too short, and the god can only wield it with one hand rather than both."

The Svartálf king spat. "That was Loki's fault! I punished those smiths severely for letting him distract them from their work."

Åsa smiled with sympathy. "I am only telling you what people say."

Dvalin's face was nearly purple. "My smiths will make an exact copy of Brisingamen, and Queen Hel can judge them. That will put a stop to this slander." Spittle showered the air. He was past the point of rationality.

Åsa tensed. She nearly had him. "Very well, I will carry your copy to her to prove that your work is superior."

"It will be done!" thundered Dvalin.

Åsa allowed herself a tiny smile.

"Come," Dvalin said. "I will show you the smithy and you can see them at work for yourself."

He took her arm firmly and led her down the steps to a narrow passageway that went deep inside the mountain.

Far down the passage she heard the familiar ring of hammer on metal, and soon they arrived at the smith's workshop. Åsa welcomed the familiar smell of hot metal and bone coal fire. As the king entered, the smiths all bowed their heads briefly before resuming their work.

There were nine of them, the sacred number, the same as Heid's apprentices. They were covered with soot from head to toe, but their eyes gleamed in their dark faces. They were dressed alike in dirty tunics and trews, each with a pointed red cap on his head.

Åsa approached their workbench and caught her breath at the blaze of gold. Two smiths forced golden rods through drawplates, making them into fine wire of thinner gauge. Though their hands were big as ham hocks, they were able to manipulate the golden wire with great skill. Others carved intricate molds of beeswax. Their focus on their work was intense, and they did not look up at her again. Åsa said nothing, only watched them work as she was accustomed to watch Ulf in Tromøy's smithy. Their quiet, serious presence made Åsa feel safe as she had with Ulf. She wished he were here with her. He would marvel at the álfar's methods.

Dvalin said, "I have a new project for you." The smiths looked up at their king, no expression evident in their dirty faces. "You will make a necklace of gold. It must be an exact copy of Brisingamen. It must be good enough to convince the most discerning person. My reputation relies on it. If you do not succeed, I will make you sorry."

The smiths said nothing, just resumed their work. They didn't seem cowed, but Åsa sensed a hint of resistance in their upright posture, as if they were forged from the iron they worked.

Dvalin turned to her with a lascivious grin. "It will take some time to forge this necklace. While you wait, perhaps we can become better acquainted."

Åsa cringed, realizing she would have to spend that time dodging his attentions. She had resisted other kings who tried to force their attentions on her—with a sword. Now she was weaponless.

But not unarmed.

Dvalin's gaze burned into her as she watched the smiths. Åsa ignored him, keeping her focus on the work.

"Come, let me show you to your chamber where you can refresh yourself before we feast." Åsa followed him, looking forward to a chance to be alone where she could drop her guard.

He guided her back down the same passage that led to the smithy and stopped in front of a rune-carved door. He pushed it open to reveal a bejeweled grotto that took her breath away. The bed was huge, its headboard and posts carved with runes and studded with gems.

Åsa stepped inside. On the wall hung a polished circle of silver the size of a platter. She could see her reflection in it, and she looked bad. Her face was almost as dirty as the smiths, and her burnt, shorn hair stood up like stubble in a field. Her clothes were ragged and filthy.

In the mirror, she saw Dvalin's reflection in the doorway, leering at her.

Gooseflesh rose on her arms. "My lord. I need some time to make myself presentable."

"Very well," he said, reluctantly. "I will come back to fetch you in a little while." When he made no move to leave, she gently pushed the door closed on him.

Åsa heaved a sigh of relief and surveyed the room. Clean clothes had been laid out on the bed—a man's tunic and breeches, but they were finely woven of a good quality wool. The tunic was a deep red and the breeches lichen green. Soft leather boots slouched on the floor beside them. A bowl of warm water steamed gently over the brazier.

After washing and doing the best she could with her hair, she pulled the clean clothes on gratefully, happy to find they were a decent fit. The baggy style was forgiving of size, and her leather belt cinched the tunic close to her body.

A knock sounded and the door opened. "Come, it is time to feast," said Dvalin. His gaze raked her up and down, making her cringe. "You clean up well." He put out his arm, and she had little choice but to take it and let him lead her to the hall for the evening meal.

He seated her beside him on the high seat as befitted a noble guest. He leaned close to her until she could feel his breath in her ear. She caught a whiff of rotting teeth. "What did you think of the work of my smiths?"

She leaned away and looked him in the eye. "They are a marvel. I so wish my own smith could be here to see their work."

The king laughed. "Be careful what you wish for, Lady. We are not so far from Helheim."

At his words, worry nipped at her. What was happening in Tromøy now? She had come far, yet had so much farther to go. She wanted the Svartálf smiths to work fast. But carefully enough to produce a replica that would convince Hel.

"You are very quiet," said Dvalin.

"It's been a long day."

"When my smiths create a copy of Brisingamen, we will present it to Queen Hel together. I can't wait to see her reaction."

This gave Åsa another worry. She would have to get away from Dvalin with the necklace and find her way back to Helheim on her own.

Her worries were interrupted when a troupe of Svartálf entertainers gathered by the longfire. Dvalin turned his attention to the entertainment. Minstrels played somber tunes on harps and bone flutes, and a skáld told the well-known tale of Völund, the smith who was kidnapped and crippled by an evil king. The king forced Völund to create precious things for him. Such was Völund's skill as a smith that he was able to fashion a pair of wings and fly to freedom, but not before taking his revenge by killing the king's sons and impregnating his daughter. It was a story Åsa had heard many times in Tromøy's hall, though in the Svartálf version Völund was an álf prince.

When the tale was told, Åsa cast about for an excuse to get away from Dvalin quickly, before he could force his attentions on her. She yawned. "I am weary. I must retire."

Dvalin looked pleased. "I will escort you to your chamber," he said with a smirk that sent a shudder down her spine. He rose and put out his arm. She hid a grimace as she took it.

They walked down the hall, Åsa avoiding Dvalin's persistent

gaze. When they reached her door, she slipped inside, eager for rest.

Dvalin made as if to follow her in, but she got the door half-closed before he could enter. "Thank you for a marvelous day, Lord King. I must rest now. I look forward to seeing you in the morning."

She shut the door on his leering face.

The down mattress was deep and luxurious, and she longed to rest. What if Dvalin came back? She didn't want a confrontation with the Svartálf king before the necklace was complete. She couldn't stay here. She must find somewhere to hide.

After waiting a sufficient interval to make sure Dvalin was gone, she opened the door a crack and peered out. The corridor was empty and she stole out into the hallway. Where could she hide? As she walked in the opposite direction from the feasting hall, the familiar ring of hammer on metal echoed down the passage-way. The smith's workshop. It was a comforting sound, reminding her of Ulf's workshop, a place where she'd always found refuge.

The Svartálfar looked up as she entered the smithy, eyes gleaming in their soot-covered faces. They sized her up, then immediately turned back to their work.

As they worked, they hummed. The sound reverberated off the cavern walls, sending chills down Åsa's spine. The humming was familiar and reminded her of chanting in the bower with Heid's apprentices while they wove.

Without thinking, she joined her voice to theirs and a great power welled up within as she uttered the words she had learned by heart, words no human understood.

The Svartálfar stared at her, open-mouthed. She was shocked to see that they had no tongues. Dvalin's punishment.

That was why they hummed. Without tongues, they could not enunciate. If she had disliked the álf king before, now a white-hot fury rose in her.

Åsa chanted the words to their familiar music, and she felt an air of acceptance from the álfar.

The smiths worked on for a while, then set down their tools and laid out pallets stuffed with straw on the hard floor of the workshop. Åsa was afraid to leave. What if Dvalin was lurking outside her door?

As if they could read her mind, the smiths presented her with a pallet of her own and a woolen blanket. Touched, she took it with a nod of gratitude and made her bed in their midst. Burrowing under the blanket, she fell asleep feeling safe for the first time since she'd left home.

The smell of barley porridge woke her. The aroma rose from a cauldron simmering over the forge. One smith approached her with a steaming bowl and a mug of small beer.

"Thank you," she said. She looked up at the others, who were watching closely. "I thank you all for your hospitality."

They shyly bobbed their heads. They were all dressed exactly alike, in dirty work clothes and pointed caps. Their soot-darkened faces were hard to tell apart. They must have names, but they would never be able to tell her.

One of them appeared to be their leader, and she marked his appearance so she would remember. He was a little taller than the others, perhaps a little thinner, though it was hard to tell beneath their tunics and breeches.

As soon as she'd finished her breakfast, she took her leave and hurried to the great hall so Dvalin would not find her among the smiths. It would go hard with them if he realized they were hiding her from him.

Dvalin looked up with a hopeful smile when she entered. "I hope you slept well, my dear."

"Yes, I did, thank you."

"I came to check on you last night, and you were not in your chamber."

Åsa thought fast. "I—I was restless, and I walked the passageway to help me get to sleep."

Dvalin frowned but let the matter drop. "Today I will show you more of the marvels of my realm."

"I would like that very much, Lord," said Åsa truthfully.

After breakfast, Dvalin called for a cart drawn by two goats. They drove down a passageway deep into the mountain, where dark álfar worked in mining silver. They were dirty, ragged, and looked half-starved. None of them glanced up as their king drove by, but kept their eyes dully focused on their work. Åsa wondered if other workers in Svartálfheim were in such a sorry state.

"Your riches are vast, my lord," she said, to mask her rising anger.

"Yes, they are almost limitless. I have all I need here, except for one thing."

Sensing she was being led, Åsa made no reply.

"Can you guess what that one thing is?" Dvalin prompted her.

There was no way to avoid taking the bait. "And what is that?"

"I have no queen."

A chill ran down Åsa's spine.

"You see, there are no female Svartálfar."

"Oh," said Åsa faintly.

"There is only one way for me to get an heir," he said.

"Oh, my, look at those gems," she exclaimed in a desperate bid to change the subject.

Dvalin was not to be sidetracked. "I can take a human queen."

Åsa's stomach heaved. She didn't dare to look at him.

"It's possible for the dark álfar to breed with humans."

She wanted to leap out of the cart and run. Instead she said nothing, swallowing hard to force down the bile that rose in her throat. Fortunately Dvalin let the subject drop.

That night, after another feast, she eluded Dvalin once again by claiming exhaustion from the active day. After he left her at her chamber door, she made her way to the smithy. The dark álfar smiled in welcome, and she joined their chants. She watched their progress anxiously, smiling encouragement while inwardly worrying about what was happening back on Tromøy. Would Eyvind still be alive when she returned?

When the smiths laid down their tools, they gestured for her to make her bed in their midst once again.

Late in the night, something woke her. Someone was creeping into the smithy. She peeked out of her bedding to glimpse Dvalin, searching through the sleeping álfar. She buried her head under the blanket and stayed very still as she listened to his stealthy footsteps. He stopped right above her and she held her breath.

After a long pause, his footsteps receded. When she felt certain he'd gone, she popped her head out of the blankets and met the stares of the smiths.

Åsa breathed a sigh of relief. Since Dvalin had not found her, he would not likely search for her here again. Still, she must be careful. After waiting long enough to be sure the Svartálf king was gone, she got up and hurried back to her room.

Far ahead in the gem-lit passage, she spotted Dvalin's stocky figure. Her pace slowed to keep her distance behind him until she reached the door of her room. When he rounded the bend, she ducked inside. She undressed and climbed into the luxurious bed. Hoping the álf king had given up his search for the night, she fell asleep.

Hours later, she woke, dressed, and found her way to the great hall where Dvalin awaited her on the high seat. He did not ask her again where she went at night, nor did he mention marriage. She dared hope he had given up. He took her on another long trip in his goat-drawn cart, careening through the narrow, winding passages of his domain to endless mines of precious stones and metals. The workers lived and worked in squalor, eking out a rough existence. They slept on pallets on the hard rock. They were thin and wiry, and food appeared to be scarce.

Åsa pretended to be impressed, but the plight of the workers stoked her fury and hatred. Outside of the royal caverns where Dvalin held court, Svartálfheim was a wasteland of poverty and squalor. The courtiers seemed to be the only ones who lived in comfort, in lavish rooms like hers off the golden hall. The guards and soldiers ranked below them, living in sparse barracks, but at least they had regular food and cots.

The smiths, with their snug workshop, were quite well-off compared to the miners. After the day spent with Dvalin, Åsa returned to the smithy where she watched them forge the necklace, link by golden link. Her chants accompanied the álfar as they hummed and engraved runes into the precious metal. Tiny gems twinkled in the gold, forming constellations.

The caverns had no day or night, though there was a rhythm of sleep and wakefulness, and regular meal times, but even so Åsa lost track of time. She feared that everyone in Tromøy would be dead by the time she got home, but there was nothing she could do to hurry things along.

Then she came into the smithy after dinner and the smiths' hammers were silent. They stood back with shy smiles as Åsa approached the worktable and caught her breath. The intricate design of intertwined serpents seemed alive, its eyes winking jewels. She reached out cautiously and touched the gold. The power surged up her arm, every bit as strong as the Irish necklace—yet different. While the Irish necklace's magic had felt foreign, strange, in a way resistant, this was familiar, comfortable...Norse magic.

The head smith nodded at the necklace. She lifted it off the table. It was surprisingly light. She lowered it over her head and laid it on her chest. Immediately, it began to vibrate with its power—warm, searing, yet gentle. Her eyebrows shot up and she stared at the smiths. They smiled and nodded in satisfaction.

At that moment King Dvalin swept in. His predatory gaze found her. Then his eyes dropped to the necklace on her chest and he stared greedily. "Good, good, I see you have completed it. Let me feel its power." He advanced on Åsa, his hand reaching for the gold. She shrank away as he fingered the necklace. "It certainly appears to be a match for Brisingamen. I can't wait to present it to Hel's court. We leave immediately."

She had to find a way to delay their departure so she could escape. "Lord, I believe the smiths have a few finishing touches." She looked at them and they nodded in unison. "Come back tomorrow and it will be ready."

"It had better be," he said, glaring at the smiths, who studied the ground. "The last time they displeased me, they lost their tongues."

How would she get away from Dvalin with the necklace and find her way to Hel's hall? She'd been pondering that all the while the álfar worked. The only way was to steal it and sneak out of Svartálfheim.

It had to be tonight.

CHAPTER 10

Odinssal, Vingulmark

King Alfgeir watched Jarl Orm of Telemark lower his bulk onto the guest seat. Alfgeir's new queen, a plump, shy girl of fifteen, served the welcome ale. Alfgeir had married for her father's property, good forestland. The girl was proving competent enough at running the hall.

Orm took the horn and drained it, the ale running down his greasy beard. Orm's once impressive strength had run to fat. Alfgeir wrinkled his nose. He himself was still as tall and fit as he'd been in his youth.

"What brings you here?" Alfgeir asked. He and Orm had never been friends, but they'd banded together as allies when it suited them. This was no social call. Orm must need something to have sailed one of his leaky buckets all the way from Grenland.

"Tromøy has sickness," Orm said, his beady eyes glowing. "I hear they are dying like flies. Now's the time to attack. I'll take the girl-queen to wife and become king of Agder."

Orm hadn't changed. He was still a greedy fool. "You remember what she did to her last husband."

Orm laughed. "Gudrød was never on his guard. He underestimated the girl. I won't make the same mistake."

"She's hardly a girl anymore. She's won a few battles. And she has a son by Gudrød," Alfgeir reminded him.

Orm grinned wolfishly. "She does right now. That can change. Children die every day."

"Olaf is her ally. You know he'll come to her defense. They fought off the Danish fleet together."

"That's why I need you," said Orm. "I can take her, but not the two of them at once. We need to split them up, make sure Olaf can't come to her aid."

Wariness came over Alfgeir. "He's my grandson."

"You took back Vingulmark from the boy after Gudrød died."

"Olaf is a boy no longer. He's proven himself in battle several times."

"Are you saying you're afraid of him?" Orm taunted.

The king of Vingulmark bristled. Who was this fat old man to call him a coward? "Of course not. As if I'd be afraid of my own grandson. But I don't want to harm him. If anything happens to my sons, he might end up being my heir."

"You don't have to hurt the boy. All I need from you is to keep Olaf occupied while I attack Tromøy. Lure his fleet up north to Borre so that he can't get back to Tromøy until I've taken it. For that I'll reward you handsomely."

The fat man's plan was beginning to interest Alfgeir. There was little risk for him, and the potential for gain. "How handsomely?"

"I'll give you your choice of a quarter of Agder's hinterlands. There's a lot of rich farmland there."

Alfgeir snorted. Tromøy's hinterlands would be worth little without access to the coast. "Half of Agder's hinterlands, and good sea access."

Orm squinched up his face until his beady eyes disappeared in rolls of fat. "I'm taking all the risk, mind you."

Alfgeir shrugged and said nothing.

After a long silence, Orm huffed. "All right, half of Agder, and access to the sea—south of Tromøy."

Alfgeir stroked his beard, pondering the offer. It would give him access to the Skagerrak sea far to the south, an advantage, but keep him away from Orm's ports. "That's a long way for my ships to sail."

Orm shrugged. "I'm not asking you to do much for it. Just distract your grandson for a day."

Alfgeir let the proposal settle. Finally he said, "We have a deal."

"On the new moon then." Alfgeir signaled for more ale and they drank to their new venture.

CHAPTER 11

Svartálfheim

Asa watched the smiths pack the necklace carefully in its oaken chest. Fortunately the chest did not have a lock. She hated what she was about to do, but what choice did she have? Lives were at stake.

After they bedded down, she lay in the dark, listening to their snores, gathering her courage. After what seemed like an eternity, she rose stealthily from her pallet. All was still, the álfar breathing rhythmically.

Feeling like a traitor, she crept to the chest and raised the lid carefully, glad the smiths kept the hinges oiled. There on a bed of wool lay the necklace, gleaming with a light of its own. She reached in and picked it up, feeling the vibration surge up her arms. She dropped it over her head and tucked it under her tunic, steadying herself while the power flooded into her chest. It both calmed her and gave her strength.

Taking a deep breath, she started across the workshop, stepping carefully over the sleeping bodies. It had to look like a theft, so Dvalin would not blame the smiths and punish them. She refused to think what he might do to her if he caught her.

Just as she reached the door, a hand snaked out and grabbed her ankle. She flailed her arms, stifling a shriek, and nearly fell. Looking down, her eyes met the álf leader's gaze.

She waited quietly while he got to his feet. The others rose and soon she was surrounded by Svartálfar. Her shoulders slumped. She hadn't fooled them at all. There was no getting away.

The lead smith held a finger to his lips. To her surprise, he reached up and took off his pointed red cap and set it on her head. Then he put his hand into the cold ashes of the forge and smeared her face with soot. He stood back and gazed at her, then around at the others. They all nodded. Åsa realized that with her short hair and dirty face, she could pass for a young álf.

Next he handed her an axe. Its blade sparked silver, engraved with runes. As she gripped the handle, her courage rose.

The smiths stepped back and bowed, clearing a path toward the door.

Åsa could hardly believe it. "Thank you!" she mouthed silently. Shy smiles lit up their faces.

With tears rising to her eyes, she turned away from her friends. They stood silently watching as she walked out of the smithy for the last time.

Outside, Åsa leaned against the wall, swallowing hard. She'd never see them again, never know what happened to them. Her heart burned with grief and fear. What would Dvalin do when he found her and the necklace gone? If he suspected the smiths had anything to do with her escape with the necklace, the álf king would go hard on them. She shuddered at the thought of how he would punish them. A poor reward for their kindness and protection. Yet she had to save Tromøy.

There was a rustle behind her. She turned to see the smiths gathered in the doorway, waving her off.

Encouraged, she squared her shoulders and set off to find the way out of Svartálfheim.

Åsa crept along the passageway, praying she would not meet Dvalin roaming the halls looking for her. She hoped he would be convinced that she had acted alone.

When she reached the entrance to the feasting hall, her shoulders sagged in relief. She paused before entering the golden cavern, which still shone light as day. Peering through the entrance, she saw no one. The high seat and benches stood vacant, and the longfire had burned down to embers. But the vast chamber cast no shadows. There was no cover.

She tiptoed in, praying no one would enter, for they would surely see her. Skirting the walls, she stole across the room. At the far end, a glimmer of silver made Åsa's heart beat faster. The silver cavern—the same one she had entered from Hel.

At the far end, a dark álf guarded the exit. He paced back and forth across the cavern's opening, a long-handled, double-bladed axe over his shoulder.

There was no sneaking past him. She would have to brazen it out. Åsa stepped into the open, trying to emulate the rolling swagger of the álfar. She was a little taller than most Svartálfar, but she hoped that since she was alone her height wouldn't be so noticeable. With her tunic and breeks, sooty face, and pointed red cap she might pass for a smith.

She approached the guard, keeping her gaze fixed on the ground.

"Evening," he greeted.

Åsa nodded her head.

"How go things in the smithy?" he asked.

Just what she needed, a chatty sentry. But the smiths were mute, so she tried shrugging her shoulders, hoping that would suffice.

But no, this sentry was obviously bored. "I hear you fellows made a grand necklace for that human queen. A match for Brisingamen."

Åsa nodded again, ducking her head in what she hoped passed for modesty.

"I haven't seen King Dvalin this excited since he presented the lady Freyja with her necklace—and collected his reward." The sentry gave a lascivious chuckle.

Åsa grunted. She could feel her face redden beneath the soot.

"Which one are you?" said the sentry, scrutinizing her. "I can never tell you nine apart. But I don't recognize you—where are you off to at this hour, anyway?"

She held her breath. Any moment now he'd realize she was no álf.

Then the sentry smacked his forehead. "Oh, that's right! You smiths can't speak, ever since old Dvalin cut out your…sorry!" He turned away, his face reddening.

Åsa ducked her head and scurried past him into the silver room. She tiptoed in and, once again skirting the walls, made her way carefully through the vast chamber. A few more steps and she would reach the exit.

"Halt!"

Dvalin's voice rang out like a bell. Åsa froze. Glancing over her shoulder, she caught sight of the Svartálf king coming through the silver hall. His running footsteps sounded on the granite floor.

Panicked, Åsa broke into a run. Despite his stumpy legs, Dvalin was swift. He was on her in an instant, barring her way with his long axe. His axe was twice as long as hers, and double-bladed.

He stared at her, open-mouthed. "You!"

She drew her own axe and smacked his long handle away. Then she swung her axe again, forcing him to jump back. She fled.

"Come back here!" Dvalin shouted.

She ran toward a dark tunnel, which she believed was the way she had entered. She could hear Dvalin pounding after her and prayed that her longer legs could outrun the álf king. Glancing back, she caught the glow of his torch. She sprinted into the dark, hoping the ground was even.

And that she was running toward Helheim.

Her foot caught on something and she fell, skidding over the rough, stony ground. Her hands and knees sent a warning sting up her limbs. She knew it was bad. In a moment it would start to hurt.

Footsteps echoed, coming closer. Åsa struggled into a sitting position and hefted her axe, ready to meet Dvalin.

A glimmer attracted her attention. The necklace had flopped outside her tunic when she fell, and now it glowed against her chest. The light it gave off was faint, but enough to illuminate the ground for a few feet ahead of her.

Åsa scrambled to her feet and hobbled away, biting back a sob. Her knees throbbed, her arms were raw, her ankles ached. And though the necklace lit her way, it also showed her pursuer where she was. She had to be faster than he was.

Dvalin's torch bobbed in the dark. He was gaining on her. She broke into a ragged jog, but his footsteps sounded closer and closer.

When she could hear his breath rasp in his throat, she turned to face him.

His gaze went to the necklace on her chest. "Those smiths betrayed me!" Dvalin's eyes had a mad glint that struck fear into Åsa's heart. "They're dead men."

"No! I took it without them knowing. They are not involved."

"Then they'll be executed for carelessness. They should never have let you steal it."

He whirled his axe and she ducked under it, swinging her own weapon as she charged him. The end of her axe blade slammed into his midsection. Though his chain-mail brynja stopped the blade, the blow drove the wind out of him. Åsa wheeled and managed another strike before he could recover. This time she sent him to the floor. She turned to run, but the long shaft of his axe swept her feet out from under her and she crashed to the hard floor beside him.

"I wanted to make you my queen!" he growled, rolling over on top of her. His body, heavy with chain mail, pressed her into the rock floor. "Did you sleep with those smiths?" He drew his knife and brought it to her throat. His breath was hot and foul. "I'm going to kill you first, then execute them all."

Memories flooded Åsa's mind of Gudrød, trapping her under him on their wedding night. Her panic spiked, igniting a fury that seared in her chest and fueled her strength. That would never happen to her again. Summoning all her strength, she yanked her axe off the floor and swung it into Dvalin's head. His helmet rang and the knife dropped from his hand. Åsa grabbed the knife and plunged it into his throat, severing the artery. Blood sprayed, drenching her.

Åsa heaved him off of her. His body flopped onto the stone floor.

She scrambled to her feet, ignoring the agony of her battered ankles and knees as she staggered toward the glimmer of gray in the darkness. It took all her will to keep moving against the pain. She wished she'd grabbed Dvalin's long-handled axe for support. But at last she reached the exit, limping out of the darkness onto the vast gray plain.

In the distance she glimpsed a familiar figure.

Heid was waiting for her.

CHAPTER 12

Helheim

"You made it," Heid said, gripping Åsa's arm to keep her from falling. "How did things go with Dvalin?"

Åsa winced and steadied herself. "He's dead."

The völva nodded. "Just as well. He treated his people brutally." She turned her gaze on the necklace. "What have we here?" Heid grasped the golden chain firmly and rubbed it between her thumb and fingers, eyes closed. "Yes, it has the feel of Brisingamen. And Hel is not as clever as she likes us to believe. It will do."

Åsa wondered how Heid knew what Freyja's necklace felt like. There was so much about the sorceress that Åsa didn't understand.

The völva opened her eyes and regarded Åsa's blood-spattered face and filthy, torn clothes. "You look a fright."

"It's been a rough journey."

"I can see that. Let's get you cleaned up."

Åsa limped after Heid across a meadow blooming with wildflowers to a copse of trees. Water trickled nearby. They entered the grove, where dappled light fell on a steaming spring. Åsa stared at Heid.

"Helheim's not all bad," said the sorceress. "The dead get what they deserve. Now get undressed and let me see if I can make you presentable."

With relief Åsa doffed the red cap and shed her clothes, now little more than rags. When she lifted the necklace from her chest, it seemed to leave a hole in her spirit. She laid it reverently on the grass.

"A necklace like that deserves a name," observed Heid. "Did the dark álfar name it?"

Åsa shook her head as she eased into the steaming pool. "No, they didn't say." She let herself sag against the moss-lined side, too tired to smile at the irony of her remark.

"Pity. But of course we must call it Brisingamen when we bring it to Hel."

Heid left her alone while the warm water soothed her injuries. Åsa closed her eyes and lay back, letting all the events wash out of her. For just a few moments she allowed herself to forget about the difficulties that lay ahead. Heid was here. The völva would guide her through.

Reluctantly, Åsa emerged from the pool. Heid appeared with a length of linen to dry her. "I've brought you some better clothes to wear when you present the necklace to Hel. I'll get rid of these rags." The sorceress held up a pale blue-gray gown, made of a material Åsa had never seen before. It had the shimmer and fluidity of silk, yet it was light as cobwebs. Åsa pulled the gown over her head and it flowed down her sides, caressing her skin. She donned the necklace and it lay gleaming on her breast.

Heid frowned. "There's not much we can do about your hair. Here, put on this headscarf." She gave Åsa a scarf of the same gossamer fabric as the dress. When Åsa draped it over her shorn head, it clung like a warm second skin.

"Are you sufficiently restored?" asked Heid.

Åsa found that she was. The soak in the pool had completely revitalized her. There was no trace of soreness anywhere in her body. "Yes." She picked up the álfar axe and tucked it into her belt.

"Let's go then." Heid took her arm and guided Åsa out of the glade. The gown whispered over her legs as she walked.

They followed a woodland trail for some time, eventually emerging from the forest onto the familiar barren plain. The sky roiled with gray clouds that spewed rain and hail, making the ground a muddy mire. In the distance Hel's hall sulked, its stationary storm cloud weeping sleet over the thatched roof.

Åsa gripped Heid's hand and they slogged across the plain. The gray sky pelted them with rain and hail while the wind tore at their clothes. But Åsa's magical dress resisted water and wind alike. Heid's cloak seemed impervious to the elements as well, and they arrived at Hel's door dry and whole.

The völva rapped on the brassbound oak door three times with her staff.

It creaked open. Hel's doleful servant, Ganglati, hovered in the shadows. "Oh, you survived," he said in disappointed tones. "And you've got the necklace. Well, I guess you'd better come in, then. Her Nibs will want to see it."

They hopped over the yawning pit and followed him through the entryway to the oaken door. "You must leave your weapon here," he insisted. Åsa reluctantly drew the axe from her belt and leaned it against the wall among other weapons.

Ganglati struck the door to scatter the snakes, then ushered Heid and Åsa into the great hall.

A gust of cold air hit them as they entered the frigid room. Icy venom dripped from the writhing serpents in the roof. The long-fire cast its gloomy light over Hel and Baldr on the high seat, Fenrir at their feet.

"Look who survived," Ganglati announced sullenly.

Hel turned her gaze from Baldr's face and regarded them. Åsa shuddered at the queen's visage, her beautiful side always toward Baldr, the other a half a black, rotting corpse.

The Irish necklace shone on her chest.

Hel's gaze riveted on Åsa's necklace, her good eye gleaming. "What have we here?"

Åsa cleared her throat, yet her voice came out as a faint croak. "Lady Hel, I bring you what you asked for." She could not bring herself to call the necklace Brisingamen.

Hel leaned forward. "Come here, let me see it."

Åsa approached, trying to still her trembling. Baldr smiled at her and her courage flooded in.

"Does Freyja know it's gone?" Hel demanded.

Åsa shook her head.

"How did you manage to get it? She's never let it out of her sight since the time Loki stole it."

Åsa's mouth opened but no sound came out. She had no idea how to answer.

"If that tale were to get out, many who are now among the living would find their way here," Heid said smoothly.

"Clever," said Hel, smiling. "Come closer. Let me see it."

Åsa stifled a shudder and approached the high seat. At Hel's nod, she mounted the platform.

Hel peered at the necklace. The smell of rotting meat arose from the dead side of her face. Åsa held her breath as the queen of the dead fingered the golden chain.

Hel cackled with glee. "I can feel its power! Let me try it on."

"Give her the Irish necklace first," said Heid.

Hel smiled, teeth gleaming on the lipless corpse side of her face. "I give the orders here. I must test it."

Åsa swallowed hard. "I cannot give it to you until I have the Irish necklace."

Hel's eyes widened. "I can take it from you." She gave Åsa an appraising glance. "Why should I not keep both necklaces?"

Heid growled, "We have a bargain."

Hel flicked her gaze to the völva. "And are you one who can bargain with the queen of the dead?"

Åsa bit back panic. "I must have the Irish necklace. It's the only thing that will convince my ancestress to lift the curse on my people. Please have pity on them."

"I take what I want. I do not bargain." Hel leaned forward and took hold of the Svartálf necklace and yanked, but it stayed in place as if stuck to Åsa's chest.

The Irish necklace dangled about Hel's neck. Åsa took a deep breath and grabbed it. As she touched the gold, the familiar vibration flowed up her arm, its power filling her with new courage. Its magic felt different than the dark álfar's necklace, though every bit as strong.

She tried to pull it over Hel's head, but the necklace would not budge.

The two queens locked eyes and hauled on the necklaces in a silent tug-of-war. The living side of Hel's face turned from red to purple. The smell of rotting meat intensified. She glared into Åsa's eyes as if trying to sear her eyeballs. Åsa refused to blink.

For all their straining, the magic chains held fast.

Baldr laid his hand on Hel's. "Please, Lady, it would cheer me so if you would give this young queen what she asks for. You know how sad I've been."

Hel looked at Baldr and the living side of her face instantly softened. "If it will make you happy, my love, then I shall." And just like that, she bent her head and lifted the Irish necklace off. Åsa took it quickly, while bowing out of the Svartálf masterpiece. As the necklace left her chest, Åsa felt a hollow where it had rested.

The queen of the underworld donned the Svartálf necklace. She closed her eyes and leaned back. Åsa held her breath.

Hel opened her eyes. "I feel the power! I am now the mistress of Brisingamen! I am mightier than Freyja. No more will the gods look down their noses on the Queen of Helheim."

Gripping the Irish necklace, Åsa stumbled down from the platform. Heid clutched her arm and dragged her out of the hall while Hel reveled in the false Brisingamen.

"Nice seeing you again," said Ganglati, opening the door to let them pass. "Sorry you have to leave so soon. Don't fall in the pit on your way out."

They stepped into the entry room and the inner door slammed in their faces.

"Quick," Heid whispered, "before she discovers there are two Brisingamen."

Åsa was relieved to see her axe still leaned against the wall. She tucked it in her belt and hurried after the sorceress toward the exit.

They leaped over the pit and dashed through the door.

"She didn't tell us where the queen's grave is. How will we find her?" said Åsa.

"I know the way," said Heid.

HEID MARCHED across the windswept plain, moving so fast Åsa trotted to keep up. Storm clouds covered the horizon, and tongues of lightning flickered to touch far-off hills that blazed with fire of their own. Thunder deafened her as they drew near the granite hills.

The völva threaded her way between the rocky mounds, dodging lightning strikes. She halted at the base of a mountain. Fire blazed from the top and its molten core shone through the granite shell.

The völva cried, "I call upon you to open!"

The rock shook with an ominous rumble but stayed intact.

Heid raised her staff to the sky and lightning snaked down to strike it. Her hair rose, undulating in the charged air. "I command you to open!" She struck the rock with her staff.

A crack sounded and a fissure split the mound open to reveal a dark passageway.

Heid started forward but Åsa hesitated.

The völva turned to her impatiently. "Come along! You've made it this far, there's no turning back now."

Åsa squared her shoulders and took a deep breath, then stepped into the passage.

The stone corridor twisted and turned. The sound of thunder faded as they worked their way deeper into the mountain. Åsa's foreboding grew with every step. She feared to meet the ancient queen again. Åsa had barely survived their battle on Midgaard. Here the draugr's power would be so much greater.

A faint light glimmered at the end of the passage. Heid increased her pace while Åsa forced herself to keep up. As they neared the opening, the light was almost blinding.

Heid stepped out of the passage and vanished into the glare. Åsa steeled herself and followed.

She emerged into sunshine. Åsa stood for a moment, soaking up the warmth as her eyes adjusted to the light.

"Come on, then," said Heid.

Åsa blinked at her a couple of times. A grove of oak materialized, and the völva led her into the dappled light beneath the trees. Birdsong filled the air. They followed a game trail to the spreading branches of an enormous oak.

A crowd of women sat in the shelter of the tree, plying their needles while they talked and laughed. Their chairs were fashioned from tree stumps.

As Heid and Åsa approached, the women stopped their chatter and stared. A smile of joy lit one fair face.

"Mother!" Åsa cried, running forward. Gunnhild smiled. In her arms, she cradled an infant. She stood to receive her daughter's embrace.

Tears ran down Åsa's cheeks as she laughed. "Oh, Mother, I'm so happy to see you." She looked down at the baby in Gunnhild's arms, the child Gunnhild had died giving birth to.

"And I've missed you, daughter. Meet your sister," said Gunnhild, handing the infant to Åsa.

Åsa took the child and gazed down into her cloudless eyes. The baby laughed and reached a tiny fist to Åsa's cheek. Åsa kissed her downy head, inhaling her clean baby scent.

"I never thought I'd see you here, Mother. How are you?"

Gunnhild smiled. "I'm well and happy here. Your father and I are very proud of you."

"Where is Father? And Gyrd?"

"They have their own work to do, just as I do with the dísir of our family. We've been keeping watch over you, all of us."

"Then you know why I've come."

"Yes, we all do." Gunnhild nodded toward a woman sitting nearby.

The queen in the mound.

She was dressed in gorgeous robes, silk embroidered with gold thread. A golden circlet crowned her silver hair. She looked young, pink-cheeked and healthy, as Åsa had never seen her.

Gunnhild took the infant back and tickled her nose, making the baby laugh.

Åsa took a deep breath and approached the queen. "Grandmother, I have traveled far through many perils to find you."

The queen stared at her. "Greetings, Daughter. What do you seek from me?"

"You have laid a curse upon my people. They're dying. You must lift the curse."

The queen's gaze sharpened. "I warned you what would happen if you sent me here, but you did it anyway. Now you come crying to me to undo the havoc you have wrought."

"Grandmother, you left me no choice when you took Eyvind."

Her voice turned petulant. "You could have let me keep him.

You who are still living are so selfish, denying the dead what little pleasure they can find."

"Men are not playthings." Åsa drew the Irish necklace from beneath her gown. "But look, I have brought what you desire."

The queen looked at the gold and shrugged. "It has no value to me here."

Åsa could not believe that all she'd gone through was in vain. "You must save my people!"

"Why should I care what happens to them?"

"They are your people too."

The queen scowled. "People who neglected me."

Åsa gave a cry of disgust. "How did you come to be this way?"

"Do you truly want to know?" The queen fixed her with a bitter gaze.

"Yes, I do," said Åsa, surprised to find that she did care about this ghoulish ancestress.

The queen stared off into the gloomy distance. "Once, long before you or your father were born, my name was Estrid, Estrid the beautiful they called me. I was a king's daughter, like you. Dagnar, king of Agder, courted me. He was young and handsome, and I loved him. We married, and when we had a son, Ivar, our happiness was complete." She was silent for a moment, as one tear slid down her pale cheek. "But before our son was out of the cradle, my Dagnar was killed on a summer raid.

"Dagnar was slain in battle, and the Valkyries chose him for Valhöll. Who would not—brave and fair as he was. But he was lost to me for all time."

The queen's grief seared through Åsa as if it were her own. The necklace warmed on her chest and began to vibrate.

The haugbui's voice grated on. "I raised our son to be a great king. He grew up to be a raider, like his father, and traveled far while I remained at home and ruled Agder. When my son returned, he tried to take over the kingdom. But I couldn't let him take it from me. It was all I had, and it was rightfully mine. I went to war with Ivar and drove him away." She sighed. "Never was victory so bitter. I ruled my kingdom alone for many years, without my husband, without my son. I trusted no man. I fought many wars and won them all. Men feared me. But I was completely alone, for I trusted no one."

Åsa shuddered, thinking how close she had come to rejecting Eyvind out of the same lack of trust, and becoming just like this lonely queen.

The queen continued. "When I died, Ivar took my kingdom. He buried me far from the living, and though I was the most powerful queen ever known, my son made sure I was forgotten. This was his revenge.

"He left me trapped alone in my mound where I lay for centuries, with no hope of ever seeing my beloved Dagnar again. At Ragnarok, he will fall with the other Einherjar, and pass from existence, while I will remain here."

Åsa quailed as the queen's crushing loss seared her veins. "I am sorry for your tragedy. Yet you should not make the living suffer for the actions of their ancestors."

"It was you who sent me here, and the shield-maiden who severed my last connection with Midgaard," the queen thundered. She loomed tall and fearsome. Then she sank back against her cushions. "Daughter, the truth is, I cannot lift the curse. That necklace was the last thing that connected me to the human world. When the shield-maiden severed that link, the curse was triggered, and I lost all power over the living. Nothing can reestablish that connection." The queen smiled at her. "I can do nothing. That is for you to undertake, daughter."

"What do you mean? I have nothing to cure this disease. The necklace has no effect on it."

"That necklace never belonged to our people. It doesn't wish us well. Return it to where it belongs. I am content here with my sisters. Let me be happy after all I've suffered." The queen turned her back, making it clear she would say no more.

Åsa's shoulders slumped. She backed away from the queen and found Gunnhild waiting for her.

"Mother, what am I to do?"

"You must go back to Tromøy and save our people."

"But there's nothing I can do. I came here to find help."

Gunnhild smiled at her. "You're not the same as you were when you set off on this journey."

"Well, my hair's a lot shorter."

Gunnhild laughed and ruffled her daughter's shorn, burnt locks. "Yes, it is. But that is not all that's different. Now hug me one more time, daughter. You must hurry."

Åsa threw her arms around her mother and baby sister, drawing all the strength she could from them.

"Come," said Heid, gripping her shoulder.

Åsa tore herself away, tears flowing down her face. "Goodbye, daughter," said Gunnhild. "We will meet again one day."

Åsa turned from her mother and looked at Heid in despair. "Now what will we do? The queen can't lift the curse."

The völva sighed. "I should have realized that when you sent that creature here, all her power in Midgaard was severed."

Rage rose in Åsa's throat, threatening to choke her. "How will we save my people?"

Heid huffed and turned her back. "There's no point in blaming the messenger."

"We'll have to figure out what to do when we get home. Let's go." Åsa set off toward the tunnel with purpose.

"I can't come with you."

Åsa's heart stopped. Her scalp prickled. She stared back at the völva. "What do you mean?"

"I have to stay here. It was the price Hel exacted."

"But Baldr said…"

"Baldr said that Hel should keep her bargain. The bargain with me. While you were in Svartálfheim, I made an agreement of my own."

Åsa's throat tightened. She swallowed hard. "But you don't need to...die."

"That is not always a bad fate." Heid turned her head. Åsa followed her gaze. A young man stood in the distance, holding a little girl in his arms.

She understood. "They're your family."

Heid nodded. "Once I found them here, I didn't have the heart to leave them again and return to a life of pain. Here I am strong and healthy, and I can have the happiness life denied me."

"But what of Tromøy? How will we survive without you?" Åsa's words came out strangled with grief.

Heid scoffed. "You don't need me. You've bested the king of Svartálfheim and outwitted Hel herself." Her expression softened. "You're ready to stand on your own."

Åsa stared at the sorceress. A lump formed in her throat and threatened to choke her. How could Heid abandon her? She wanted to plead with the völva to return with her, but that wasn't fair. Heid deserved to be happy.

Heid turned away. Then she stopped and looked back at Åsa. "Remember this. The necklace is only a finely crafted tool. All power comes from within." The völva turned again and walked toward her family.

Åsa bit back tears. Somehow, she would have to find a way to get along without her mentor. Stunned, she walked away. The tears came then, hard and fast like a rainstorm burning trails down her face.

She couldn't help but look back one last time.

Heid was in her husband's arms, holding their child. She was smiling in a way Åsa had never seen before.

CHAPTER 13

Odinssal, Vingulmark

A dozen ships lay on Vingulmark's beach, figureheads of dragons and wolves mounted on their prows, crews bristling with spears and shields, their helmets glinting. King Alfgeir was deploying his entire fleet to sail across the narrow fjord separating Vingulmark from Borre. This couldn't look like a normal, friendly trading visit such as he had made to Borre numerous times past. His sham attack had to be convincing enough to bring Olaf's fleet north to defend Borre.

Alfgeir was certain that Olaf would take the bait. When he took Vingulmark back after Gudrød's death, Alfgeir had purposely kept his grandson uncertain of his intentions, leaving the possibility of attack as a threat over Olaf's head. He wanted to keep the young pup off balance.

With any luck Borre's lookouts would light the signal fires as soon as they sighted Alfgeir's war party heading their way, and Olaf would set out to defend his territory, a day's sail from Tromøy, while Orm sailed south to attack Åsa's island kingdom.

By the time Olaf realized the ruse, he would be more than a

day's sail north of Tromøy. Too late for him to come to the rescue.

A niggle of guilt over betraying his grandson was quickly brushed away with thoughts of the rich farmland he would gain from a grateful Orm. Besides, it was the young queen he was betraying, not Olaf. No harm would come to the boy.

"Prepare to launch!" he shouted, and his sailors slid their ships into the sea.

~

Grenmar, Telemark

ORM WADDLED down Grenmar's beach, inspecting his fleet. Seven ships lined the shore. There were three small, dilapidated vessels surviving from his father's day that Orm's warriors had dragged out of the boatshed and hastily refitted, each carrying twenty-five men. Beside them lay three newer ones that Orm had commissioned in recent years, crewed by thirty-five sailors apiece. Lastly, one captured from the Danes years ago on a raid, its stem and stern much battered by axe marks but still seaworthy.

With its limited shoreline, Telemark had never been a great sea power like Vestfold and Agder. When Åsa's fleet was fully manned, Orm could never hope to conquer her, but now he had a good chance to overcome whatever feeble defense the stricken island could mount.

His ships were crammed with men, enough to overrun Tromøy's weakened forces and crew their ships when he captured them. Orm would broaden Telemark's access to the sea and double its fleet, making it a maritime power for the first time. He imagined the riches trading and raiding would bring him. And as he gained power, he could challenge Vestfold. If he could take the Shining Hall...

One step at a time, he reminded himself.

Alfgeir should have sailed at dawn to attack Borre. Orm had only to wait for the chain of signal fires running down from the north to reach Skiringssal, sending Olaf to dispatch his fleet to defend Borre, a day's sail to the north.

Orm had stationed a fishing boat off the headland that separated his property from Skiringssal, watching for the signal fire and Olaf's departure. The fisherman would hurry back to report to Orm as soon as Olaf's sails were sighted and confirmed to be heading north.

Today's wind was from the north, promising a fast run for Orm's fleet south to Tromøy while Olaf would be forced to beat his way against the wind all the way to Borre. Once he arrived and found out it was a false alarm, he would be at least a day's sail from Tromøy. Orm would have plenty of time to overrun the island.

Of course, the pup could try to win Tromøy back, but Orm would be ready for him. By the time Olaf made it to Tromøy, Orm would have wedded and bedded the girl-queen and taken legal possession of the kingdom. He would be a king at last.

Skiringssal

THE NORTHERN SIGNAL FIRE FLARED. The lookout jumped on his horse and rode to the steading. He found Olaf in the stable, binding a horse's strained foreleg.

"Trouble in the north, Lord," the lad gasped. "The beacon's lit."

There was no way to know exactly what the trouble in the north could be, but if it was serious enough to light the beacon, it must be bad. Heart drumming, Olaf hurried to the hall where he took his war horn from the wall. Striding to the entrance, he blew a mighty blast that echoed throughout the steading.

In the practice field, his warriors dropped their wooden swords and ran to the hall.

When they had mustered, Olaf said, "The north beacon has been lit. Get ready to sail today."

The húskarlar began arming themselves for a sea battle, donning varnished battle jackets, taking up their spears and axes.

They were ready to go when a rider arrived from Borre. The boy flung himself from the saddle, exhausted from his frantic ride thirty miles over the moraine that formed a rough road from Borre to Skiringssal. "King Alfgeir's fleet is heading for Borre," he gasped. "His crews are fully armed."

Olaf's stomach clenched. Alfgeir's kingdom of Vingulmark had been his mother's dowry. After she died, Gudrød had retained the dowry. Alfgeir had probably been loath to go to war with his powerful son-in-law. But when Gudrød died, Alfgeir took the territory back. As an untried new king with few allies, there had been nothing Olaf could do at the time. Since then, Olaf had gained support and attracted many followers. Skiringssal was strong now, and he'd hoped his trouble with Alfgeir was over. He should have known the wily old king would interpret his lack of response as a sign of weakness. Olaf was surprised Alfgeir waited so long to attack Borre, a tempting target just across the fjord from Vingulmark.

Borre had been Gudrød's hall, and Olaf had no love for the memories it held, but he couldn't let his grandfather just sail in and take it. If Olaf gave Alfgeir any more ground, the old man wouldn't stop until he'd taken all of Vestfold.

Olaf had to stand up to him now.

"I never did trust that old fox." He sent the lad to the cooks to be fed and rested in the stable along with his horse.

Olaf finished donning his battle jacket, strapped on his sword, Bear Biter, and loaded his sea chest onto the cart. He strode down the trail to the shore, followed by his war band. They laughed and chattered, eager to set sail and see some action.

Though he hadn't made any long voyages since his marriage, Olaf had kept his fleet in good shape. He liked to work on the boats while he dreamed of far-off ports. Now his pastime was paying off.

His flagship, *Sea Dragon*, was moored to the pier, always ready to sail on the many local trips he made. His crew ran the other vessels out of the boathouse onto the beach. The ships were ready for war, needing only to be loaded and provisioned. They would set sail within the hour.

The warriors heaved their sea chests aboard the ships, along with kegs of ale and water, barrels of dried fish and meat, and stacks of flatbread carefully wrapped in waxed linen. They shoved the vessels off the beach and clambered aboard. The oarsmen seated themselves on their sea chests, racked their shields along the rails, then fitted their oars and began to row. Olaf took *Sea Dragon*'s helm, leading his fleet out of the harbor.

Once out of the headland's shelter, the wind proved to be against them. Olaf gritted his teeth. Vestfold's fleet would have to tack their way up the narrow Fold, not reaching Borre until late evening. Alfgeir had a day's lead, time in which the old king could have wreaked all kinds of havoc.

Steering as close to the wind as he could, playing the eddies to coax more speed out of his ship, Olaf played the attack out in his mind. Borre didn't have a harbor, just two jetties and a hard shingle beach for landing. The defenders could hold Alfgeir's ships offshore with arrows and spears shot from the jetties, a ploy Åsa had used effectively when the Danes attacked Borre two years before.

But Alfgeir knew this. What other tactic might he take that would be more successful? Olaf closed his eyes and pictured Borre's shoreline, the approaches to the steading. His grandfather knew the area well. If an attacker beached his ships farther down the shoreline, out of sight of the lookouts, and marched overland, he might be able to reach the steading unchallenged.

But even if he reached the steading, Alfgeir's attack was unlikely to succeed. Borre was well manned with experienced warriors who had defended the steading against many seaborne attacks. Olaf had no doubt they could hold out until he arrived, and then they would crush his grandfather's forces between them. The best Alfgeir could hope for would be to make it out of there with his ships and forces intact.

What was the cunning old king playing at? It didn't make sense.

As the ships beat north-east through choppy waters, Olaf's gut churned, telling him something was not right.

CHAPTER 14

Tromøy

R agnhild dampened the linen cloth and gently wiped the sweat from Murchad's forehead.

Tova entered the guesthouse. Ragnhild looked up at her hopefully. "You've found Halfdan?"

The girl shook her head in defeat. "We've searched everywhere for him, but he's nowhere to be found."

Where had Halfdan gone? Ragnhild imagined the little boy escaping the bower, and suddenly a memory surfaced of herself, a little girl escaping her fóstra, Katla, to run to her own mother, who was sick.

But Katla had caught her and dragged her back to the bower to keep her safe from the disease. Ragnhild's mother died without saying goodbye.

She jumped up. "I know where Halfdan is. I must go find him. Will you tend Murchad while I'm gone?"

"I will stay by his side," said Tova, sliding onto her stool.

Ragnhild nodded in relief. Tova would take good care of him.

She ran from the guesthouse, past the evil-smelling byre with the dead stacked up inside. She hurried down the trail to the shore and turned up the beach toward the forest—toward the mound of the ancient queen.

Soon she spotted a small figure marching sturdily down the beach, the wolf at his side. Ragnhild sprinted to catch up with them.

Halfdan wore his wooden sword strapped to his hip and carried his tiny wooden shield.

She slowed to catch her breath and tried to make her tone casual. "Hello, Halfdan. Where are you off to in such a hurry?"

"I'm going to find Mama," he said shortly, not missing a step.

"How do you know where to find her?"

"I dreamed it," said the little boy. "I saw her in a scary place."

Ragnhild shuddered. "Your mama is on a very important journey. We shouldn't bother her."

"Mama needs help." Halfdan fingered his sword hilt. "She's scared."

Ragnhild's neck hairs rose. She had known her mother needed her too. Her heart went out to the little boy. "There's not much we can do. Vigdis is there, and Halla, and Runa. They're helping your mama."

"Mama needs me," he insisted.

If she picked Halfdan up and took him back by force, he'd scream and fight her. It would only traumatize him more. And who was she to argue with his dream? What if Katla had let her go to her mother, all those years ago? Would it have made a difference, at least to her? She could have said goodbye, and that would have meant a lot. "Then I'll go with you."

The little boy put his hand in hers.

They marched down the beach, the blind wolf shambling along beside them.

Ragnhild spotted the break in the trees and veered off into the forest, following the game trail to the burial mound. The sound of women chanting came eerily on the wind. The mound loomed among the trees and she stepped into the clearing, leading Halfdan by the hand. The wolf trailed behind.

The women fell silent and Vigdis's eyes snapped open. "What are you doing here?" she demanded.

"Mama needs me," said Halfdan.

Ragnhild said, "Queen Sonja wants to take Halfdan back to Skiringssal. But he ran away to find Åsa. I couldn't stop him, not without hurting him. You know what a fight he can put up."

"Sonja had the right of it," said Vigdis. "Tromøy is not safe for Halfdan right now. No matter what precautions are taken, he could fall sick."

"He has a right to be with his mother," Ragnhild said firmly.

"But you're interrupting our work," Vigdis protested. "Åsa is deep in a trance, and we must focus all our concentration to support her."

"He's had a dream about her."

"A dream?" Vigdis squatted down and fixed her gaze on the little boy. "Tell me."

"Mama's in the dark. She's scared."

Vigdis nodded. "Yes, she is. We are trying to help her. If I let you stay, can you be very quiet and let us work?"

Halfdan nodded solemnly. He seated himself on the ground, and Fylgja flopped down beside him. The little boy laid his hand on the wolf's head.

Vigdis looked at Ragnhild. "You were right to bring him here. His presence may lend her some strength."

Ragnhild nodded, reassured. She took a seat on a log.

Vigdis studied her face. "What about you? You look a little pale."

"I'm fine. The stink of the guesthouse has made me lose my breakfast a few times, but no fever or anything else."

Vigdis's eyebrows shot up. "Have you considered you may be pregnant?"

Shock coursed through Ragnhild. "I take precautions," she protested.

Vigdis gave her a knowing smile. "They are not foolproof."

Ragnhild's mind reeled as she grappled with the possibility of a child. A burning need to get back to Murchad gripped her. She must tell him, even if he couldn't hear her. She needed to touch him.

In the distance, horns blared.

War horns. Ragnhild's heart thudded. She had to get to Murchad.

Vigdis looked up at the sound. "Go back to the steading, Lady. You'll be needed. Halfdan will be safe here with us."

Ragnhild nodded in relief. If Tromøy was under attack, then this place, hidden in the woods far from the steading, was the safest place for Halfdan.

Heart hammering, she scrambled through the woodland trail to the beach, where she broke into a run, driven by the need to get back to Murchad.

By the time the steading came into view, she was out of breath. She ran to the guesthouse and found Murchad, still unconscious. She leaned close to his ear and murmured, "My love, I am with child." She kissed his pale forehead and rose. Her sword was needed in the shield wall.

With one last look at Murchad, she rushed out the door to the guest quarters assigned to *Raider Bride*. Burrowing in her sea chest, she pulled out her battle jacket and helm and donned them, then got her shield and sword. She hurried to the great hall, where the húskarlar were arming themselves by firelight.

The lookout burst in. "Seven ships," he gasped.

Jarl Borg gave him a keen look. "Whose?"

"The shields are red and yellow."

"Telemark." Olvir scowled. "Orm. The old rat must have heard about our sickness."

Jarl Borg finished strapping on his swordbelt and nodded grimly. "Send a messenger up the hill and tell them to light the signal fires for Skiringssal. Olaf will come to our aid."

"Even with this breeze, it will take him hours to get here," said Olvir. "We'll have to hold them off that long."

"We can do it," said Borg. "Orm's warriors spend more time in the drinking hall than on the training field. They're poorly disciplined and they run more to fat than muscle."

Sonja came in, wild-eyed. Olvir took her arm and tried to guide her back out. "You need to get back to the bower, Lady."

"Halfdan is still missing! You must help us search for him," Sonja demanded, shaking Olvir off.

Ragnhild said, "Halfdan is with his mother at the burial mound, hidden deep in the forest. He's in the care of three apprentices. He'll be safer there while we fight off this attack."

Sonja stared at her, took several deep breaths, then nodded. "My crew are trained warriors. They'll fight with yours."

Sonja's crew would add about thirty fighters. "That would be a big help," said Ragnhild. "Svein, can you and Thorgeir take Queen Sonja to her ship and muster her crew?"

They nodded and hurried out. Ragnhild turned back to Olvir. "How many healthy warriors do you have?"

"I can scrape up maybe eighty of Tromøy's fighters. All of Eyvind's crew are too sick to be of much help. I doubt any of them can rise from their benches, let alone wield a weapon."

She looked at Einar. "What of *Raider Bride*'s crew?"

"We have twenty healthy fighters, plus Unn and her sisters."

Ragnhild's stomach twisted. With seven fully crewed ships, the enemy would have twice their number.

Jarl Borg said, "The healers need to stay with the sick, but we can give them weapons in case the attackers break through our lines and they need to defend themselves. And we'll arm any of the sick who can hold a blade. They can at least take some raiders with them to Valhöll. Give weapons to the women in the bower and every servant who can wield a pitchfork."

The warriors mustered in the yard with *Raider Bride*'s crew. They were so few to stand against the raiders.

Ragnhild longed to run to the guesthouse to see Murchad. It could be the last time. But she was needed here.

Sonja arrived with her crew of thirty, led by Thorgeir and Svein. "I'm no battle commander," she said. "Give me a weapon and I'll join the women in the bower."

Ragnhild handed her a spear, relieved that Sonja was not going to interfere with their battle plans.

Sonja hefted the spear. "I hope I won't have to use it. Good luck to you." She hurried off to the bower.

Jarl Borg surveyed the troops. "We're still outnumbered, but we have a chance." He dispatched the twenty best archers to the headlands flanking the harbor entrance. "See how many you can pick off in the ships before they reach shore. Then run back here as fast as you can. I need you in two places at once."

Olvir gathered all the able-bodied servants and workers. Everyone got a weapon of some kind, even if it was only a pitchfork or a hoe. Their numbers swelled to one hundred and seventy. "Enough to make a good show if the enemy doesn't look too closely," he said.

Ragnhild herded Tromøy's makeshift army down the trail, where they took up a position on the high ground above the beach. She nudged her way into the warriors at the forefront while the common folk and reserve archers gathered behind them.

Her heart pounded as she watched the fleet of seven ships enter the harbor, sails full and drawing. Jarl Borg's hand-picked archers had reached the headlands at the entrance, and they rained arrows and spears down on the invaders. Screams echoed as the missiles found targets, but the ships came on. The sails dropped and rowers ran out their oars, bearing down on Tromøy's beach.

As the first longships grated onto the beach, Ragnhild's blood heated. Behind her, bowstrings creaked as Tromøy's reserve archers nocked and drew.

"Loose!" shouted Jarl Borg. The arrows rose in the air as Orm's crews scrambled over the gunnels. They hastily flung their shields up, but the hail of arrows hit some who fell screaming into the water. Those who survived trod over their shipmates' bodies to line up on the shore and slam their shields together.

Ragnhild felt the familiar exhilaration rise in her, flooding her veins with power stronger than she'd ever felt before. She knew in her bones that she could take on all of them and beat them. They were dead men. Her vision sharpened as she scanned for a target.

Orm's banner fluttered in the prow where the jarl watched the battle, surrounded by his húskarlar. Ragnhild's focus latched onto the stout warlord.

Orm bellowed an order and his archers, sheltered behind the shield wall, nocked their arrows. "Draw!" he roared. "Loose!" Arrows darkened the sky.

"Shields up," said Jarl Borg.

Ragnhild snugged her shield tight to Einar's and Thorgeir's. The shield wall rattled down the line as Tromøy's defenders racked shield to shield and flung the wall overhead. There were thwacks and grunts as arrows rained down, but no death cries came from Tromøy's ranks.

"Shields front," said Borg.

Still locked, the shield wall came down in front just as Orm screamed, "Charge!" His warriors surged forward, their own shields before them. The two forces clashed, each side shoving while blades flicked out from behind shields. In the front line, Ragnhild rammed her shield into the mass of churning bodies. She drove her spearpoint into an enemy, finding a seam in the man's battle jacket and worrying it. The seam gave way and she shoved hard, feeling her point slide deep into soft flesh beneath. His shriek cut short and he sagged amid the crush of bodies, dragging her spearhead down. She jerked it free, then thrust it back into the horde, jabbing in and out, searching for an opening. The screams of men mingled with the cries of the gulls as spear and seax found their marks. The throng was so tight the dead could not fall, jammed between the living.

The formations broke up and the battle degenerated into a melee. The dead thudded underfoot, corpses tangling the combatants' feet. As the shields parted in front of her, Ragnhild thrust her spear into an enemy's gut and let it stay, quivering, while she drew her sword, Lady's Servant. She hacked it hard at the assailant in front of her just as he swung his axe at her. Her blow hit first, catching him in the neck, and he fell, his axe flying out of his hand and landing at her feet.

Shouts and screams rang out, punctuated by the clash of steel. The air reeked of blood and bowels and the sea ran red. Bodies bobbed in the shallows while shrieking gulls wheeled above.

Ragnhild turned as an axe swung at her head in a murderous arc. She ducked under it and rammed her metal shield rim up under the attacker's chin. His head snapped back and he fell backward, slamming into two of his comrades. They all went down in a tangle. Ragnhild waded in, jabbing her sword into them, ripping flesh.

Her peripheral vision caught a flash of steel, and she flung her shield up to deflect a blade. A hand snaked out from the bodies at her feet and grabbed her ankle. She wobbled and went down just as another blow missed her head. She landed hard on the hand that gripped her ankle and she heard bone crack. The man shrieked and let go of her ankle. She scrambled to her feet and danced away from the writhing mass on the ground.

The fighting went on into the afternoon. The ravens joined the gulls in their feast, turning the shore into a carrion field.

Orm's forces still outnumbered Tromøy's, but they were ill-trained and poorly disciplined, and the defenders were able to hold their own. The warriors on both sides were tiring, becoming sloppy.

Ragnhild thrust her blade into an enemy's throat and parried another with her shield. Where was Olaf? He must have seen the beacon hours ago. He should arrive any time.

They just had to hold out until he got there.

Skiringssal

As OLAF DROVE his ships north toward Borre, he couldn't stop the niggling feeling in his gut that something wasn't right.

He gazed back to the south. In the distance, a signal fire flared.

Tromøy. Tromøy was under attack.

Sonja was on Tromøy. Åsa and Halfdan were there. Olaf froze, gripping the tiller.

If he didn't fight Alfgeir for Borre, his grandfather would be emboldened. He'd look on Olaf as the timid boy he'd been, and try to take more land from him. The day would come when Olaf would have to meet Alfgeir in battle and check him. It would be better to do it now rather than let him take more ground, more power.

But Alfgeir knew full well that he couldn't take Borre. It was too well defended. Why would the old warrior waste his men and his ships on an attack doomed to failure?

All of a sudden it dawned on him. Alfgeir was purposely luring Olaf away from Skiringssal.

Or from Tromøy.

Olaf cursed himself for a fool. And for his grandfather thinking he was so naive as to fall for a trick like that.

"Turn!" he cried. "Head for Tromøy!"

He thanked the gods he'd seen the signal fire. The tide was against them, and it would take his fleet long enough as it was to get to Tromøy.

Olaf's gut told him that he might be too late.

CHAPTER 15

Helheim

The ever-present thundercloud began to sleet down on Åsa as she trudged alone toward the parched plain. The weather outside reflected the storm in her soul. Even if she could find her way home, what would life be like without Heid?

A horse whinnied.

Svartfaxi trotted up to her. Åsa's heart beat fast with relief at the sight of him, still saddled and bridled. She stroked his neck. "My old friend, I am so grateful to see you. Are you willing to take me back the way we came?"

He tossed his head and pawed the ground, then stood quietly while she mounted. Tucking her axe in her belt and the Irish necklace beneath her gown, she clucked and Svartfaxi began to walk.

Horse and rider emerged from the sleet storm. Svartfaxi shook the moisture off his coat and set off at a brisk trot across the parched plain, toward the flaming gate of Hel. As they approached, the horse broke into a canter, gathering himself to leap the flames, but before they reached the gate, it creaked open. Svartfaxi came to an abrupt halt, nearly throwing Åsa.

The jotun Fjolsvith peered at them with a grin. "I'm surprised to see you, Lady. How was your mission?"

In the tree above him, the sooty red cock crowed and shook his tail feathers. Åsa's shoulders sagged. "It was not a success."

Fjolsvith shrugged. "Still, you survived. That's something. Few leave Hel alive. How about one last riddle for the road?"

The jotun looked so hopeful, Åsa couldn't refuse. "Very well."

Fjolsvith cackled and rubbed his hands together, a strange motion for such a hulking creature. "Are you ready?"

Åsa sighed. "As ready as I'll ever be."

The jotun screwed up his face in concentration. "Here goes: They sleep on a bed of stone, dark in sunny weather, but the lighter they are the less one can see."

Åsa didn't have the heart to disappoint the jotun. She pretended to think long and hard. "I give up. I don't know."

Fjolsvith's craggy face broke into a delighted expression. "I got you!" he crowed.

"Yes, you did, old friend. Now, tell me the answer."

The jotun hugged himself with glee. "It's a really hard one. They are ashes! Understand? Their bed is a stone hearth, and they blacken in the flame, until they turn white and disappear."

"Very clever! I hope I can remember it and tell everyone back in Tromøy."

Fjolsvith's smile drooped. "There may not be many left there."

Åsa's heart lurched. "How many?"

The jotun shook his head. "You'd better hurry."

With a heaviness in her chest, Åsa clucked to Svartfaxi.

"Wait, Lady," said the jotun. "I have something for you."

Åsa turned back. Fjolsvith held out his hand.

In it was the feather from the sooty red cock's tail.

"This is yours, fairly won."

Åsa took the feather. It flashed iridescent, colors flowing like the Northern Lights.

"What powers it may give you in your world, I don't know. May it bring you good luck, Lady, until I see you again."

"Thank you, Fjolsvith," said Åsa, touched by the jotun's gift. She tucked the feather into her belt pouch.

Svartfaxi set off into the dark. In the distance, they could hear the Helhound, Gorm, his howls echoing through the cavern.

Åsa shivered at the sound. But this time, she was prepared for him.

"Ready?" Åsa said to Svartfaxi. He tossed his mane.

As they neared the entrance, Åsa took her axe from her belt and gripped it close to the horse's side. In the glare of daylight, the black hound loomed, nearly as big as the horse, growling and gnashing his teeth in fury. Svartfaxi broke into a run. Åsa stayed low in the saddle. As the ferocious dog lunged, she swung her axe at him. The blade bit deep into the creature's chest, and his weight threatened to drag her from the saddle. She was determined not to lose the álfar weapon. Clenching the horse's sides with her legs, Åsa jerked the axe with all her strength. The blade stuck fast in Gorm's chest as he fell, bloody and snarling. Her hands were slick with sweat, and the handle slid in her grasp. Åsa struggled to hold on. Gorm thrashed, trying to get at her. He wrenched the handle from her grip and fell away, howling.

Svartfaxi didn't miss a beat as he ran into the iron forest. A hot wind funneled through the branches, making the blades swing through the air. The wolves set up a howl, scenting them.

Åsa timed the swing of the blades as they dashed through the trees. She grabbed hold of a sword branch and snapped it off, then another. She crouched low on the horse's back, a weapon in each hand, gripping Svartfaxi with her legs.

The wind of the whirling blades ruffled her cropped hair. Dark shapes loped alongside, snapping at her feet. A wolf lunged and she swung her sword, sending him flying up into the trees.

Pieces of bloody flesh rained down. More dark shapes loped alongside. Åsa jabbed and slashed with the other blade while the horse dodged through the forest of swords. Svartfaxi neighed in alarm as a wolf nipped at his hind leg. The horse lashed out with a hoof, catching the beast in the head. The creature dropped with a yelp.

Svartfaxi thundered into the clearing where Angrboda sat, wearing her gloom like a cloak. Åsa reined the horse in beside the jotun woman. Svartfaxi skittered nervously, eyeing the dark shapes among the trees.

"Good lady, call off your children," Åsa cried.

Angrboda barely looked up. "Why should I? They need the exercise."

"I must get home to my people."

"What's the point? They're all dying anyway."

Åsa swallowed hard. "If my people must journey to Helheim, I will lead them there."

"Wait here and you'll meet them soon enough. There's a battle going on and they are sorely outnumbered. Most of them will be on their way here by the day's end."

Åsa's heart lurched while Svartfaxi pranced anxiously. "Please, Lady, I beg you. I must get home and help my people. Your daughter let me go. Now you must allow me passage as well."

Interest flickered in Angrboda's eyes. "You saw my daughter? How is she?"

"I saw all of your children," said Åsa. "Jörmungandr swims the river, fishing for men. Your daughter rules on her high seat, Baldr sits on her right hand, and Fenrir lies at her feet."

"Fenrir is fettered," said Angrboda glumly. "The poor boy. The gods, curse them, flung my children down to the underworld."

"They are all well, and together in Hel's realm," said Åsa. "You know what pain it is to be separated from your children. Don't make me suffer the same way you have. All I wish is to see my son alive and well, and die with my people if I must." Åsa cast about in her mind for something that would persuade the woman to favor her request. "I brought your daughter the power of Brisingamen."

Angrboda looked up at this remark. "Is this true?"

It wasn't exactly a lie. Åsa chose her words with care. "No longer is Hel a mere jotun cast down into the underworld. She wears the glory of a goddess."

"Sit," Angrboda commanded, and the wolves hunkered down, never taking their eyes from horse and rider. She waved her hand and the wind dropped. The blades slowed, then hung inert from the iron trees. "Go, then."

"Thank you, Lady," said Åsa. She clucked to Svartfaxi, who set off briskly lest the jotun woman change her mind.

The clamor of battle reached them long before they saw the glint of the gold-roofed bridge. She glimpsed the terrible river it crossed, full of clashing blades and hapless people struggling to reach the shore where the wolves awaited them with sharp teeth. The stench of sulphur rose from the waves, stinging Åsa's nose with its rotten-egg smell.

Svartfaxi increased his pace as they neared the covered bridge where the battle still raged. Armed now, Åsa was ready to fight her way through the melee. "Well, boy, do you want to jump or fight?" she said.

She drew the swords from her belt. The blades disintegrated to a gray powder. She stared at the limp branches in her hands with dismay. "I guess we jump. Are you ready?"

Svartfaxi whinnied and tossed his head. Åsa felt him gather his hindquarters to jump. She wrapped her arms about his neck as he sprang into the air. The horse's power surged through her and they flew up as one.

They landed on the golden roof with a clatter and Svartfaxi skidded across it, then stretched out to leap to the ground. Åsa laid herself along his neck, clinging tight to keep from flying over his head as he soared down.

He touched down in front of a startled Modgud. "So it's you," the jotun shield-maiden exclaimed. "I thought it was Loki, up to mischief. Did you achieve your goal?"

Åsa hung her head. "No, I have failed."

Modgud nodded, scratching Svartfaxi behind the ear. "We can't always win."

"I return now to my people, that we can meet our fate together."

"I fear you'll be meeting quite a few of them along the way. Some have died in the battle and gone on to Valhöll and Sess-rumnir as well."

Åsa turned Svartfaxi's head toward the dark valleys.

They entered the endless night and Svartfaxi plodded forward, taking comfort in the necklace's glow, though it was not bright enough to light their path. Åsa was anxious to return to Tromøy, yet dreaded what she would find. She worried about the battle. Who had attacked Tromøy when they were so weakened? Visions of the dead and dying tortured her. Would anyone be left alive when she returned home?

Svartfaxi trudged on with determination. The journey through the dark valleys seemed to take much longer than nine nights, but at last a gray light shone ahead and they emerged into Niflheim's chill mists.

A band of half a dozen people shuffled toward them, heads hanging. They did not look up as they drew near, but Åsa recognized them and her heart lurched. They were Tromøy folk.

"What has befallen you, my people?" she asked.

"Hail, Åsa, Queen," they said.

A woman stepped forward. She recognized one of Heid's apprentices. "We go now to Helheim, to be with our ancestors. We bid you farewell."

"What of the battle?"

"We are sorry, Lady, we know nothing of it. We died of sickness. When we departed Midgaard, no one had attacked Tromøy."

Åsa scanned the group, her sorrow mingled with relief that she did not see Eyvind or Halfdan, or Brenna, or Ulf. "May the lady Hel bless you," she said. "I will miss you all."

"Thank you, Lady." They shambled on toward the bridge. Åsa prayed that Modgud would allow them safe passage to Helheim, and that Hel would treat them well.

She nudged Svartfaxi onward, passing the icy spring, Hvergelmir. Beyond it loomed the dark root of the world tree, the cave beneath it like a yawning maw ready to swallow them. Without hesitation, Svartfaxi ducked beneath the root and started up the dank, winding trail. The air had a rich, earthy scent. Far below came the sound of the serpent Nidhogg gnawing at the roots of the tree. Åsa shuddered. When the serpent finally chewed through the root, the world tree would die, and the nine worlds would end. The wolves would catch the sun and swallow her, sending the worlds into darkness. Gorm and Fenrir would break their chains and loose terror on the nine realms. The armies of Hel would march out to clash with the Einherjar. There would be nowhere to hide for the living or the dead.

Åsa hoped that day was far off.

A faint light glimmered ahead, signaling the end of the passage. Svartfaxi emerged from beneath the root to the field at the base of the Yggdrasil, where stood the hall of the Nornir.

The three jotun sisters sat outside at their weaving, running men's entrails through the warp with swords and spears to form their grisly tapestry. They stopped work and watched Åsa approach.

"So, you have returned," said Verdandi.

"As I said she would," said Skuld.

Urdr was silent beneath her hood.

"What tidings, daughter?" said Verdandi.

Åsa hung her head. "I have failed in my quest. My foremother

143

cannot lift the curse. My people are doomed, and I go to share their fate."

The sisters broke into laughter. Åsa stiffened. "I know you deal in life and death every day, but what can be funny about the demise of an entire community?" she demanded.

Skuld stopped laughing. "It's true your ancestress lost her power over the living when she died out of Midgaard. But your quest was never to get her to lift the curse. It was to gain the power to banish it yourself."

Åsa stared at the Nornir, stunned. "What are you talking about? I have no power."

Verdandi said, "Daughter, you've been to Helheim and back and survived. You've bested the Svartálf king and Hel herself."

Åsa stared. The Norn used the same words Heid had spoken.

"You've grown on this journey, and gained everything needed to set things right. Think on what you take with you." Skuld gave her a gentle shove that broke the spell. "Now go, your people need you."

Dread fell on Åsa. "I've been gone too long. I passed a crowd of the dead on my way here. How many can yet survive? Is my son still alive? Or any whom I love?"

Urdr's voice emanated from the depths of her hood. It was the first time the Norn had spoken, and her laughter seemed to come from far away. "Daughter, time flow passes differently in the Otherworld. In Midgaard, you haven't been gone so long."

At these words, new hope lifted Åsa's sense of doom. There was still a chance. "Thank you, Lady."

Urdr said, "That necklace is not friendly to you. It must be returned to where it belongs, or it will cause more mischief to your people."

"I will see it done," said Åsa.

"Good. Now you must hurry. You are beyond the Otherworld, and time is passing."

Svartfaxi nudged Åsa with his nose. Sorrow gripped her. He

could not come with her either. She laid her face along his cheek, stroking his soft mane. "Brave friend, you have faced the terrors of Helheim with me, and performed feats that no other horse could accomplish. Now your mission is ended, and I release you. May you find the green pastures you deserve." Svartfaxi snorted gently. "Until I see you again." She took off the saddle, then the bridle. The black horse stamped his hoof, shook his mane, then wheeled and trotted off without a backward glance.

Another friend lost. Åsa watched Svartfaxi as he disappeared into the distance. She heaved a sigh, then turned to the Nornir. "How do I get back to Midgaard?"

Skuld shrugged. "The same way you got here, I suppose." The three sisters returned to their weaving, making it clear Åsa was no longer their concern.

Åsa sighed and set the saddle on the ground. She'd lost the álfar axe and the ironwood swords. All that was left was the rooster's tail feather. She made sure it was tucked safely in her belt pouch. Feeling a bit foolish, she mounted the saddle. Holding the bridle in one hand, the other touching the necklace, she began to chant.

ÅSA COULD SEE nothing at all. It was as if she were back in the dark valleys, though this was utter silence as well as utter darkness. At least the air was dry, and there was no drip of water as there had been in the valleys.

The floor was solid beneath the soft soles of her boots. Was it rock? She had no idea which way to go. She rose from the saddle and started walking. The necklace cast its faint, comforting light, but did little to illuminate her surroundings.

She walked for a long time, with no sense of how much time had passed. Was she going the right way? In this darkness, she could wander forever and never find her way out. With nothing to guide her, she was lost.

Was this like the dark valleys? If she kept going, would she finally come to the end?

A cold draft on her right cheek indicated a side passage. Should she take it? Åsa passed it by, but her nose bumped a hard surface. Pivoting, she retraced her steps to the side passage. After a few steps her nose found another rock wall. The passage branched again in both directions. The main passage had ended, and she was standing in a node with side channels.

Åsa stopped in confusion, not daring to proceed.

HALFDAN SQUIRMED out of Halla's lap. He jumped up and ran to the mound. "Mama!" he cried.

Halla stopped chanting and hurried to pick up the little boy. "You mustn't disturb your mother."

Halfdan nimbly evaded her and started to scramble up the side of the mound. "Mama!" he cried.

Halla reached for him.

"Let him go," said Vigdis. "He has a right to be with her."

"But he'll break her trance."

Vigdis peered into the mound. Åsa's breath was coming in gasps, as if she were afraid. "Something's wrong." The apprentice climbed into the mound, taking the boy with her.

Halfdan squirmed out of Vigdis's grasp and climbed onto his mother's lap. "Mama!" He grabbed her hand. Åsa's breathing seemed to calm.

ÅSA HEARD SOMETHING, a voice, faint and far away, coming from the right-hand passage. She entered the passage, moving toward the sound.

"Mama!" It was Halfdan's voice. She hurried toward it.

"MAMA! WAKE UP!" Halfdan was bouncing on Åsa's lap, pulling on her hand. Vigdis reached out to pick him up, but something stopped her.

The queen was no longer restless. Her breathing was regular.

IN THE DARKNESS, Åsa felt a tiny, warm hand take hold of hers. Halfdan! Hope flared in her chest. She let him pull her into a passage.

Far off, a little light flickered. Desperate, she hurried toward it.

"Mama!" echoed down the passage. The faint voice was gaining strength. She could feel him gripping her hand, pulling her forward toward the light.

CHAPTER 16

Tromøy

"Mama!" Åsa's eyelids fluttered and she clutched Halfdan's hand. Her eyes opened and she swept the little boy into her arms, inhaling the pine scent of his hair.

Keeping a firm grip on her son, she scrambled up from the floor. A wave of dizziness washed over her and she sagged against the timber walls, waiting for it to pass.

"Lady!" said Vigdis in alarm, reaching out to steady her.

"I'm fine," Åsa said. "We must hurry."

Vigdis put an arm around her waist. Clutching Halfdan, Åsa staggered to the opening and handed him out to Halla. Vigdis helped her struggle through the opening, then scrambled out after her.

"You still have the necklace," said Vigdis, staring at her in horror. "Did the queen refuse to lift the curse?"

"The queen had no interest in the necklace and said she has no power to lift the curse. The Nornir told me I have what I need to set things right."

"But what do you have?" said Vigdis.

148

Åsa showed the apprentice the tail feather from the rooster. "It may be that it holds the power from the Otherworld. But we must hurry. Every moment means another life lost." With a firm grip on her son, Åsa staggered off down the trail.

"Lady, you must ride," said Vigdis, catching Åsa as she stumbled, and taking Halfdan from her. "Hitch up the horse to Heid's wagon," she said to Halla, keeping a grip on Åsa's arm.

The apprentices helped Åsa into the cart, then handed Halfdan up to her. Vigdis climbed in beside her and took up the reins. They set off, the other two acolytes following on foot.

Vigdis drove the horses as fast as she could on the rutted track through the woods. When they reached the beach, the cart made better speed. Above the rumbling of the wooden wheels, the wind carried the sound of shouts and clashing steel.

As they got closer, Åsa could see the battle raging on the beach. She was in no condition to join a fight. Her legs were rubbery and she was weak from lack of food. Yet she had to help somehow.

"Take me up the hill to the bower," she ordered. Vigdis veered from the beach and drove the cart up the hill, coming to the side of the steading away from the battle. The apprentice pulled up to the bower door.

Åsa scrambled down from the cart and held her arms out for Halfdan. The little boy climbed into her embrace.

Brenna met them at the door. The fóstra seized Halfdan and hugged him close, covering him in kisses. "You spawn of Loki. You gave me such a scare." She turned to Åsa. "Oh, Lady, thank the gods you're here."

Sonja stood behind Brenna. Åsa met her gaze hesitantly.

At the sight of Sonja, Halfdan began to wail. "No!" he cried. "You can't take me away from Mama!" His cries grew louder.

Sonja's face creased in distress. "No," she said. "I won't take you away!"

Unconvinced, Halfdan howled inconsolably.

Åsa took him from Brenna. He buried his head in her shoulder and clung to her with a death grip, sobbing. "Don't worry," she soothed. "She won't take you away. You can stay right here with me."

Sonja stepped back out of his line of sight. The little boy's cries moderated to a steady wail that gradually subsided. He hiccupped and Åsa patted his back.

Sonja spoke softly. "You were very brave to undertake such a journey. I don't know that I would have the courage. I'm glad you are safe." Her tone was guarded.

"Thank you for coming," Åsa replied stiffly. "Our people are fighting the enemy on the beach, but they are sorely outnumbered. I must make another soul journey to help them. Will you join the other women in the vardlokkur? I need everyone's strength."

"I will do whatever I can to assist you," Sonja said, and Åsa believed her.

"Lady, you must not leave your body again so soon," Vigdis protested.

"I have no choice. Every moment I wait costs more lives. Are you going to help me?"

Vigdis nodded in resignation.

Åsa carried Halfdan to her chamber, followed by the other women. The little boy's tantrum had worn him out and he was fast asleep. Åsa laid him gently on the bed. He moaned when she withdrew her arms but didn't wake.

Stormrider drowsed on her perch beside the bed. Åsa removed the falcon's hood and untied her lashings. She withdrew the iridescent rooster's feather from her belt and tucked it into Stormrider's jesses, then lay on the bed beside her son while the women gathered around her.

Sonja stood among them, her head down. She raised her head and met Åsa's gaze with a forlorn look. Åsa's heart went out to her. The woman was only trying to do what she thought was right. "If I do not return, will you raise Halfdan?"

Sonja nodded, a smile ghosting across her face. "Of course," she said warmly. "I would raise him as if he were my own. Olaf and I would keep Tromøy safe for him."

Åsa nodded, reassured. Taking a deep breath, she nodded to the women. "Begin the vardlokkur." She settled herself against the pillows as they began to chant. Vigdis cast herbs onto the fire, filling the air with intoxicating smoke. Åsa slipped once again into a trance.

The necklace vibrated on her chest. Power surged through her like nothing she'd felt before.

As the women sang, Åsa flowed into Stormrider's body. The iridescent feather sparked against the falcon's feathers. She flapped her wings, lofting into the air and out the smoke hole. Soaring high above the steading, she could see the curse lying over the island like a gray fog. The stink of death rose from it.

On the shore below, the battle raged. She flew down closer to get a better look.

Ragnhild was fighting beside her crew. Olvir led Tromøy's forces while Jarl Borg stood on the rise behind them, directing the battle. From her vantage point, Stormrider could see that with great skill and courage, Tromøy's forces were holding out, but the enemy's sheer numbers were grinding them down and eventually would overcome them.

She spotted Orm in the prow of his ship beneath his banner, bellowing orders at his men.

She hovered, beating the air with her wings. What could she do? She could harass the enemy, attack them with her beak and talons, but how much could she accomplish by herself? She needed more warriors.

Beneath her, bodies bobbed in the water while carrion birds wheeled and dove, plucking choice morsels from the dead. If only she could get the birds to attack the enemy. Would they heed her if she called to them?

It was worth a try.

She uttered a sharp, commanding cry. The ravens and gulls stopped their feeding and fixed their gazes on her.

Encouraged, she focused her mind and sent a silent message. *Muster to me!*

Nothing happened.

Perhaps words did not work with birds. She focused inward, forming an image in her mind of birds flying to her.

For a moment, nothing happened. She hovered, keeping the picture vivid and sharp in her mind.

A single raven flew up to her side. He cawed and another raven joined him.

A few at a time, the carrion birds abandoned the dead and flocked to her. Soon she was surrounded by dozens of ravens, crows, and gulls, milling in the air above the battle.

With all her power, she visualized the birds attacking the men below. Holding the image, she dove at the enemy. She set her sights on a bearded warrior who closed on Ragnhild, swinging his axe. His weapon knocked her shield away and slammed into her gut, sending the shield-maiden reeling. Stormrider flew straight at the enemy's head, flapping her wings in his face while she lashed out at his eye with her talons. He dodged away, but it gave Ragnhild time to recover and get her shield up. As the warrior waved his arms to fend off the attacking falcon, the shield-maiden drove her sword into his unprotected throat. He dropped like a stone and Ragnhild charged the next opponent, while Stormrider winged away.

The birds flocked to her. When she dove at the enemy, they followed. Dozens of birds mobbed the attackers. They flew at heads and beat wings in faces, pecking eyes with dagger-like beaks and clawing with talons. Orm's men tried vainly to beat the attack off with weapons and shields, but the rapacious birds were fast and lethal.

Tromøy's warriors rushed in and attacked the distracted enemies. They brought down a dozen foes, but the defenders were still outnumbered and Orm's men cut them down.

A horn sounded. Stormrider hovered in the air, watching the harbor's mouth, where a fleet dropped their sails and rowed in. Friend or foe?

Olaf.

The new arrivals surged down on the raiders and attacked from the rear. Caught between two forces, Orm's warriors fell in great numbers while Tromøy's warriors pressed their advantage. The tide of battle turned and soon the shore was clogged with enemy corpses. Orm's surviving men fled to their ships, trying to launch while fending off the attacks of birds and Olaf's crews.

Only Orm's flagship succeeded in fighting their way through Olaf's line into the bay. They rowed away, leaving their shipmates to their deaths.

Stormrider watched the battle from high above. She spiraled up into the sky until the combatants looked like swarms of ants. Her keen falcon's vision picked out Orm's figure, standing on his prow beneath his banner. She folded her wings and dove straight at the enemy.

She hurtled down on him with blistering speed. Just before she struck, she let out a cry as she flung out her wings and spread her tail feathers to break her furious dive. She flipped in the air, reaching out with her talons. Orm looked up at her as she hit his face hard enough to snap his head back. A crack sounded as his neck broke.

The falcon dropped to the deck.

She lay there, struggling to regain her strength. Her work was not finished yet. She had to deal with the plague.

Before the enemy sailors could get to her, the falcon righted herself and flapped her wings, lofting into the air, high over the fog. She called again to the ravens and gulls, who left off their feeding and mustered to her. Stormrider worked her wings, fanning the deadly mist. The other birds surrounded the cloud of sickness and flapped their wings in unison.

Slowly, the fog began to coalesce in response. The birds continued to round up the disease, consolidating it into a dense cloud. When the curse formed a compact mass, the flock drove it toward the sea. The sickly mist gradually drifted away from the steading, out over the water, where it descended on Orm's fleeing ship, enveloping them as they rowed out of the bay.

When the last of the fog was gone, Åsa gave a call of thanks and dismissed the birds to return to their carrion. She beat her weary way toward the beach, reaching shore just before she dropped out of the sky.

CHAPTER 17

Tromøy's forces had vanquished the last of the enemy and now the warriors turned toward the steading, looking for rest and healers.

Ragnhild limped up the trail, gripping her stomach where the axe had hit her. She spotted something lying on the beach. Her heart stopped as she recognized Stormrider. She bent and gently picked up the still form. She couldn't tell if the bird was alive or not, but she tucked it in her battle jacket and turned toward the hall.

As she trudged up the hill, pain seared her stomach, making her double over. There was no outward sign of injury, but something was wrong.

Unn and her sisters would sort it out. Bent over to ease her gut, she headed toward the guesthouse.

She burst through the door just as another wave of pain surged through her. Hot blood gushed down her legs.

"My lady!" Unn caught her as she collapsed.

Ragnhild mutely held out the falcon. "It's Stormrider," she managed to gasp before she lost consciousness.

IN THE BOWER, Vigdis sat by Åsa's inert form, chanting the vardlokkur. Halfdan lay in the bed beside his mother. The little boy refused to leave her side, but thankfully he was now asleep. The blind wolf lay at the foot of the bed, head resting forlornly on his paws.

Åsa still breathed, but her face was pale. She was locked in the trance. Vigdis prayed to the gods that Stormrider would fly in through the smoke hole and bring her lady's soul back to her body.

The door banged open and young Tova rushed in, cradling something in her arms. Vigdis stopped chanting. Fylgja roused, but when he scented the girl, he lay back down dejectedly.

Vigdis's heart skipped a beat when she recognized Stormrider. She took the falcon's still form, fearing the worst. If Stormrider died, Åsa would die too.

"The bird is alive," said Tova. "Her heart beats faintly. She does not seem to be injured anywhere that can be seen or felt. My sister does not know whether she'll recover. Keep her warm and in a dark, quiet place and hope she wakes again."

Vigdis nodded her thanks. She rose from the stool and wrapped the bird in a wool blanket. She tucked the falcon under the covers beside Åsa's still form. Tova was right. All she could do was wait and hope the bird regained consciousness and brought her lady back.

INSIDE THE GUESTHOUSE, the air filled with coughs and groans. The sick were beginning to recover, embraced by loved ones.

Murchad sat up in bed, strength flooding into him. Across the room he glimpsed Ragnhild lying on a bench. His wife was unconscious, her face a pasty white. Unn and Ursa had taken off her battle jacket and wrapped her in a linen sheet. It was spotted with blood.

Murchad leaped up from his bench. His head swam and he steadied himself against the wall until the dizziness subsided. Then he staggered across the room. "Where is her wound?" he demanded.

Unn looked up at him, her eyes filled with sympathy. "She's lost the child."

Murchad sat down abruptly on the bench beside his wife. "Child?"

"You didn't know?"

Murchad shook his head. "She didn't tell me."

"She wasn't very far along. She may not have realized she was pregnant. I'm sorry."

He swallowed hard as the loss seared through his chest. "Will she live?" He hardly dared to speak the words.

Unn nodded again. "I think so. The bleeding has stopped. She's young and very strong. Her fighting spirit will keep her alive. It will help if you sit here and speak to her."

Murchad took Ragnhild's hand and stroked the calloused palm. "It's all right, *a chroí*. I'm here and I'm well. Rest and recover." He glanced up at Unn questioningly. "Will she be able to have other children?"

Unn shook her head. "I wish I could say, but I can't see inside her. Only time will tell."

Murchad stayed beside his wife, praying to every saint he could think of. Ragnhild had always been so strong. He'd never seen her look helpless. The sight shook him to his core.

RAGNHILD KEPT HER EYES CLOSED, though she heard Murchad's words and took comfort from his touch. She didn't want to face him. She'd lost their child. Perhaps she would never be able to have a baby now.

Isn't that what she wanted?

Her stomach felt hollow where the child had been. She'd barely known of its existence when it was taken away. Yet now the loss crushed her. She didn't ever want to open her eyes and join the empty world. The baby was lost and she'd never see it, never know if it was a boy or girl. Never hold it, watch it grow, share the joy with Murchad.

Murchad. What would he do? He wanted a child so badly. Would he find another wife who would give him what he longed for? He deserved it.

It was all her fault. If she had it to do over again, maybe she'd behave herself. Stop fighting everything so hard. Do as she was told.

That would never happen. She wasn't going to change. She had to face the world as she was.

She sighed and opened her eyes to meet Murchad's worried gaze.

"Oh, *a chroi*," he breathed.

"I'm sorry," she said. "I can't change. You should find a different wife, one who will give you what you long for."

He gathered her in his arms. "*A mhuirin*, never say that. You are who I want. I don't care if we have a child, as long as you are all right. I could never live without you by my side."

She rested her head on his shoulder and closed her eyes.

OLAF LED HIS WARRIORS ASHORE. Sonja waited on the beach. The sight of her filled him with hope. He swept her up in his arms and buried his face in her hair, inhaling her herbal scent.

"Thank the gods you're safe," she murmured. Relief flooded Olaf at her tender words.

She pulled away. "I must go assist the women. Åsa's soul has not returned to her body. Stormrider has been found, but the bird is near death, and if we lose the bird, Åsa will die too. We are going to try to bring her back."

Worry savaged Olaf's heart, but he didn't let Sonja see his distress for fear it would threaten their fragile reconciliation. He took her arm and walked her up the hill to the bower.

Sonja stared at the ground. "She is so brave. I understand why you love her. I don't know if I could find such courage if it was required of me."

"You are brave too, my love," said Olaf, meaning it. "You came here to help, despite the danger. I call that true courage."

"Your words mean a lot." At the door, she stopped and looked up at him. "I promised Åsa if anything happened, we would raise Halfdan."

His heart lurched. "Of course. Of course we would. But we won't have to. You'll get her back. I have faith in you."

She slipped inside the door. Olaf swallowed hard and hurried back to the shore where he busied himself bringing the wounded up to the guesthouse. Carts had been dispatched, and stretchers made from blankets stretched over saplings.

He helped a wounded man hobble into the guesthouse and found Eyvind bandaging a crew member's gashed arm. All traces of the sickness had left the trader, as with everyone else. Those who had been writhing with fever a few hours ago now cared for the wounded.

"What have you heard of Åsa?" Eyvind asked when he saw Olaf. "I tried to see her, but those women turned me away."

"They are tending to her," said Olaf cautiously.

Eyvind paled. "What's wrong with her? If she's injured, why isn't she here with the wounded?"

Olaf did not want to tell the newly revived man how dire Åsa's situation was. "The women will take good care of her. Vigdis is there, and Sonja."

Eyvind finished bandaging the sailor and started for the door. "I'm going to her."

"They won't let you in," said Unn, shooting Olaf a warning glance. "Men aren't allowed."

"They'll have to make an exception for me." Eyvind hurried out the door.

Unn gave Olaf a helpless look. "He mustn't disrupt their work."

"I'll go after him," he said.

He caught up with Eyvind and reached out a hand to grip his arm gently. "The women in the bower are doing everything they can to help her. We shouldn't disturb them."

"I can't lose her," Eyvind said, a desperate look in his eye.

"And you won't. Vigdis and Sonja will save her. Come, help me with the wounded. There's nothing we can do for her right now."

Reluctantly, Eyvind followed Olaf back down to the shore where the wounded lay thick on the ground, groaning.

Sonja chanted with the other women. She watched as Vigdis lifted the blanket. The falcon lay there, still unconscious. She knew it was better not to handle an injured bird. But there must be something they could do to help the falcon recover.

Vigdis lowered the blanket and shook her head.

As Sonja sang, she noticed that the iridescent feather had dropped to the floor. She stooped to pick it up and handed it to Vigdis. "Where did this come from? I've never seen one like it."

Vigdis took the feather and stared at it. It shimmered with the gleam of the Northern Lights. "It's from the Otherworld. Maybe…" Lifting the cover once more, the apprentice laid the shining feather on the comatose bird's breast.

The feather glowed and seemed to vibrate while a faint hum

emanated from it. The falcon's feathers ruffled as if in a breeze and the bird's head stirred. Stormrider's eyes snapped open. Vigdis threw the cover aside and backed away.

The falcon got to her feet and swiveled her head, gazing about the room. After a few moments, Stormrider picked up the iridescent feather in her beak and lofted up to the headboard of Åsa's bed. The bird perched there, and let the feather drop onto her mistress's face.

Åsa wrinkled her nose, blowing the feather away. She blinked her eyes open and gazed at the chanting women. She tried to sit up, but Vigdis gently pushed her back down. "Lady, you must rest."

"I must see to the sick and wounded. Halfdan—"

"Here is Halfdan. He is well, see?" Sonja gestured to the sleeping boy. "Eyvind is recovered. The others are in good hands. Rest a little longer and take some broth. Then I promise I will help you down to the guesthouse."

Åsa nodded, and Vigdis helped her into a sitting position and fed her spoonfuls of broth. Halfdan woke. "Mama!" he murmured. Åsa put her arm around the little boy and pulled him close. He snuggled down against his mother and went back to sleep.

When Åsa had finished half the bowl of broth, she insisted it was time to go to see the sick.

"Very well," said Vigdis. "I know I can't keep you here."

"I'll take her," said Sonja. "You need your rest." Vigdis nodded wearily. Sonja helped Åsa from the bed and bundled her in a cloak. Åsa clung to her as they traversed the room to the door. Sonja pushed it open and together they staggered across the yard to the guesthouse.

"You are the bravest woman I know," Sonja said. "I don't know if I could ever find the courage to take such risks for my people."

Åsa smiled at her. "I know you could. You will do whatever you have to. It was very brave of you to come here and risk your life to help us, and I am grateful that you were willing to take Halfdan to safety."

Sonja hugged Åsa closer. They reached the guesthouse door and she pulled it open, flooding the dim interior with light.

"Lady!" cried Tova, jumping up.

All around the room, the sick were up and tending to the injured, looking pale but well. There was no sound of coughing, just the moans of the battle-wounded.

Ragnhild lay on a bench, still and white-faced, wrapped in a bloody coverlet. Murchad bent over her, his face a mask of grief.

Åsa let go of Sonja and hurried over. "What's happened?" she asked Murchad. At the sound of Åsa's voice, Ragnhild's eyes flickered open.

"We lost our child," Murchad whispered.

Åsa gasped. "I'm so sorry."

Ragnhild said nothing, but her face bore an expression of defeat the likes of which Åsa had never seen on the shield-maiden. Her stomach knotted with worry.

Murchad hung his head, and Åsa laid a comforting hand on his shoulder. "Unn says she will recover."

Across the room, a still, linen-shrouded body lay on Heid's sick bench. At the sight, despair fell over Åsa like a dark cloak.

"I'm sorry," said Unn, following her searching gaze. "The völva died a few hours ago."

"She's with her family," said Åsa, fighting the grief that crushed her chest and clogged her throat. "She'll be with us always. Watching over us, guiding us. But she has the peace, and freedom from pain, and happiness she deserves. She's earned the right. Leave her there. She will not burn with the others. We will build her a mound to rival my father's, so that she can watch over Tromøy forever."

The door burst open and Olaf entered, carrying the front end of a stretcher with a wounded sailor on it. Sonja hurried to him.

The other end of the stretcher was hefted by Eyvind. When he saw Åsa, he handed off his end to a waiting nurse and rushed to his lover's side. He swept her into his arms and held her tight. She laid her head on his chest. "Welcome back, my love," he murmured. "You saved us."

"But Ragnhild has lost her child." Åsa choked on the words. "And the völva is dead."

Eyvind cradled her. "I know, I know, her death is a great loss to us all." Everyone in the room fell silent in grief.

From across the room came a groan.

As they all watched in horror, Heid's linen winding sheet quivered.

The shrouded figure sat up. Halla screamed.

"Damn the Nornir!" Heid ripped the fabric from her face.

Everyone stared at the sorceress, speechless.

"You were dead!" Åsa blurted.

The völva glared at her. "The Nornir sent me back. They said my work was not finished here."

Åsa stammered, "But you had a deal with Hel."

Heid scowled. "The Nornir trump all."

CHAPTER 18

Åsa woke the next morning in Eyvind's arms. She lay looking around the room. Stormrider drowsed on her perch. Beside them, Halfdan slept in his bed.

Utter joy filled Åsa. She stroked Eyvind's face, and his arms tightened around her. He ran his hands over her shorn, burnt hair. Eyes sparkling, he drew her in for a kiss. "Good to see you back from Hel," he said, "even if you are a little scorched around the edges."

"Good to see you back from the dead," she replied. He was still a bit weak from his illness, and she exhausted from her ordeal, so they left it at a kiss. Halfdan woke and was out of his bed and climbing into theirs. After a brief tussle with the little boy, they rose and dressed, and emerged from their chamber to find an empty hall. The outer door stood open to sunshine. Laughter beckoned.

Outside, the yard was filled with people seated at long tables. They were passing bowls of steaming porridge and cups of small beer. The scent of food made Åsa's stomach rumble. She gazed around at those who had risen so miraculously from their deathbeds. Many were thin and pock-marked, but everyone smiled and shoveled in their breakfasts as if they were starving. Which many of them were.

Åsa led Eyvind and Halfdan over to take their places beside Murchad and Ragnhild. The shield-maiden was still pale, physically recovered from her ordeal, but with a haunted look in her eyes. Åsa sensed a lingering gloom hanging over Ragnhild. She put a hand on her friend's shoulder.

Ragnhild frowned and shrugged her off. "I'm fine."

Murchad shot Åsa a despairing glance.

His gaze fell to the necklace gleaming on her chest. "Lady, how did you manage to get out of Helheim with the necklace, yet still lift the curse?" He looked at his wife, but Ragnhild didn't seem to hear.

"That is a story, Lord," said Åsa with forced cheer, "which I will relate this evening, over a cup of ale." In truth, she needed the day to gather her thoughts. Her head was in a whirl right now, and she hardly knew where to begin. She wished she had a skáld to help her tell the tale, but old Knut no longer traveled, and his apprentice was hard put to visit all the steadings in a season.

From across the table, Olaf and Sonja smiled at them. Åsa hesitated. She was not sure where she stood with them. "Olaf, King of Vestfold, and Sonja, Queen," she said formally. "I thank you for coming to our aid."

"Your gratitude is not necessary, Åsa, Queen of Agder," Olaf replied with equal formality, but his smile was warm.

"Tromøy is safe," Åsa said. "I owe you both so much."

"It was the least we could do," Sonja said with a warm smile. "You were brave to make your spirit journey, and how strong you were to have survived the dangers of the Otherworld and come back to us. I hope to hear all about it."

Åsa heard the forgiveness in Sonja's voice. A load lifted off her shoulders. "If you and your crew will join us for a feast tonight, I will tell my tale."

"Gladly!" said Olaf.

Halla plunked a bowl down in front of Åsa, and she fell to eating along with everyone else—all except Ragnhild, who sat there as if carved from wood.

After breakfast, Eyvind took Åsa by the hand. Halfdan clung to her skirt as they walked through the steading. She relished the sun, the scent of green spring grass, the gentle breeze, and the touch of her son and her lover. She silently thanked the gods for her good fortune.

That afternoon, a much-recovered Heid and her apprentices presided over the ritual as they burned the outbuilding that contained the dead. The women gathered around and crooned the vardlokkur, asking the Valkyries to guide those slain in battle to Valhöll and Sessrumnir, and the gatekeepers of Helheim to grant the sick entry to the land of the dead. Åsa knew firsthand where they were going, and what they would encounter on their path. As the funeral smoke rose into the sky, Åsa sent a personal prayer to Hel to be kind to her folk in the afterlife, and gave thanks to the gods for sparing those who still lived and for victory over Orm.

She showed the feather to Heid. "This is what gave me the power to command the birds in battle."

Heid smiled. "It's just a feather, even if it's from the rooster of Hel. Remember what I told you. All power comes from within. You can focus it on anything—a stick, a stone, a staff...a necklace." She nodded toward the necklace that hung around Åsa's neck.

Åsa touched the gold and felt its familiar vibration. "But I feel it."

"Yes, of course you do. It's a finely crafted vessel. The power comes from you. That's why not everyone can feel it."

Åsa stared at the völva, mentally chewing on her words.

Evening fell, and they gathered around the remains of the fire to drink the minni cup, honoring their departed loved ones. Eyvind's crew had been greatly reduced, and Tromøy had lost twenty, some to illness, some fallen in battle. *Raider Bride*'s crew had lost three sailors.

When all the dead had been honored, the time came for Åsa and Heid to tell of their journey.

Heid did not speak of her lost family, though she said, "All of Helheim is not a gruesome place. Those who deserve punishment receive it. But there are lush pastures and green forests, and those you love await you there." Heid's description of the pleasant parts of Hel's realm gave the bereaved fresh hope for their loved ones.

Murchad turned to Åsa. "Lady, did you find Svartfaxi in Helheim?"

She nodded. "He was waiting, and I might not be here had he not come to me. He carried me far and braved many dangers. He took me over the golden roof of the Gjoll bridge, through the iron forest, and leaped the flaming gates of Hel. Now, I hope he is grazing in green pastures as he deserves."

"Tell us of your adventures," said Sonja. "I long to hear of the Otherworld."

The words poured out of Åsa as she related her adventure to a rapt audience. She told them of Modgud standing guard on the bridge over the river of knives and swords, Gorm the Helhound in the Gnipa cave, Angrboda in the iron forest, and the jotun Fjolsvith guarding the gates of Hel. They marveled at her descriptions of Svartálfheim and her adventures with the dark álfar. Ulf questioned her eagerly about the Svartálf smiths and their techniques.

When the tale was told, Åsa turned to Murchad. She took off the necklace and presented it to him. "Lord Murchad, I now return this to you."

"Lady, if anyone has earned this necklace, it's you," he protested.

Åsa smiled. "The Nornir told me it must be returned to where it belongs, or more evil will befall us. I'll be glad to see it gone. I don't need it anymore. I have everything I require within me. Take it back to Ireland."

Murchad took the necklace and gave Ragnhild a searching gaze. "We brought this curse down on you, and now we will remove it. *A chroí*, it looks as though you will keep this promise."

Ragnhild did not smile, but only stared at the necklace listlessly.

～

RAGNHILD WALKED ALONE along the water's edge. Her body had healed, but inside she felt heavy and dark, like sodden wool, ready to tear at the wrong word. She felt best when she was alone, without having to respond to anyone.

The waves lapped peacefully along the shore. The soothing sound was broken by uneven footsteps grating along the rocky beach. Ragnhild turned to face the völva, unable to muster any feeling but defeat. She waited while the sorceress hobbled up alongside her.

Heid kept walking. After a moment Ragnhild fell in with her.

"Loss is part of life," said the völva, her gaze trained on the ground.

What did Heid know about it? Ragnhild did not have the energy for a retort. She kept walking.

"I lost my child," said Heid.

Ragnhild halted and stared at the sorceress.

"Raiders took my child, my husband, my home, and left me to live my life alone, a cripple." Heid kept up her labored pace, and Ragnhild hurried to catch up.

"I didn't know."

"I saw my family again in Helheim. I wanted to stay with them. But I had to leave and come back here." The völva stabbed her staff into the sand, pulling herself along. "I know you feel as though losing the child was your fault. But the Nornir determine the length of each of our lives. It is they who bear the blame," she said bitterly.

She halted, breath wheezing in her chest, and fixed Ragnhild with a fierce gaze. "We each have a destiny to fulfill, even you. So stop moping around here and get after it."

The völva resumed her labored steps, leaning heavily on her staff.

Ragnhild stared after her.

PART II: THE QUEEN'S NECKLACE

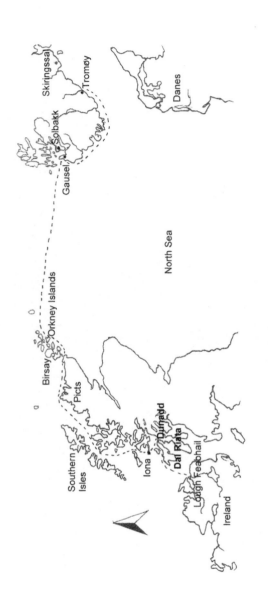

Skiringssal

Tromøy

Solbakk

Gausel

Birsay

Orkney Islands

Picts

Southern
Isles

Iona

Dunadd

Dál Riata

Lough Feabhail

Ireland

North Sea

Danes

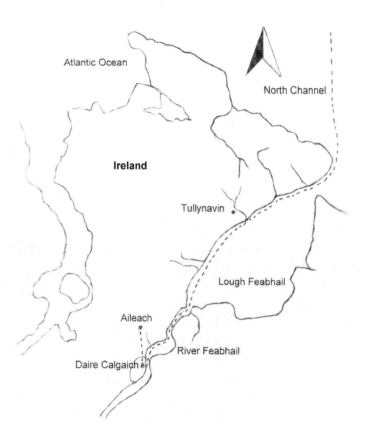

CHAPTER 19

Tromøy
June, AD 824

It took Murchad, Ragnhild, and those of *Raider Bride*'s crew who had been ill or wounded another three weeks to recover enough to resume their journey.

Gradually life returned to normal. Folk went about their chores. *Raider Bride*'s crew made ready for the voyage to Ireland. Three of Tromøy's warriors volunteered to join them in the voyage to fill the places of those who had died.

On a long summer evening, Murchad and Ragnhild strolled the beach together. He put his arm around Ragnhild and murmured, "When we get back home in the fall, perhaps we can try again to have a child."

"Perhaps," said Ragnhild. She thought of Åsa, who longed to sail with Eyvind, but must stay behind to be with Halfdan. To Åsa the exchange was worthwhile. Ragnhild could imagine loving a child, but would it change the person she was forever?

And what if she lost another child? Could she bear it?

Ragnhild was eager to set sail and leave the sadness of the

miscarriage and the decisions behind her. "A long voyage is just what I need, perhaps with a few battles to cheer me up."

Murchad said, "I hope we will get to Ireland in time to replace the necklace before Niall knows it's gone."

"You said there was a way to replace it without anyone seeing us."

Murchad nodded. "The treasury is located underground, in a souterrain. It is also a way to escape from the fortress in times of attack. I know where the secret entrance lies, outside of the fortress. We can sneak the necklace in there without Niall knowing."

Ragnhild said, "We have to get to Ireland first. What kind of reception do you expect from your cousin?"

"Regardless of how he feels about me, Niall has no choice but to treat me with the honor due my royal blood, and that extends to you and our crew. The laws of Irish hospitality require it. If Niall were to violate these customs, he would be put to eternal shame and he knows it."

"Niall seems pretty shameless to me, betraying you and taking the kingship for himself."

Murchad protested, "Niall did what he had to do, with the full backing of the brehon council." He grinned. "If he fails to show us proper hospitality, I could fast outside his door in protest, and he would never live that down. Such an embarrassment could even topple him from the kingship."

"Would you really do that?"

"As long as Niall thinks I might, that's all that matters."

Ragnhild nodded. The Irish had tricky laws and customs that baffled the Norse mind. As a scholar and a former king, Murchad knew them well, and how to use them to his advantage. Like the Norse, the Irish had their law speakers, called brehons, and their skálds, called bards, keepers of ancient history, all committed to memory and passed down painstakingly from one generation to the next. Murchad had been trained by these scholars, and Ragnhild trusted him to guide them through the perilous waters of Irish law.

She packed the necklace carefully in its leather satchel. It had caused so much trouble for her and those she loved. It would be good to get rid of it. Yet as she closed the satchel on the golden links, she felt a twinge of regret. It was natural to be reluctant to give up such a valuable prize. But what use had she for it? She couldn't tap its power, and she was not given to wearing extravagant ornaments. She shook off her reluctance and shoved the satchel to the bottom of her sea chest.

The morning of departure arrived, and a crowd gathered on the shore to bid them farewell. They helped *Raider Bride*'s crew load the ship with their belongings, weapons, and Åsa's generous provisions. When all was ready, the sailors scrambled aboard and seated themselves on their sea chests while Ragnhild took her place at the helm.

At her command the crew fitted their oars and raised them straight up in the air, waiting to be launched.

"Give my best to Behrt," Åsa called from the shore. "Tell him we miss him here and he's always welcome back."

"Be careful what you wish for," said Ragnhild, holding the steering oar out of the water while the folk of Tromøy heaved *Raider Bride* off the beach. "The man is now a Christian monk. He'll try to lead your folk astray."

Åsa smiled and shrugged. "On Tromøy, all may worship as they wish."

Raider Bride's keel grated over the bottom, then the ship was floating free. "Row!" shouted Ragnhild. Her crew brought down their oars and began to propel the ship out of the harbor. She unlashed the steering oar and dipped it into the water. As the tiller came to life in her hands, the last of her grief blew away.

Ragnhild's spirits soared as *Raider Bride* surged through the glittering waters. It was perfect summer weather, with the solstice just ahead and the days long. Beside her, Murchad grinned. He loved the sea as much as she did. This was where they belonged.

The ship emerged from the harbor's shelter and the breeze freshened. Ragnhild gave the command, and the crew boated their oars and scrambled eagerly to hoist the sail.

The seas were calm enough for them to stay outside the skjaergaarden, the rocky archipelago that provided shelter from heavy seas. To travel in the tortuous channels, fraught with hidden shoals and treacherous currents, required painstaking navigation under oar. Today they ran free with a following sea, making excellent speed. The crew, at their leisure now under sail, chattered excitedly as they trolled fishing lines in hopes of catching dinner.

That night they put into a sheltered cove just before they reached the treacherous southern cape. They would navigate Lindesnes during daylight hours. While they dined on fresh fish, Thorgeir and Murchad resumed their tale-telling contest, vying to see whose stories could most amaze the audience. The Irishman had an advantage over his Norse opponent, firstly because Murchad had been schooled in the art of storytelling by the best bards in Ireland, and secondly because he had an inexhaustible store of Irish tales his Norse audience had never heard. His exotic stories held his audience spellbound with his lilting cadence.

But Thorgeir had his own advantages. His booming voice and humorous antics kept his audience amused, and they loved the familiar stories they'd known since childhood.

"How about the tale of Idunn and her golden apples?"

His offer was greeted with a cheer. Thorgeir rubbed his hands together and launched into the story.

"The gods stay young because the goddess Idunn lets them eat of her golden apples. Any time they see a wrinkle or a gray hair, they ask her for an apple, and their eternal youth and beauty are restored.

"One day Loki got himself into a scrape with the jotun, Thjazi." Everyone groaned at the mention of the trickster's name. "Thjazi, in the form of an eagle, got hold of Loki and flew him high into the air. He threatened to drop the trickster unless he promised to kidnap Idunn and bring the goddess and her apples of youth to Jotunheim. Naturally, Loki promised what he must to keep from being smashed on the rocks.

"Now, Idunn is beautiful and kind, but not too cunning. Loki managed to lure her out of the safety of Asgaard where Thjazi, in his eagle form, swooped down and carried her off.

"In a few short days, the gods began to age, and when they sought Idunn and her apples, she was nowhere to be found. Naturally, they suspected Loki was the instigator, and they caught him and tortured the truth out of him. They demanded he go and rescue Idunn and her apples and bring them back to Asgaard.

"Loki had no choice but to try, unless he wanted to suffer the gods' horrible punishments. 'I'll rescue her, but I'll need to borrow your falcon cloak, Freyja,' he said.

"'You use that cloak more than I do,' the goddess of love and beauty grumbled. But the sight of a few gray hairs convinced her to agree.

"Loki put on the falcon cloak and flew to Thjazi's hall. He found Idunn sitting alone in the garden, her basket of apples in her lap. He changed her into a nut and carried her away in his talons."

"What about the apples?" asked Murchad.

Thorgeir frowned. "The apples were changed along with her."

"Into nuts? Was there one nut, or several? Did the basket get changed into a nut too?"

"Oh, for Thor's sake, they were all changed into a cluster of nuts. Loki carried the cluster off in his beak."

Mollified, Murchad smiled and stayed silent.

Thorgeir resumed his tale. "Thjazi quickly discovered the

escape. He took his eagle form and pursued Loki. Falcons are fast, but they can't outfly an eagle. Loki was nearly within Asgaard's walls, but Thjazi was upon him. When the gods saw Loki coming with the eagle on his tail, they built a huge bonfire out of a pile of wood shavings. Loki made it over the fire, but Thor blew on the flames with his bellows just as Thjazi flew over. The fire flared high into the air, singing the eagle's feathers. Thjazi plummeted to earth inside the walls of Asgaard. Thor dealt him a mighty blow with Mjölnir, and the jotun died.

"The gods thought all was well. They ate Idunn's apples, and their youth and beauty were restored. But Thjazi had a daughter named Skadi. She was a fierce shield-maiden. When she learned of her father's death, Skadi put on her armor, picked up her weapons, and stormed Asgaard, seeking vengeance.

"She came before the gods and demanded justice for her father's killing. 'Fight me if you will,' she said.

"The gods were filled with admiration for the brave jotun maiden. Nobody wanted to fight her. 'I think we can reach a suitable compensation for your father's life,' said Odin.

"'Very well, what do you offer me?' Skadi said.

"For hours, the gods bargained with her over Thjazi's wergild, but nothing satisfied the bereaved maiden.

"Finally Odin said, 'We will let you choose a husband from among us. That will make you one of us, entitled to all the bounty of Asgaard.'

"'That's a good start,' said Skadi, eyeing Baldr, the most beautiful of the gods. 'What more do you offer me? My father's death has saddened me. I've lost all my merriment—you have taken it from me.'

"'What if we make you laugh again?' said Thor.

"'Fine,' said Skadi. 'I can't imagine how you might accomplish that.'

"'I am certain Loki will find a way,' said Thor, casting a meaningful look at Loki.

"'I will let you try, if you also ensure that my father is never forgotten,' said Skadi.

"'Very well, I will think of a way to do that too,' said Odin. 'Now, choose your husband.'

"Skadi smiled eagerly at Baldr. 'Very well, line up all the eligible gods and I will choose.'

"But Odin lined the gods up behind a curtain so that all Skadi could see was their feet. When she complained, Odin said, 'We did not say you could choose them by their faces. Where's the fun in that?'

"Skadi examined the gods' feet. One pair was more attractive than the rest. 'Those must belong to Baldr,' she thought, and chose their owner for her husband.

"But when the curtain was pulled back, the feet were revealed to belong to Njord. He was not exactly ugly, but he was no match for Baldr.

"Skadi scowled and gripped her spear. 'I've been tricked!'

"Odin soothed her, saying, 'Njord will make an excellent husband. He's among the wealthiest of gods, he rules the wind and storms, and he's the father of Frey, the god of peace and plenty, and Freyja, the goddess of love and beauty. You could not make a better choice.'

"Skadi grumbled, 'Very well, you have gotten the better of me in that bargain, but I still haven't laughed.'

"'Loki will make you laugh,' said Thor, brandishing Mjölnir in Loki's face.

"The trickster skulked out to the yard and returned leading a nanny goat by a rope tied around its beard.

"'I fail to see the humor,' said Skadi ominously.

"'You will,' said Loki glumly. He doffed his breeches."

Thorgeir loosened his belt as if to drop his own pants, but the audience protested. "We don't need you to demonstrate. Keep your breeches on!"

Thorgeir looked offended, but he resumed his seat and

complied. "When Loki stood, bare-assed, before the gods, Skadi admitted, 'I'm beginning to see the humor.'

"'You haven't seen anything yet,' said Loki. He tied the other end of the goat's lead rope around his own scrotum.

"'Is he mad?' said Skadi.

"'That's a certainty,' said Thor.

"Loki yanked on the rope. The indignant goat tugged back, and Loki shrieked. The gods roared with mirth, but Skadi did not crack a smile."

Thorgeir leaped up from his driftwood seat, sloshing the ale in his wooden cup as he pantomimed the action. He grabbed his crotch and pretended to yank on his privates, then lurched forward, as if the goat jerked back. The audience howled with laughter.

"The tug-of-war continued, with the goat protesting and Loki shrieking, but still Skadi did not laugh. Finally Loki gave a mighty yank on the rope, and the goat took off running, pulling Loki off his feet. The rope snapped and Loki fell into Skadi's lap.

"When she looked down at the whimpering mess in her lap, Skadi broke into laughter. Loki sighed in relief. 'Can I stop now?'

"Skadi pushed Loki off her lap and stood. She gave Odin a stern gaze. 'Now, All-father, how will you keep your final promise? What will you do to ensure my father is never forgotten?'

"Odin went to the fire where Thjazi had burned. He reached into the embers and pulled out two giant, glowing orbs. 'These are your father's eyes,' he said, and he gave them to Thor, who flung them high up into the sky. You can see them to this very day." Thorgeir pointed up to the night sky, where two bright stars glowed side by side.

"And so Skadi was at last appeased, though she and Njord found they could not live together. When they stayed in Njord's home by the sea, Skadi longed for her mountains. And when they visited her mountain home, Njord could not sleep because he craved the sound of the waves crashing on the shore. At last they agreed to live apart."

"That is a fine tale, brother," Murchad admitted. "The next night we spend ashore, I will tell you an even better one."

"That's a wager I will take," said Thorgeir. "If your story is better than mine, I will take your turn as the lookout on the bow."

By now the fire had burned low, and many had already taken to their hudfat. Murchad and Ragnhild crawled into theirs and lay in each other's arms, too tired to do more than nuzzle before they were fast asleep.

Ragnhild woke in the night, as she so often did these days. Murchad stirred beside her. "I wonder if it would have been a boy or a girl?" she murmured. "Would the baby have had your dark hair and green eyes?"

Murchad said nothing, only held her close and stroked her hair. She knew there was no point in wondering. They would never know.

CHAPTER 20

Lindesnes

Next morning, in preparation for rounding the southern cape, Ragnhild had the crew reef the sail while they were still in the shelter of the cove. While it was possible to take a reef while under sail, it was a dangerous operation, with the huge expanse of tarred wool flapping, threatening to sweep crew members overboard. If the wind died down later, it was far safer to shake out the reef in calm winds.

A dozen sailors manned the halyard, raising the massive sail, while eight more hands gathered the heavy fabric at the base and tied it off with the reefing pennants that dangled from the cloth, shortening the sail by an eighth.

Once the sail was properly reefed, they spent one more night in the cove, and in the morning before the land breeze filled in, they got underway. For the first leg of the journey, they rowed in the narrow, skerry-littered shelter of the skjaergaarden.

By midday the skjaergaarden thinned, and the rocky headland of Lindesnes lay ahead. As *Raider Bride* emerged from the shelter of the last scatter of islets, a brisk wind hit them, kicking up choppy seas.

"Ship oars," Ragnhild cried. "Make sail!"

The crew unlashed the sail and hauled it up the mast, sheeting it in hard. The wind freshened, coming across the beam as they neared the cape, and Ragnhild was glad she had taken the reef. *Raider Bride* had plenty of weather helm as it was, and it took all her strength on the tiller to keep the ship from rounding up into the wind. Shortening the sail more with another reef would be even better, but it wasn't worth the risk to the crew to have them manhandle the sail in this breeze. She pointed the bow as close to the wind as the ship could go, taking them well away from the lee shore with its treacherous currents and hidden rocks.

The wind gained force and the ship heeled over, dipping her rail in the water and throwing up spray. The crew members grinned as they clung to the rigging, enjoying the ride. They'd all rounded Lindesnes more than once and knew *Raider Bride* could weather the rough seas.

The ship roared around the cape and Ragnhild came onto a northwesterly course. As soon as she turned downwind, the following seas settled down, pushing the ship with a soft, steady whoosh up the Jaeren coast. Ragnhild sailed due north until she sighted the headland of Solavika, where they put in to the bay to wait for sunrise.

At sunrise, the wind was flat calm. They waited all morning for the wind to fill in, but when it did, it came from the west, so they waited another day. The next day, the hoped-for northerly came. Ragnhild headed due west on a beam reach for the Orkney Islands.

That night Einar and Ragnhild marked the sun's angle as it set on the prow. After dark, he woke her and together they took a bearing on the pole star, using their clenched fists held at arm's length to measure the height of the star, to make sure they were on track. They steered a modified course just a little north of west to compensate for the southerly set of the wind and current. As long as they were set to the south, and kept their westerly heading, they ran little risk of missing the Orkneys, or at the worst, the Shetlands to their north. To miss those islands spelled disaster for a ship, doomed to wander the vast open ocean without landmarks until they ran out of food and water. This deadly misfortune was known as hafvilla and could be brought on when the ship lost its course due to fog or foul winds.

For now the winds were strong, blowing away all danger of fog and setting them toward the mainland of Pictland. *Raider Bride* romped across the seas like a horse let out of its byre in the spring. A sense of freedom welled up within Ragnhild, vast as the crisp blue expanse, tinged with a delicious thrill of the unknown that lay ahead. The ship's planks creaked as they flexed in the seaway, always taking on a little water between the seams. She loved being so close to the water, as if she were a whale or a fish.

Her crew was seasoned and none were seasick, a far cry from their last passage to Ireland, when so many were green farmhands. They were rosy from the wind and laughing at the ship's motion.

They sailed out of sight of land all afternoon and into the evening. The crew gnawed on dried cod and flatbread when they were hungry. As the sky's blue deepened to cobalt, Ragnhild set watches to let everyone get some sleep. Einar took a bearing on the setting sun, then relieved her on the helm, and she climbed into her sheepskin. Murchad was sound asleep and barely moved when she wriggled in beside him. She gazed up at the stars, listening to the hiss and gurgle of water creaming past the hull while *Raider Bride* rose and fell rhythmically in the seas. Sleep came easily at sea, and she didn't wake until the watch roused her to take her turn at the helm. She felt refreshed and full of energy.

When dawn broke, the wind strengthened, sending *Raider Bride* racing over the waves. The crew, used to living with the perpetual slant of the ship's heel, fell into a comfortable rhythm of sleep and work, taking their turns as lookouts, washing down flatbread and dried meat with a cup of ale, burrowing under the furs for a nap in the shelter of the bow. The endless work of coiling lines, bailing the bilge, and trimming the sail to suit the breeze made the time fly by.

EINAR WOKE Ragnhild to a world enshrouded in mist. The wind had died completely in the night, and they made their way cautiously under oars. Ragnhild could see no further than the ship's prow, but the raucous calls of seabirds, changes in the motion of the seas and the color, heralded land. Hidden in the impenetrable fog were the rugged cliffs and treacherous tides of the Orkneys, home of their enemies.

Even though the fog imperiled navigation, Ragnhild was grateful that it hid *Raider Bride* from their foes. The previous year, as *Raider Bride* sailed home from Ireland, Orkney pirates had attacked. Murchad had killed Kol, their most dangerous adversary, but the chieftain of Birsay had survived along with many of his war band.

Ragnhild, Einar, and Svein each took short turns on the helm. Thorgeir, who had the best eyesight, was stationed on the bow with a white signal flag, peering into the mist for sails and scanning the waters for submerged rocks and tide rips, using the signal flag to point out hazards. Gradually the sun burned away the fog, and Thorgeir guided them through the treacherous currents to a deserted bay on the south side of an eastern island, far from Birsay.

As the keel grated on the shore, Ragnhild's shoulders relaxed. She realized she'd been clutching the helm tightly. It was good to be on land again and out of sight of enemies. She broke out a keg of ale in celebration.

It was Murchad's turn to tell a tale. "I will tell you of Ireland's greatest queen. In ancient times, Ireland had shield-maidens and warrior queens just as the Norse do. The most famous of them was Medbh. You have heard of her in the great cattle raid of Cooley.

"Medbh was a daughter of the king of Connacht. His sons had rebelled against him. When they fell in battle against their father, he swore no son would rule in Ireland after him.

"Medbh's father killed the high king and took the kingship of Tara. As compensation, he gave his three daughters in marriage to Conchobar, the high king's son, and made him king of Ulster.

"Medbh was far too proud to be one of three wives. She divorced Conchobar and returned to Connacht. Her father, now High King of Tara, had left the kingship of Connacht vacant, and he decreed that no man could be king of Connacht without becoming Medbh's husband.

"Three men were rivals to become king of Connacht: Fidig mac Feicc, Tindi mac Conra, and Eochaid Dala. Fidig gained the high king's permission for Medbh's hand, thereby gaining the kingship, but Tindi ambushed him. They fought a great battle and Fidig was killed. For killing his favorite, the high king drove Tindi into the hinterlands and set Medbh up alone on the royal seat of Connacht. But Tindi secretly became Medbh's lover, and they plotted to overthrow her father. Medbh gathered all the king's sons to her.

"The high king held a fair at Tara, and when Medbh did not attend, he sent his messenger to fetch her. While Medbh was at Tara, Conchobar waylaid her when she was bathing in the Boyne River and raped her.

"At this, the kings of Ireland rose up together and declared war on Conchobar. Tindi challenged Conchobar to single combat, but Conchobar set Tindi's own brother to fight him, and Tindi fell in that duel.

"Then the kings of Ireland made war on Conchobar. The armies met at the River Boyne, and Conchobar was the victor.

But Eochaid Dala rescued Medbh. She agreed to marry Eochaid and make him king of Connacht provided he should have neither jealousy, fear, nor niggardliness, for it was *geis* to her to marry a man with these faults.

"Medbh's sister, Clothru, was still married to Conchobar, and when Medbh discovered Clothru was carrying Conchobar's child, she drowned her sister in a stream. Clothru died but her son survived. He was called Furbaide, for he was cut from her womb.

"Medbh fostered a young boy, Ailill, son of Mata. Ailill grew to be a warrior of great skill and valor. He defended Connacht against Conchobar's incursions, and he became the head of Medbh's household guards. In due course, Medbh took him as her lover. Medbh's husband, Eochaid, became jealous and tried to banish Ailill. When Medbh forbade that, Eochaid challenged Ailill to fight for her, and the kingship. Though Eochaid fought bravely, Ailill killed him, some say through Medbh's magic. Ailill became her husband and, with her consent, king of Connacht.

"Medbh bore Ailill seven sons. Their marriage was a happy one, but Medbh still hated her first husband, Conchobar. She asked her druid which of her children would kill Conchobar, and the druid answered, 'By Maine he shall fall.' Medbh had no child of that name, but to make sure Conchobar would be killed, she renamed all her sons so that their first name was Maine.

"It so happened that one of her sons killed a man named Conchobar. He was not Conchobar, the king of Ulster, but the son of Arthur, king of Scotland.

"Furbaide mac Conchobar, the son of Medbh's murdered sister, Clothru, grew to manhood and swore vengeance. Medbh was well protected, but Furbaide laid a trap for his aunt. He knew that Medbh bathed in a certain pool each day, and he hid there and watched her. When she left, he marked the place where she stood to bathe, and measured the distance between her spot and the shore. In secret, he set up a pole the same height as Medbh and set an apple on top of it. He measured the distance with the rope and practiced with his sling every day until he could hit the apple nine times out of ten.

"When Furbaide was ready, he lay in wait for her one morning as she bathed, and slung his rock at her head and killed her.

"Some say Furbaide killed her with a piece of cheese, but that story was started by satirists, seeking to steal Medbh's glory.

"Queen Medbh was buried in a tall stone cairn on a mountain summit. At her command she was buried standing up, facing her enemies in Ulster."

Everyone was silent, absorbing the tale. At last Thorgeir said, "Well, Lord, I think you have bested me for tonight. But next time I will tell a story that will make yours seem tame by comparison."

When they got underway in the morning, Thorgeir took Murchad's turn on the bow with the signal flag as they worked their way south through the Orkney Islands. The hard-running tide flushed the ship between the islands, allowing the rowers to rest their oars while Ragnhild kept *Raider Bride* on course with the steering oar. Thorgeir once again guided her through the maelstrom of submerged rocks and riptides. Ragnhild thanked the gods there was no fog.

After several intense hours the current gradually slackened, and Ragnhild turned the helm over to Einar. The crew fitted their oars and rowed hard through the slack. Thorgeir still kept a close lookout, but it was much easier to navigate the shoals without the current threatening to dash them on the rocks. By midafternoon, the tide strengthened against them, and they put into a deserted cove to wait out the contrary current.

They stayed on board, eating a cold meal of dried meat and flatbread, washed down with a ration of ale, and took turns napping while the others kept watch on the current as it raged against the rocks. As soon as it slackened, they raised anchor and fitted their oars once more. This time Einar took his place on the bow with the signal flags, giving Thorgeir a rest from the intense concentration. Through the long summer evening, the ship skimmed across the calm water until Einar directed them into another cove for the night.

They slept aboard that night and spent the next working their way through the islands, then put into a protected bay that evening. They beached the ships, making camp and building a proper fire to cook a hot meal of barley porridge. Afterward, the crew lingered around the campfire, sipping their ale in silence, too tired from the day's work for their usual chatter.

"I'm worn out," said Thorgeir. "Our story competition will have to wait until our next night ashore." Though there were disappointed groans, everyone turned in early.

Ragnhild and Murchad snuggled into their hudfat and slept like stones. At dawn, they climbed out of the sheepskin to join the crew around the campfire for steaming bowls of porridge. Then they struck camp and loaded the ship.

It was a fine morning. Sail set and drawing, they skirted the rugged north coast.

"This is the land of the warlike Picts who tattoo their bodies," said Murchad.

They followed a southwesterly course to thread the archipelago that sheltered the southern passage. The wind died off and the crew plied their oars once more, though the currents here were less treacherous than in the Orkneys. Dolphins, eagles, and seabirds of all descriptions teemed the waters, reaping the rich harvest of the sea.

Late in the day they broke out of the islands into ocean swells and hoisted sail to a good northerly breeze, running across the open water. Murchad searched the coastline. "There is the sacred Isle of Iona," he said, pointing out an island in the distance. "Would that we could pay them a visit." The longing in his voice was palpable.

Ragnhild stared at the rugged seaway. "Is this what your heart is set on, husband?"

Murchad nodded, gaze fixed on the speck of land. "It has been a holy site since long before the coming of Christianity. It is said that a druid colony inhabited the island when the blessed Colm Cille made the voyage in a coracle, with twelve brethren. The druids were so impressed with the saint's teachings that they adopted Christianity. The colony thrived, and they produced many treasures. Colm Cille loved to illuminate sacred texts, and Iona had one of the greatest scriptoriums ever established. The monks created beautiful manuscripts on smooth-scraped calf-skin. It is writing, like the runes, but far more glorious. The volumes are painted like the carvings on the high seat pillars, full of serpents and angels in colors made from precious pigments, lapis lazuli, silver and gold. Each page is a precious work. It is here that the Dal Riata kings are anointed by the abbot, and their fleet protects the monastery."

"This voyage is for your sake, *a chroi*. Let's see this sacred isle," said Ragnhild.

Murchad smiled, then said, "We must be cautious. Eighteen years ago, the Danes attacked Iona. They burned the settlement and martyred sixty-three monks. The survivors have rebuilt, but the sight of us will cause them alarm."

"I thought the Dal Riata protected Iona?"

Murchad sighed. "Originally the Dal Riata was ruled by the Irish of Ulaid, but the Picts defeated them in battle many years ago and have ruled the Dal Riata ever since. Though blessed Colm Cille converted the Picts to Christianity, they still cling to their druids and the old ways. It is they who defend Iona, or are supposed to. It was under their protection that the blessed isle was laid to ruin."

Ragnhild altered her course and called out to the crew. "We're going to land on that island. Take down the prow beast and leave your weapons in your sea chests. We don't want to frighten these Christ-priests."

As they approached the shore, a warning cry echoed from the settlement. Men scurried into the enclosure and the gate closed behind them.

Raider Bride landed and the crew leaped out onto the white shell beach. The monastic settlement was fortified by an earthen bank topped with a dry-built stone wall. Outside the walls was a scattering of outbuildings. Ragnhild made out a cowshed, barns, stables, a carpenter shop, a smithy, and a kiln.

Monks with tonsured heads peered over the walls. *Raider Bride*'s crew halted, looking to Ragnhild for guidance.

Murchad advanced toward the walls, holding up a white shield. "We are not *dubh gaill*," he shouted, using the Irish name for Danes. "I am Murchad mac Maele Duin of Cenel nEoghain, and these are my wife's people. We come in peace."

Sounds of a muted discussion could be heard behind the walls. After a moment, the gate opened and a robed monk strode out briskly. His graying hair and weathered features placed his age around fifty. He eyed the Norse suspiciously. "Greetings, Lord Murchad. I am Blathmac Flann, acting abbot here."

Ragnhild translated for her crew, who had learned only a few words in Irish on their previous visit.

"Greetings, Father Abbot," said Murchad. "We have met before, I believe, when we were younger."

"Indeed, I remember when you were but a boy. And then when King Aed was killed, I attended your election to king." Blathmac gave Ragnhild a hostile glance. "But I heard that Niall deposed you for refusing to renounce your heathen wife."

Ragnhild groaned inwardly, realizing she must be prepared for such a reception throughout Ireland.

"That is true," said Murchad, his arm around Ragnhild. "I married to form an alliance with the *finn gaill*, but I would not be parted from my wife now. We have established our own kingdom in Lochlainn and have formed alliances with my wife's kin to protect Ireland from attack."

Blathmac frowned as he took in Ragnhild and her shield-maidens in their salt-stained breeks and tunics. "Women are not allowed on the holy isle."

"We are on our way to Ireland, to offer our pledge of protection to Niall. When I sighted your isle, I had a longing to see it again, and so we stopped. I am sure you can make an exception for my wife and her warriors, all sworn to defend Ireland."

Blathmac paused, looking as if he were tasting something unpleasant. Then his expression smoothed out and he nodded. "Please enter as my guests."

They followed him through the gate. Within towered two Celtic crosses hewn from rock beside a stone-built church. The other buildings were also stone, though crowned with thatched roofs. Blathmac pointed out the abbot's house, the guesthouse, as well as a cookhouse and refectory.

The yard was dotted with little beehive-shaped cells built of stone. "Each monk has a cell, and here they seek solitude to sleep, pray, and meditate," said Blathmac. "Some also venture out into the wild."

By now a dozen or so monks had gathered to stare at *Raider Bride*'s crew. They were wire-thin and weather-beaten from years of hard work and self-denial.

Blathmac gestured to the brethren. "After the *dubh gaill* destroyed this colony, Abbot Diarmait fled to Kells with most of the surviving monks. They took many of the treasures with them, including Saint Colm Cille's reliquary and many of the precious books that had been created in the scriptorium. These brethren had the courage to stay on and rebuild, in spite of the danger."

"You are very brave indeed," said Murchad, nodding to them.

One of the monks said proudly, "After the raid, we quarried

rock from the hillside to build an abbey that the *dubh gaill* could not burn."

Blathmac continued, "When I heard these good men were without an abbot, I agreed to come here to lead them. I brought the blessed Colm Cille's remains back to the island, to be buried here where he wished to be."

"Aren't you afraid the *dubh gaill* will return?" asked Murchad.

Blathmac's expression turned stern. "I am certain they will, and soon. But we have no fear. This isle has been sacred to my people for hundreds of years, long before the coming of Christianity. We choose to stay here and defend it from the *dubh gaill*. We are ready to become martyrs for Christ. We will guard Saint Colm Cille's remains with our dying breath. Now, go and refresh yourselves." Ragnhild wondered if the rest of the monks were as eager for martyrdom as their abbot.

A monk showed them to the guesthouse and brought them water. After they had washed and rested, another brother appeared to bring them to the hall for a meal.

They joined the monks around a long table lined with benches. The brethren gave Ragnhild and her shield-maidens a friendly if shy reception, making room for them with polite nods and lowered eyes.

After the abbot had offered a prayer, a simple meal of barley porridge, bread, milk, eggs, and fish was served. It tasted wonderful after days of dried fish and flatbread.

When they had eaten, Blathmac turned to Murchad. "Lord Murchad, will you join me in sunset prayers on Sithean Mor?"

Murchad nodded eagerly. "Gladly. It's been a long time since I've prayed with a man of God." He looked at Ragnhild. "Will you and the crew be all right while I go with Father Blathmac?"

Ragnhild nodded. "We'll be glad of the rest." She rose and led the crew to the guesthouse.

~

IN THE EVENING LIGHT, Murchad followed Blathmac to a smooth, grassy hill. They climbed to the top and seated themselves on the stones, still warmed from the late afternoon sun. From here, the sea stretched endlessly to the west.

They watched in silent awe as the sun dipped into the sea. Blathmac said, "The blessed Colm Cille chose this island because he could not see Ireland from here, for when he went into exile, he swore never to set eyes on his homeland again. It is said that he came here every night at sunset to pray. One evening, a brother followed him and watched. As the sun set, he saw angels of light descend on the saint. We call it the Hill of the Angels."

The last light of day flared and Murchad felt the spell of this place fall over him. His druid teachers had also told him of the spirits that swept across this holy island at sunset. He wondered if these were the same beings that the Norse called land spirits, who lived in sacred rocks and waterfalls. They seemed to be universal, not the property of one religion or another, but part of the earth.

Murchad sat silently beside the abbot as the sun sank below the western horizon, far across the sea. He let himself settle into the peace of the place.

When the last of the light was gone, Blathmac rose. They walked back to the abbey in silence, neither of them willing to break the spell. The abbot found his way surefooted despite the darkness. At the guesthouse door, Blathmac nodded a mute parting.

Murchad climbed under the covers beside Ragnhild, and she roused enough for a good-night kiss. He relished the fresh, salt-free bedding as he drifted into sleep, still feeling the spirits shining around them.

In the morning one of the younger brothers, Eoin, gave them a tour of the settlement. "I wish the scriptorium had survived," he said wistfully. "But the *dubh gaill* burned it. The sacred texts which had been hidden from the raiders were taken to the abbey of Kells for safekeeping. Now the scriptorium is there as well."

A young monk came running into the fortress. He was gaunt and dirty, with matted hair and beard. "Father Abbot!" he cried.

"Why do you break your vow of solitude?" Blathmac demanded.

"I was meditating out on the Dun when I spied a *dubh gaill* longship heading this way," the young monk gasped.

The other brothers crossed themselves.

"Close the gates!" shouted Blathmac.

Ragnhild grinned at Murchad. "I haven't killed any Danes in a while."

"You can't think of fighting them," said Blathmac.

Ragnhild gave him a look. "Why not? They're only one ship's crew. The odds are fairly even, and defenders have the advantage. We have an excellent defensive location here. With any luck they'll already be laden with treasure."

"But you're a woman! Half your crew are women."

"That's never stopped us killing Danes before," said Ragnhild.

"Father Abbot," said Murchad. "The Norsewomen are more like the Irish queens and warrior women of old. Think of the tales of Scáthach and Queen Medbh."

Blathmac glowered at Ragnhild's shield-maidens. "If I'd known they were such an abomination, I'd never have shown you hospitality."

Murchad stiffened. "You can't be thinking of refusing hospitality to a son of Niall?"

The abbot clamped his mouth closed.

Ragnhild retorted, "Fear not, as soon as we've taken care of these Danes, we'll be on our way." She turned to her crew. "To arms!"

She swept away. Murchad smiled at the abbot's shock as the crew formed a disciplined line behind her. They marched down to *Raider Bride* where they retrieved weapons and armor from sea chests, taking shields from the gunnel racks.

As soon as everyone was armed, Ragnhild shouted, "Shield wall! Archers to the rear!" Murchad took his place beside her along with Einar, Thorgeir, and Svein. They locked their shields, spears ready at their side. A dozen crew members joined them while the archers crowded behind their protective wall.

As the Danish ship approached, Ragnhild cried, "Archers! Nock!" She waited, letting the enemy get closer, until Murchad could see the Danish archers nock. A quick head count confirmed that their crew outnumbered *Raider Bride*'s by a dozen. Their first flight of arrows had to thin the enemy's numbers before they reached shore.

"Draw!" shouted Ragnhild. Behind Murchad, bows creaked as the strings were dawn. He tensed as the Danes came into range. *Now.* "Loose!" she cried.

The Danes loosed their arrows at the same time. The two volleys crossed in midair. A few arrows collided and fell harmlessly in the water, but the rest came down in a deadly hail.

"Shields up!" shouted Ragnhild. The locked shields flew overhead as the enemy arrows descended, thwacking into the wood. The shields caught them all. None of *Raider Bride*'s crew was hit.

There were no cries from the Danish ship either. The enemy had succeeded in fending off the first volley. They closed the shore, still outnumbering *Raider Bride*'s crew.

"Archers!" Ragnhild shouted again. They had already nocked, and Murchad heard the bowstrings creak as they drew. "Loose!" The archers sent another flight toward the enemy. They had managed to get their volley off while the Danes were still regrouping. The closer range paid off and the arrows struck with more force. This time the enemy shrieked as the arrows found their marks. Men fell and shields dropped.

"Nock!" cried Ragnhild again.

Abruptly, the Danes sheered off. Their big sail backed and filled on the other side as they tacked away from shore.

"Cowards," Ragnhild scoffed.

"They're not interested in a battle. They thought the monastery would be easy pickings," said Murchad.

Behind the walls, the monks cheered. But when Blathmac came out of the gate, instead of thanking them, he scowled. Murchad realized that the abbot was serious about his martyrdom, and a woman had robbed him of it today.

Ragnhild glared at the ungrateful abbot. "We sail at dawn," she growled.

It saddened Murchad that they were unwelcome, but he had to agree with his wife. It was time to leave. He'd had the opportunity to visit the legendary holy isle, and found it much reduced.

CHAPTER 21

The Dal Riata

After delaying a day for a favorable wind, they departed. Despite Blathmac's sourness, the monks had provisioned them generously with ale, bread, and dried meat that would last them far beyond the three-day journey to the Lough Feabhail.

The open sea stretched out before them. "Colm Cille chose this island because he could not see Ireland from here," said Murchad, "but it will come into sight before day's end."

Before they could unfurl the sail, a fleet of currachs emerged from the shelter of the Isle of Mull. The hide-covered boats headed straight for them.

"They're going to overhaul us," Einar reported from the bow.

Ragnhild nodded, her stomach tightening. She turned to Murchad. "Who are they?"

"The Dal Riata," he said. "Now they appear, when the fighting is done."

"From your tone, they're not good friends."

"The wind blows fair and foul between Ireland and the Picts," he said. "Their king is called Domnall mac Caustantin. Just go along with what I say until I see how things are with them."

The ships were smaller than *Raider Bride*, but there were a dozen of them and their hide-covered hulls looked stout and seaworthy. Each currach was manned by seven warriors whose speartips and helms glinted over the thwarts. The small boats swarmed down to surround *Raider Bride*. Ragnhild calculated the odds of fighting their way out if Murchad's diplomacy failed. *Raider Bride* might be able to smash through the smaller boats. But the Dal Riatan craft were swift, and escape was far from certain.

Murchad carried the white shield to the prow and declared his name and titles. "We come in peace," he said.

Ragnhild held her breath, watching the Dal Riatans closely. "Stand by your oars," she muttered to the crew.

"I am called Sotal," said their leader. "Captain of the Dal Riatan fleet. I am surprised to see an Irish lord on board a *dubh gaill* longship." He spoke a dialect of Gaelic that was different from the Irish Ragnhild knew, but she could follow his words. The man's bare arms were tattooed with flowing, intricate geometric designs with a dye that looked like woad. The tattoos continued from beneath his tunic and curled up his neck. The others bore similar designs on their skin.

"This is my wife, the lady Ragnhild, a queen of Lochlainn," said Murchad.

"We have reports that the abbey at Iona was attacked by a *dub gaill* longship," Sotal said.

"Aye, and it was we who fended them off. I did not see any Dal Riatan ships coming to their defense."

Sotal colored at Murchad's implied insult. He blustered, "If that's true, then we owe you thanks. We are spread thin these days. I must take you to our lord."

Murchad frowned. "We had not planned to stop at Dunadd, but rather sail to Aileach where I have business with my cousin,

King Niall."

The Dal Riatan captain shrugged. "I have my orders. All foreign ships must be taken to Dunadd."

"But we defended Iona from attack."

Sotal spread his hands in a gesture of helplessness. "I will dispatch a boat to the blessed isle to verify your story. Meanwhile, I must bring you to my lord."

"Very well." Murchad turned to Ragnhild. "Do as he says. I'll be able to clear this up with Domnall."

Ragnhild explained to her crew that they must follow the captain's boat. They grumbled fearfully. Ragnhild didn't blame them, considering how they had fared when they had been prisoners of the Irish. The Picts were a complete unknown.

"Don't worry," she reassured her crew. "Lord Murchad's status will ensure they treat us well." She looked at her husband for confirmation.

Murchad said, "I don't know what terms my cousin is on with the Picts these days. I myself was always on friendly, if wary, terms with Domnall."

His dubious tone did not instill confidence in Ragnhild. However, if anyone could talk their way out of this situation, it was Murchad. She smiled at her crew with supreme confidence.

Sotal dispatched one of the boats to Iona to confirm their story. The remainder of the Dal Riatan fleet surrounded *Raider Bride*. Ragnhild did not think they appeared to be spread thin. She wondered if they were purposely avoiding confrontation with the Danes.

Raider Bride was escorted to a sheltered cove on the mainland, where they tied up to a pier and disembarked. A peat bog stretched ahead of them. In the distance, a huge rocky promontory rose like a leviathan ascending from the deep.

"The trail is steep and narrow," said Sotal. "You will have to leave your sea chests with your ship. Take only what you need for a short stay. You must also leave your weapons here. They will be well guarded."

The crew muttered at leaving their arms behind and Ragnhild echoed their concern.

"You'd best bring the necklace," Murchad murmured into her ear. She gave a quick nod.

While the crew dug necessities from their sea chests and stowed their weapons, Ragnhild withdrew the leather satchel that contained the Irish necklace and slung it over her shoulder along with her bag containing her comb, clean linens, and other things.

When *Raider Bride*'s crew were ready, Sotal's men herded them along a wooden causeway that crossed the peat bog. As they neared the promontory, white dots of sheep stood out on the hillside where stout walls enclosed three terraces. The thatched roofs of roundhouses poked up above the lower wall. Heavy smoke billowed from the distant second level. The top of the hill formed the third terrace, crowned by an enormous roundhouse that nearly filled the enclosure. Ragnhild marveled at the vast, thatched roof.

The causeway ended at the base of the hill, where a narrow trail rose steeply. Single file, they wound their way through the rocks to the first enclosure. Massive earthen ramparts were topped by a formidable stone wall, its gateway crowned with a wooden watchtower.

Tattooed spearmen watched as they passed through the gate onto the lower terrace. Here roundhouses and byres clustered around a well. Children herded geese and ducks on the hillside, and chickens scratched in the yard. Women looked up from their work, eyeing the newcomers warily.

Two trails led out of the settlement, each leading to one of the remaining levels. From the smell of burnt metal and the clang of hammers, the second terrace housed a smithy.

"The Dal Riata is famed for its metalwork," said Sotal proudly.

"King Domnall has some of the finest silver- and goldsmiths in the world, and our ironwork is second to none."

Sotal's men ushered them up the other path that led to the great hall. Along the way they passed flat rocks carved with animals and spirals. Cup marks indented some of the stones, rimed with crusts of sacrificial milk and blood. One outcropping had been hollowed into the shape of a footprint. "Here is where our kings are acclaimed by the people," said Sotal. Ragnhild imagined standing on the rock, one foot in the footprint of kings, gazing out over the land below.

Murchad joined her. From here they could see beyond the bog to the sea, a river that snaked its way across the plain and wooded hills. "Look there," said Murchad, pointing to a vast glen in the north. "See the monuments." Miles of standing stones, stone circles, and hundreds of cairns, all half-buried in the peat marched across the landscape. "They form an ancient processional to the sea. There's old magic here," he murmured.

Ragnhild's thoughts went to the necklace in its leather satchel. Did this ancient power call to its own? She wished she could feel it.

Sotal coaxed them away from their vantage point and led them on to the highest terrace. It was dominated by the vast timber roundhouse with its immense thatched roof. Ragnhild couldn't help feeling a sense of awe as they approached.

A steward waited by the open door. The doorposts were carved with Ogham runes and set with jewels and precious metal. The steward bowed and led them into a room that glimmered with the light of dozens of torches and candles, the white-washed walls twinkling with more gems and bronze. The lofty ceiling, supported by a forest of rune-carved timbers, vanished into the peaty smoke.

At the far end, nearly lost in the gloom, the high seat stood on its platform. As they approached, Ragnhild made out a long-haired man who boasted a full beard and a moustache to rival

Murchad's. He looked to be close to Murchad's age, with dark hair and brown eyes. His deep-purple robes glinted with silver embroidery, and his arms and throat were covered with tattoos even more intricate than those of Sotal and his men. Swirling abstract designs intermingled with stylized animals: a wolf, an eagle, a horse, and a boar. Around his neck he wore a massive silver chain. Ragnhild couldn't take her eyes from it.

The steward conducted them to the dais, where Murchad halted and bowed his head respectfully.

The king spoke first. "Greetings, Murchad mac Maele Duin. It has been long since I have welcomed you in my hall."

"Greetings, Domnall mac Caustantin, king of the Dal Riata. I am honored to be your guest. I bring my wife, Ragnhild, a queen of Lochlainn, and our followers."

Domnall nodded to Ragnhild. "Welcome, Lady." He turned back to Murchad. "What brings you into our waters?"

"My lord, we have come from Iona, where we repelled a ship of *dubh gaill* raiders."

Domnall stared at Murchad. "If this is true, then I owe you a great debt."

Sotal stepped forward. "My lord, I have dispatched a ship to the holy isle to verify Lord Murchad's story. In compliance with your orders, I have brought their longship here and presented them before you."

"You have done well, Sotal," said Domnall. "Lord Murchad, I apologize for inconveniencing you and your followers. Things do not stand well between me and your kin, and so you must be my guests until we verify your claim. You will be made comfortable for the duration of your stay."

Ragnhild exchanged a dismayed glance with Murchad. No matter how politely Domnall put it, they were prisoners. Her crew would not be pleased. She met Einar's gaze, noting the consternation in his eyes. He understood enough of their language to be worried. She tried to give him a reassuring smile, but she could tell he was not comforted.

"Thank you, Lord," said Murchad, his tone gratified, as if they had just received a sought-after invitation.

"Please, refresh yourselves, and then we shall feast."

Sotal ushered them out to an adjacent roundhouse. It was a typical guesthouse, whitewashed walls inside and out. The walls were lined with alcove beds, allowing each person privacy. In the center was a hearth whose smoke filtered through the thatched roof. An iron cauldron simmered on its hook.

Servants drew wash water and served them ale. A man brought Murchad a clean robe and helped him change. "Have you no torc, my lord?" the man inquired.

Murchad shook his head. "I don't take my gold to sea with me."

The servant quickly stifled a look of disdain.

Meanwhile, a woman had entered with a robe of fine woad-dyed linen over her arm. Like the men, her arms were covered with designs in blue, intricate swirls and circles. She headed for Ragnhild.

"My name is Deirdre." She gave Ragnhild's salt-encrusted tunic and breeks a contemptuous glance. "I was told you were royalty."

Ragnhild shrugged. "We've just made a long voyage."

Deirdre sighed and shook her head. She helped Ragnhild change out of her sea-stained clothes and wash, then helped her into the linen gown. Deirdre stood back and ran an appraising eye over her handiwork. "That's a little better."

Ragnhild bristled at the woman's disapproval. Who was she to judge their appearance?

Deirdre gestured toward a stool. "Please sit, Lady, and I will dress your hair. That's bound to help."

Ragnhild stomped over and took a seat with an injured air, while Deirdre attacked her ratty braid.

When Ragnhild's salt-encrusted hair had been washed, dried, and combed into a glossy upsweep, Murchad's eyebrows lifted in appreciation. "You look every inch a queen, *a chroi*," he said.

"We are accustomed to royalty wearing jewelry," said Deirdre. "Surely you have something in your bags?"

The woman's disparaging tone was beginning to grate on Ragnhild. It was past time to put her in her place. She shot Murchad a questioning look, and he nodded, obviously annoyed by the servants' airs.

Ragnhild burrowed into the satchel and pulled the golden necklace out. "Will this do?" she inquired.

Deirdre's eyes widened and she swallowed hard at the sight. Even the serving man gaped. "Yes, yes, that will do."

Ragnhild gave her a smug smile and donned the necklace. "Shall we go?"

"Please, this way." The serving man ushered them out with new reverence.

As they entered the hall, the scent of cooking meat roused Ragnhild's stomach. They mounted the platform and were seated next to Domnall.

The Picts king's gaze fastened on the necklace, tracking it as she moved. "That is a marvelous piece of jewelry you wear, Lady," he remarked, the admiration evident in his tone.

"Thank you, my lord," Ragnhild said with satisfaction.

"I am intrigued by the workmanship. I would have my chief druid examine it if you don't mind."

Ragnhild smiled. "Certainly." She glanced at Murchad, who was looking a bit uncomfortable. She shrugged. She could hardly refuse.

Domnall nodded to a bearded elder dressed in white robes. "May I introduce Art, the Archdruid of Dal Riata. He is very knowledgeable in goldsmithing."

The druid bent down and fixed his gaze on the necklace. He sucked in his breath. "It is very unusual workmanship."

"It's very old," said Ragnhild.

Art shot her a piercing look that made her squirm. "The gold-smithing techniques are most advanced. I have seen nothing like it except the work of the ancient Sidhe."

Something in his tone stirred the hairs on the back of Ragn-hild's neck. Fortunately, the food arrived, distracting everyone's attention. A platter of venison was set before them, and Domnall became an urbane and hospitable host. Murchad appeared to relax, and Ragnhild attacked her food with appetite.

After the meal, Domnall's bard brought out his harp and performed a long, mournful ballad that Ragnhild only half followed. She watched her crew, knowing they understood few of the words, but the lilting melody cast a spell over them, and they listened, mesmerized.

When the bard sang his last lament, armed guards escorted them back to the guesthouse. Though the bracken-stuffed beds were comfortable enough, Ragnhild could not sleep.

"I wish we could leave now," she murmured to Murchad.

"Don't worry, *a chroí*," he said. "As soon as their boat returns with word from the sacred isle, we'll be on our way." He stroked her hair, soothing her into sleep.

In the morning, Sotal appeared at the door to the guesthouse. "My Lord and Lady, my currach has returned from Iona," he said. "King Domnall is waiting for the two of you to join him and hear their report."

Ragnhild and Murchad dressed hurriedly. "You'd best wear the necklace," said Murchad. "I don't trust these people." Ragnhild donned the necklace over her gown. They followed Sotal to the hall, where the captain of the currach stood before the high seat.

Domnall began, "Good morning, Lord Murchad, Lady Ragn-hild. The report from Iona is as you say, and I thank you for your defense. The holy isle has long been a protectorate of the Dal Riata."

The captain bowed his head. "Please also accept my gratitude.

It is my shame that our fleet was not there to defend it." Ragnhild looked sharply at the man, wondering again if their neglect of the isle was purposeful.

Murchad said, "We accept your thanks, Lord, and now we would be on our way to Ireland to see my cousin."

Domnall smiled genially. "I'm sorry to say you have missed the tide. The currents around here are treacherous. You will have to wait until tomorrow."

Ragnhild shot Murchad a sharp glance. He knew as well as she that they had not missed the tide. But Murchad shook his head slightly. She clenched her jaw. It was not polite to argue with their host, and from the look in Domnall's eye, it would do them no good.

"Since you will remain as my guests for another day, Lord Murchad, I will entertain you with falconry," Domnall said. "I have the finest birds of prey in seven lands."

Murchad nodded. "Thank you, Lord, I have heard that your falcons and hawks are a marvel."

"Go with my falconer to choose your bird. I will join you shortly. Lady Ragnhild, my women will make you comfortable while your husband is occupied."

Ragnhild was surprised to be left out, but perhaps Picts women did not hawk. Murchad nodded to her reassuringly and followed the falconer out the door.

THE BIRDS WERE HOUSED in a mews behind the great hall, on a rocky outcropping that jutted out over the valley.

The falconer said, "Wait here, my lord. I will return with a falcon I recommend."

While the falconer was gone, Murchad surveyed the valley. The view was stunning, and it would be a thrill to fly a bird of prey from here.

Footsteps approached and he turned, expecting to see the falconer. Instead, a hefty stranger strode toward him. Murchad didn't like the look in the man's eyes, and when he broke into a jog, Murchad's whole body went into alert. As the man reached out to shove him, Murchad stepped aside and gave the attacker a push, adding to the man's momentum to carry him over the edge.

Murchad watched the man plunge, stunned by what had nearly happened.

As he fell, the man grabbed Murchad's ankle, yanking him off the cliff. Murchad hurtled into the air.

CHAPTER 22

Afeter Murchad had departed, Domnall nodded at Art. The druid approached Ragnhild, his gaze riveted upon the necklace. Ragnhild did not like Art's greedy gaze, or that of Domnall. Her hand went to her belt for the blade that was not there.

Art examined the necklace closely. "I have consulted the ancient lore and I have identified this necklace. It is an amulet of great power, fashioned centuries ago by the Tuatha de Danann for the warrior queen Medbh, she who was wife of five kings in succession. While she lived, no man could become king unless he was Medbh's husband. And now, the woman who possesses Medbh's necklace bestows sovereignty on her husband."

Domnall looked at Ragnhild in a way that made her squirm inside her skin. "Lady, you will marry me, and I will rule as king in Ireland as well as Dal Riata."

Ragnhild eyed the exits, all guarded. "My husband will object to that."

"You have no husband, Lady," said Domnall.

A wave of horror flooded Ragnhild. She fought to keep her expression deadpan. "You lie!"

Domnall gave her a smile that made her stomach churn. "I'm afraid not. You see, my falconer took him to the highest eyrie, and there instead of flying hawks, Lord Murchad flew himself."

Ragnhild gritted her teeth to keep her face expressionless. With enormous effort, she turned the despair that threatened to overwhelm her into a fury that seared her veins. She fixed Domnall with a murderous glare. "Then you are a dead man."

The Dal Riata king laughed. "You are not the first to make such threats."

Ragnhild filled her voice with venom, as if she could kill him with her words. "Perhaps not, but I will be the last."

"And how do you propose to accomplish that, my lady?" Domnall spread his hands, indicating his guards stationed about the room. Ragnhild vowed silently that she would find a way to kill this man, and if she died in the act, so be it. The future stretched dismally ahead without Murchad. All that was left to her was fury at his murderer, and once that was done, she need live no longer. First she must get back to her crew.

Domnall spoke. "If you will not marry me, then I will have the necklace, and bestow it on a woman more willing, and you may join your husband." He nodded to the burly smith beside him. "Take it."

The smith approached Ragnhild and reached for the necklace. Ragnhild steeled herself not to flinch as he took hold of the links and lifted to pull it over her head.

The necklace stayed on her chest. The smith jerked hard, pulling Ragnhild toward him, but the necklace did not move. He tried again, but this time Ragnhild was ready for him and she yanked back with all her strength. The links dug into her neck, but it was worth it when he stumbled a few steps toward her before regaining his balance. "I can't move it," he said. "It must have some kind of enchantment on it."

"Art, take the necklace," Domnall ordered.

The druid came forward and reached out one finger to touch

the necklace with great caution. He muttered a few words under his breath, then gingerly tried to lift it. The necklace stayed as if stuck to Ragnhild's chest. He turned to the king. "I cannot remove it," he said in awe. "This necklace is cursed."

～

THE TWO MEN plummeted through the air. Murchad grabbed hold of a gorse bush growing out of the vertical rock. The bush jerked Murchad up short and he delivered a hard kick to his assailant. The man lost his grip on Murchad's ankle and flew off into space, screaming.

The spindly shrub broke and Murchad slammed into the cliff face. He gripped the rough surface with his hands and feet to slow his descent as he skidded down the rock. He landed on his belly on a narrow rocky shelf and dragged his feet and hands to stop himself from rolling off.

He lay catching his breath while his hammering heart slowed. His body felt battered and bruised, and blood seeped from myriad cuts and abrasions. Tentatively, he moved his limbs. Nothing seemed to be broken.

With utmost caution, he turned his head and hazarded a glance down where his assailant lay sprawled on the rocks far below. The height made Murchad's head whirl and his gut roil. He averted his gaze abruptly, fighting nausea.

Stuck on a shelf high above the valley and far below the hill-top, he had no viable way up or down. The ledge was narrow, barely wide enough for his body. Just getting to his feet without falling would be a major accomplishment. But that he must do, and soon, before his survival was discovered.

Setting his jaw, he put his hands flat on the rock and drew his legs under him. Slowly, carefully, he brought his knees under his chest, then pushed up with his arms and legs. His body trembled with the effort, and sweat poured down his face. He shuffled his feet, body still tight against the surface, and turned to face the cliff. Pressing his hands and body into the rock face, he straightened into a standing position.

He took a few breaths, clinging to the stone, while his stomach settled.

When his trembling stopped, he craned his neck and scanned the cliff face above him, seeking out crevices and handholds.

Reaching up, he found outcroppings and began to climb. The soft soles of his boots cleaved to the rock, and he gritted his teeth against the pain in his skinned hands as he gripped the hard surface. He crept up the cliff, searching out the next hold, balancing his body carefully, fully aware there were no second chances and that he was many years older now than the last time he'd performed a feat like this.

The sun seared into his back, but he was grateful there was no rain or mist that day to make the rocks slippery.

He had not gone far when he heard voices above. He froze, hoping his body didn't stick out far enough for them to see him clinging to the cliffside.

"I see his body down there."

Murchad hoped that his clothing was similar enough in color to his attacker's so that at this height they could not tell who lay at the bottom.

"We'll never be able to retrieve him."

"We don't need to. King Domnall can see for himself."

"Where's Drust? He should be here."

"He's probably drinking his reward right now."

"Well, we can report to the king that the job is done."

A rock worked free beneath Murchad's hand and skittered down.

"What's that?"

Murchad hugged the precipice, holding his breath, willing himself to be invisible.

"Loose rocks fall here all the time. Come on, all the ale will be drunk."

The men's voices faded as their footsteps retreated, and Murchad resumed his ascent.

~

RAGNHILD'S NECK HAIRS PRICKLED. Cursed? This was a new twist to her. When she'd tried to wrest it from the dead queen, she had assumed it was the haugbui that held the necklace fast, not the other way around. But thinking back, she had never seen the necklace taken by force until she whacked off the corpse's hand. Even then, the hand had kept its grip until Hel possessed it.

Perhaps it was the power of the necklace that had cursed Tromøy, not that of the dead queen.

"Take the necklace off and give it to me," Domnall demanded. "I am sure I can find a woman who wants to be queen of Ireland."

Ragnhild had to keep the upper hand. "Perhaps I could, if I wanted to. But you tell me you have murdered my husband. That does not make me too well disposed to do as you request."

The Picts king regarded her. "Perhaps it will be easier to take the necklace from your corpse."

Ragnhild stifled a shiver and kept a stone face. "That has been tried before. If you try to take it from me by violence, its curse will fall on you and all your people." She hoped what she said was convincing.

"She's telling the truth, Lord," said the druid. "I felt the latent power of the curse when I touched it. I would not harm her while she wears the necklace. You must marry the wearer of the necklace to claim kingship, and while she possesses the amulet, that must be her."

Domnall gazed at Ragnhild speculatively. "Your crew are my prisoners. I'll fling them after your husband, one at a time, until you marry me or hand over the necklace."

Ragnhild racked her brains to think of a way to outwit this man. She couldn't get Murchad back, but she would make his murderer pay. "How can I be sure you won't kill them all anyway if I comply?"

"You have my word as king."

Ragnhild snorted. "What good is the word of a treacherous beast like you?"

The Picts king shrugged. "As my prisoner, you have little choice. The first of your crew dies in the morning, unless you are my wife or have given me the necklace by then." He turned to his guards. "Lock her in the storehouse."

Svein tried to force the guesthouse door open. "They've barred it. We're trapped."

Einar said, "We've fought our way out of captivity before. We outnumber these Picts guards. At some point, they must bring us food. Be ready to overwhelm them then. With no weapons, we'll have to be quick."

Einar and Thorgeir stationed themselves on either side of the door with a couple of stout lads, ready to disable whoever came through it. The rest of the crew arranged themselves in their alcoves, slumping and wearing dejected expressions.

They waited. Hours passed, and the door remained closed. There was no sound outside.

"Surely they will feed us, bring us water," said Unn.

"Perhaps not," said Tova glumly. "If their plan is to kill us all, why waste the food?"

They set watches by the door through the night, though no one slept. When dawn sent shafts of light through the thatch, they heard the bar scrape.

The door opened.

Einar and Thorgeir were on the man like lightning, wresting

his spear out of his grip and stabbing him in the gut. More guards filled the doorway, but the crew of *Raider Bride* crowded them, wrenching weapons out of their grasp and trying to drag the guards into the guesthouse.

"Retreat!" The Picts backed out of the doorway and managed to slam the door on *Raider Bride*'s crew. The bar dropped in place with an ominous clunk.

"They won't give us another chance," said Thorgeir.

"Perhaps not, but we're still alive," said Unn.

"Unn is right," said Einar. "We've gained ground on our enemy. We have four spears. We must be ready for them next time."

THE HARDEST PART of the climb came when Murchad reached the top and had to drag his full weight up over the edge of the precipice. He reached his arms overhead, scrabbling for purchase until one hand found a tree root. Praying it was sturdy, he gripped it hard and pushed with his legs, his feet finding new holds while his other hand patted the ground above. His fingers found a tree root. He took hold with both hands and heaved his body up, pushing with his feet, praying the root was a sturdy one.

At last his head topped the cliff edge and he raked his gut over the stone, squirming onto the ground.

He lay clinging to the tree root for a while, but he was too exposed to rest here long. He had to find cover. Gathering all his remaining strength, he squirmed his way toward some brush and worked his body under it as far as he could. He had a good view of the guesthouse below, where the crew of *Raider Bride* had slept.

The sound of a skirmish reached his ears. From behind a bush, Murchad watched *Raider Bride*'s crew try to fight their way out of the guesthouse, only to be subdued by the guards.

Murchad counted twenty guards. Most of them retreated to

the guardhouse after they slammed the guesthouse door and barred it, leaving four of their fellows guarding the door.

He had to get to them without being seen. He lay waiting as the evening shadows fell over the yard.

When dark descended on the settlement, he started working his way down the hill on his belly. He reached the back of the guesthouse and he got to his feet. A wave of dizziness swept over him and he leaned against the wall until it passed.

Murchad searched the ground until he found a fist-sized rock. He cocked his arm and hurled it as far as he could across the yard.

"What was that?" Two of the sentries left their posts at the door to investigate. The two who remained watched their fellows. Murchad crept up along the shadows, two more rocks in his hands. When he was close enough to do some damage, he straightened to his full height and hurled one of the rocks at the nearest guard's head. He hit dead on, dropping his target, and as the other turned in alarm, Murchad charged him and bashed his head with the other rock. The man gave out a cry as he fell. Murchad clapped his hand over the man's mouth and lowered him to the ground. He snatched up their spears.

By then the other two guards had started back. Murchad lifted the bar from the door and flung it wide open. "*Raider Bride*, to me!" he rasped.

The crew was quick to respond. Spears leveled, Einar, Thorgeir, and Svein led the way as they poured through the door into the yard and swarmed over the remaining two guards, dispatching them silently. Murchad took two spears and hurried over to the guardhouse, where he used them to brace the door shut. It would not hold against a determined assault, but it would slow the guards down long enough for the crew to escape.

Murchad's stomach dropped as he surveyed the crew. "Ragnhild is not with you?"

"She never came back from the great hall," said Einar.

"Then I pray she's still there. We must free her. All of you, scatter and hide in the shadows. When you hear my owl hoot, muster to me." Murchad nodded at the three húskarlar. "You three, stay with me." The crew split up into pairs and trios, sprinting across the yard for cover. Thorgeir, Einar, and Svein helped Murchad drag the guards inside the guesthouse. They took the men's knives and hurried out, barring the door behind them.

Keeping to the shadows, the four of them crept up to the wall of the uppermost keep.

The gate to the great hall was not as formidable as the outer gate. It appeared to serve a ceremonial purpose rather than a defensive one, manned by six warriors who appeared undisturbed by the activities below. Their spears leaned against the wall, and they were throwing dice. Exclamations of victory and loss covered any sound.

Murchad gave the owl hoot and the crew materialized from the shadows. Three húskarlar came into casting range and hurled their spears, catching two guards in the throat. As they dropped, gurgling, their fellows looked up in alarm. The crew fell on three of them, cutting their throats.

Murchad kept his man alive. "If you wish to survive with your manhood," he told his captive, brandishing the man's own knife at his throat, "you'll tell me where my wife is."

"She's locked in the storehouse behind the great hall," the man stammered.

"How many guards?"

"Four," he whispered.

Murchad left him bound and gagged.

He handed out spears from the guards' stock and described where Ragnhild was being held. "Einar, Thorgeir, Svein, come with me to take down the guards and free her. We need to do it quietly, or we'll bring the entire Picts army down on us. The rest of you, hang back in the shadows in case we need help. Be ready to fight. Once we have Ragnhild, head to the ship. We'll meet there."

Raider Bride's crew melted into the shadows.

Murchad and the three húskarlar, armed with the guards' knives and spears, stole into the yard and circumnavigated the great roundhouse, keeping close to the wall. Murchad halted when he sighted the storehouse, guarded by four men just as his captive had told him. He and the three húskarlar crept up on the guards and cut their throats before they could make a sound.

Murchad threw off the bar to the shed door. Ragnhild charged out of the darkness, wielding a stick like a spear.

Murchad dodged just in time. "It's me, *a chroí*," he whispered urgently. She lowered her weapon and threw herself into his arms. "Are you hurt?"

She shook her head. "Just angry. I need to kill Domnall."

Einar hissed, "We have to go! The guards will break out of the guardhouse soon." They grabbed up weapons from the fallen guards and ran down the trail.

Murchad gave his owl hoot and the crew materialized from their hiding places. "To the ship!"

As he spoke, the spears propping the guardhouse doors gave way and the imprisoned guards burst out, sounding the alarm.

The crew fled down the trail as fast as they could in the darkness. Shouts and pounding feet could be heard on the trail behind them.

The shore guard, consisting of a dozen men, had formed a hasty shield wall in front of the pier. If their pursuers caught up, the crew of *Raider Bride* would be trapped between the two forces.

"We have to get through them!" cried Ragnhild. "Charge!"

Spears outthrust, the crew barreled through the Dal Riatan shield wall, sending the shore guards stumbling into the water.

The crew ran down the pier. "Cut the lines!" shouted Murchad. Einar and Thorgeir slashed at the mooring lines of the currachs, shoving a number of them loose to drift free and tangle with the other lines.

Ragnhild vaulted onto *Raider Bride* and unlashed the steering oar. The rest of the crew followed and got their oars in the water faster than they ever had.

"Row!" shouted Ragnhild. "Your lives depend on it."

"Archers!" cried Murchad. Everyone not manning an oar snatched up a bow and nocked. "Loose!" he cried, and they sent a volley into their pursuers as the guards charged onto the pier. A few of their arrows hit their marks while sowing chaos among the enemy as they scrambled to form a shield wall.

While the Dal Riatans regrouped and untangled their boats, *Raider Bride* cleared the harbor, surging into the moonlit sea.

CHAPTER 23

Tullynavin

As the sun set over the water, Murchad stared into their wake anxiously. They had spent the day crossing the North Channel to Ireland and the sails of the Dal Riatan fleet remained tiny flecks in the distance.

"It looks like we've outrun them," said Einar. "They can't catch us before we reach Irish waters."

Murchad heaved a sigh of relief and looked at his wife. "*A chroi*, what happened back there? I understand they wanted the necklace, but why try to kill me?"

Ragnhild's gaze flicked from the horizon to him. "Domnall's druid claimed he identified the necklace from his lore. He said it was created by the Tuatha de Danann for the warrior queen Medbh. It's his belief that the woman who wears the necklace bestows sovereignty on her husband. And Domnall shares that belief."

Murchad looked stunned. "That lore has been lost to my people. The druids taught us that the necklace was to be worn by the ruling queen of Cenel nEoghain. But Medbh was queen of Connacht. My ancestors must have taken it, perhaps a war prize."

Ragnhild gave him a pointed look. "If what the Picts believe is true, it means that as long as I possess the necklace, you are still the rightful king."

Murchad stared out to sea, his thoughts clashing within. He tasted the bitterness of being deposed, the pain of betrayal by the man who had always been his brother. None of it was enough to send a kingdom into turmoil. "I won't go to war with Niall, nor will I go against the will of the brehons. We must return the necklace to be rid of the curse, and we need to do it before Niall discovers it's missing."

"That is your decision, husband," said Ragnhild. "I hold no desire to be queen in a foreign land."

Murchad went to the prow, where he stayed all day in silence, peering into the distance, straining to catch sight of the familiar cliffs.

At midday flocks of seabirds appeared, and finally the rugged bluffs of Inis Eoghain rose from the sea. They rounded the rocky headland and sailed through the narrow cut into the inland sea of Lough Feabhail. Melancholy flooded him. This had been his home, his land. No longer.

At least they were safe now, well within his kin's territory. The Dal Riatans would not dare pursue them here.

It was full dark, and the northerly wind fought the ebb tide, raising a nasty chop. Ragnhild had the crew anchor in the lee of the north shore. They ate a hasty meal, set watches, and slept.

Murchad did not sleep. As the sun rose, he gazed at the familiar landmarks. A stone cross was silhouetted on the headland, speaking of home. The deepest part of him yearned for this land, but closer to the surface his feelings roiled like the tide rips that surrounded them.

After sunrise, the tide slackened and the choppy seas calmed. They raised the anchor and set the sail to a favorable breeze.

Soon the flood tide joined the wind to carry *Raider Bride* down the estuary.

Murchad sighted the mouth of the river that led to Tullynavin. The crew dropped the sail and took to their oars, following the withy markers through the sand bars. He knew the crew harbored bad feelings about landing here. "I know the last time you were at Tullynavin, you were prisoners and ill-used. But I assure you that this time you will be treated as honored guests."

As they neared the dock, the shore guards blew horns and hefted spears. Murchad sensed the tension run through the crew. "We come in peace," he called, holding up the white shield. "I am Murchad mac Maele Duin, and these are my people."

At that, the guards put down their spears and stood by to receive the mooring lines. The crew relaxed as they moored *Raider Bride* among an assortment of vessels, from tiny hide-covered currachs to larger seagoing ships built of wood planks. *Raider Bride* was still the largest vessel by far.

The leader of the guards came forward and bowed. "Greetings, Lord Murchad."

"Thank you," said Murchad. "Take us to see Aed."

They followed the guards up the trail to the walled fortress. Murchad was alert for signs of tension among the crew, but to their credit, they showed no fear.

As they passed the corral, a whinny made Ragnhild turn her head. "Brunaidh!" she cried. She hurried over to her pony, left behind a year ago. The shield-maiden stroked the pony's mane while Brunaidh nuzzled her. "I'll be back to see you soon, old friend," she promised, and ran to catch up with the others.

The anxiety seemed to have dissipated with Ragnhild's happy reunion, and Murchad felt the crew relax. Shoulders eased, heads went up, smiles hovered.

The gate opened, and an honor guard conducted them inside while the dock watch returned to their posts.

Tullynavin had been rebuilt after the previous year's fire. The thatched dwellings that had been reduced to embers had sprung up like toadstools again in the yard, and folk scurried among them with flocks of chickens and geese.

Aed greeted them at the door of his hall. "Hail, Murchad mac Maele Duin, Lady Ragnhild. Your visit does me honor. You and your followers are welcome." He gestured for them to enter.

The crew was silent, staring at the Irish lord who had held them captive in a cow byre, starved them, and worked them near to death. Murchad had a bad moment, fearing a confrontation, but when he took Ragnhild's arm and led her inside, they followed peaceably.

Aed entertained them with fair grace, as if the crew had not been his slaves the year before. Servants brought bowls of warm scented water to wash with and clean linen towels. Porridge and bread were served along with ale.

The taste of Irish ale sent a wave of emotions washing through Murchad. When the bard struck his harp, Murchad's soul quivered. He laughed to hide his feelings from the others and from himself.

As the meal went on, Murchad broached the subject that had worried him for weeks. He strove to keep his tone casual. "Tell me, Aed, has Niall taken a wife yet?" He held his breath while Aed swallowed his ale.

Aed smiled and shook his head. "No, the king is still possessed body and soul by his mistress. It's too bad she's not of noble birth, then he could marry her and have done with it."

Murchad smiled and breathed easy again. "When I visit him, I will see if I can persuade him to do his duty."

"I wish you luck. Many have tried. But you and Niall have always been close as brothers."

"We were," said Murchad with a sigh.

After the meal, Aed conducted them to the newly rebuilt guesthouse. Their gear had already been brought up from the ship. Ragnhild and Murchad were given a partitioned chamber dominated by a huge feather bed, their sea chests sitting at the foot, the necklace secure in its leather satchel at the bottom of Ragnhild's chest.

They were alone for the first time in days, and Ragnhild gave him a welcoming smile. He took her in his arms and embraced her tentatively, alert for signs it was too soon. She returned his kiss with enthusiasm and his heart beat faster. They slowly undressed each other.

A cauldron of water warmed on the hearth and they bathed each other with linen cloths. After so many nights at sea, Murchad relished salt-free skin and clean hair, basking in the warm room. They climbed into the soft bed and Murchad ran his hands over her warm, smooth skin. He let Ragnhild take the initiative, making sure that she knew she could call a halt at any time. Carefully, gently, they made love for the first time since the miscarriage.

In the morning he woke to find her smiling at him. She embraced him and they made love again.

"And what would you like to do today, *a chroi*?" Murchad murmured into her hair.

She beamed at him. "I want to see Brunaidh!" She got out of bed and pulled on her tunic and breeks. Murchad followed and they hurried to the corral where the pony was already waiting at the gate to greet her. Murchad's horse, Aenbarr, stood beside Brunaidh.

They mounted and rode out through the countryside.

"It's good to breathe Irish air again," said Murchad. "We must go to see Niall as soon as the crew is rested, and restore the necklace. We can sail down to Daire Calgaich. Aed will have men bring Brunaidh and Aenbarr to the monastery."

"It will be good to see Behrt," said Ragnhild. "I promised Åsa to give him her greetings."

"We'll spend a few days at Daire Calgaich while we wait for Niall to send horses for the rest of the crew. When we ride to

Aileach, we can leave the ship at Daire. It will be safe there." He was not ready to face Niall quite yet. A brief stay at Daire would settle his emotions.

"As long as we make our way back to Gausel by the end of summer," she cautioned.

"Yes," Murchad said absently, gazing at the Irish countryside. The rolling hills and lush greenery of his homeland soothed his eyes, and a vast peace came over his heart.

CHAPTER 24

Daire Calgaich

After three days' rest at Tullynavin, they loaded *Raider Bride* and set sail for the monastery of Daire Calgaich. Though Aed had treated them well, Ragnhild and her crew were more than ready to leave the place of their captivity, and eager to see Behrt.

Ragnhild remembered the forceful currents of the river well. They hugged the western shore as they sailed south down the lough, staying out of the main current. Fishermen's currachs plied the waters, keeping a cautious distance from the longship. Fishing camps clustered on the beaches while cattle and sheep grazed the highlands. Small farmsteads dotted hilltops, each encircled by woven fences or earthen banks, their conical thatched roofs peeking above the enclosures.

The ship neared Culmore Point, the sharp bend where the lough narrowed and became a river. The swift current of the flood tide overcame the river's natural northerly flow and carried them along for an hour, then the waterway broadened once again into a bay. For a time the sailing was good, but soon enough the river narrowed again and swung to the east. At the bend, a sturdy wooden palisade rose from an earthen embankment.

Daire Calgaich.

The monastery stood on a hill crowned by a grove of ancient oaks. "It is said that those oaks were sacred to Colm Cille," said Murchad, his eyes misted with memory. "He would not allow them to be cut down."

The river fronted the hill, and all other sides were surrounded by an impenetrable bog that could only be crossed by a causeway of wood planks. It was an ideal defensible position for a fort.

"Daire Calgaich was originally under the rule of our enemies, the Conaill clan," said Murchad. "Many years ago, my father drove the Conaills out and destroyed the monastery. Since then it has been rebuilt by my kin."

Ragnhild turned the prow toward the shore, but the current was still swift and threatened to sweep *Raider Bride* past their landing place.

"Man your oars," Ragnhild ordered. Her crew pulled hard as the strong current dragged *Raider Bride* downstream. She brought the ship around sharply to assist the rowers.

With one final stroke, the oarsmen drove the longship hard onto the beach and shipped their oars. Those in the prow jumped over the side to steady the vessel as it swayed in the current. The rest of the crew racked their oars and climbed down to help drag *Raider Bride* up the beach out of reach of the tide.

Ragnhild shipped the steering oar and vaulted over the side to join Murchad, who was already striding up the hill. He held his white shield high, shouting his name.

The gates creaked open and a middle-aged monk appeared. "I am Brother Padraig." He inclined his tonsured head, seemingly undisturbed by the crowd of Norse at his gates. "Welcome, my lord and lady."

They followed the brother inside, where monks went about their work in the garden, glancing up curiously at the Norse party. It was a typical Irish stronghold, so different from the austere Iona colony. Chickens pecked and strutted among round huts with their thatched, conical roofs. The church was the only structure built of stone, rectangular in shape, with a carved stone cross before it.

Brother Padraig led them across the yard to a roundhouse larger than the others. Inside, the guesthouse was big enough to house the entire crew. Straw-stuffed sleeping pallets were piled against the whitewashed walls, and a table with benches stood in the middle. The ever-present cauldron of warm water steamed over the central fire, and linen towels were piled on the bench beside it.

"Please refresh yourselves," Padraig said with a bow, and backed out of the door. "I will fetch you something to eat."

The crew of *Raider Bride* took turns washing. Brother Padraig returned, followed by two younger monks carrying a bucket of ale, wooden cups, and a huge platter of bread and cheese. They set the meal on the table. "Please, eat," said Padraig.

Ragnhild tried not to fall on the food like a ravenous wolf, but her stomach commanded otherwise. Padraig stood by in silence while they ate, his hands folded serenely on his belly.

When they'd finished their meal, Brother Padraig said, "Lord Murchad, Lady Ragnhild, I must take the two of you to the abbot. He is eager to see you. Your crew can rest while we are gone."

The crew members made themselves comfortable while Ragnhild and Murchad followed the monk back out into the yard. He led them along a flagstone path across the courtyard to another roundhouse, nearly as large as the guesthouse.

The door stood open to the sunlight. A gentle voice greeted them from within. "Come in."

At Padraig's nod, Ragnhild and Murchad ducked inside the low doorway. The dim interior was lit by a single candle on a table. Ragnhild recognized the plump, middle-aged man who sat behind it, a book open before him. He gave her a kindly smile, so different from Blathmac's hostile glare.

"Greetings, Father Abbot," said Murchad, bowing low. Ragnhild inclined her head in respect.

"It is good to see you again, my son, and your bride," said the abbot. "Please have a seat." He motioned toward two low stools that stood before his desk. "What brings you here? The last I heard you had sailed to Lochlainn."

"That we had, Father Abbot, and many adventures we had there. But we have business with my cousin Niall."

The abbot frowned, a look of consternation creasing his brow.

"Do not fear, Father, I have no plans to contest his kingship. My wife and I have come to give him our oaths."

The abbot's expression smoothed. "Very well, then. I hope you and your crew will spend a few days with us to rest after your voyage."

"Thank you, Father Abbot, we gladly accept your hospitality. My horse and my wife's horse will arrive this evening from Tullynavin. I would be grateful if you could dispatch someone to Aileach to inform Niall of our arrival and ask him to send horses for our crew."

"Say no more, it shall be done."

"Thank you, Father."

"Now tell me of your travels." The abbot's eyes sparkled in anticipation.

"We stopped at Iona, and Father Blathmac sends his greetings."

Father Ennae sighed. "Ah yes, Blathmac. I fear he is determined to become a martyr for Christ."

"If we hadn't been there, he would have succeeded already," Ragnhild muttered.

The abbot raised his eyebrows in query.

Murchad explained. "While we were there, the *dubh gaill*

attacked, and we fended them off. Father Blathmac was less than grateful."

The abbot nodded. "I am sure he was disappointed. But I am equally sure that the other brethren were grateful to you."

"That they were."

"And you have my thanks as well. It is so sad what befell that blessed place."

"Yes," said Murchad, "I was sorely disappointed that so much had been destroyed. When I was a boy, I dreamed of seeing the scriptorium."

"That has been reestablished at Kells now, and it is a splendid place," said Ennae. "I pray it will be safe."

A monk had ducked in through the doorway and stood waiting to be recognized. Ragnhild turned, expecting to see Brother Padraig, but the robed form was silhouetted against the doorway's light.

"Ah, there you are, Brother Becc," said the abbot.

The monk bowed his head. "Welcome, Lord Murchad and Lady Ragnhild," said a familiar voice. A monk stepped out of the doorway and the candlelight illuminated his face.

Ragnhild leaped up in delight. "Behrt!" she exclaimed.

"I am so glad to see you both in such good health," Behrt said with a smile. "Here they call me by my Irish name, Brother Becc."

"We are so glad to see no matter what you call yourself. Åsa sends her greetings. How is life here?"

Behrt said, "It's not too exciting here since your brother stopped the *finn gaill* raids. We work in the scriptorium, tend the vegetables and livestock. We pray." He shot a glance at the abbot. "I do train the brothers in arms, in case the Norse return."

Father Ennae sighed. "I try to tell Brother Becc that violence does not become holy men."

Behrt gave a wicked grin. "It's not really violence. It's exercise."

Ennae threw his hands up in mock despair, but Ragnhild

detected a twinkle in his eye. He looked at Behrt. "I am sure that you have much to tell each other. Please rest now, and we look forward to seeing you at the evening meal."

"Thank you, Father Abbot." Behrt bowed low and conducted Ragnhild and Murchad out through the low door into the sunshine.

As soon as they were out of earshot, Ragnhild said, "Tell me, how are you? Are you happy here?"

Behrt looked around the yard where the monks worked in the gardens. "I am where I belong. Here I have work, comradery, and my faith."

"Do you ever miss your life as a warrior?"

Behrt looked up at the sky. "Honestly, no. I am content here. The days pass by in peace, and I am happy for that, though we are ready for a fight if need be. As a matter of fact, it's time for our training. I wonder if you and your crew would like to join us?"

"We'd like nothing better," said Ragnhild.

"Excellent," said Behrt. "We could use your expertise. Please meet us in the yard when you are ready."

Raider Bride's crew was well rested and eager to see some action, even if it was against monks. When they spilled out of the guest-house into the yard, they were confronted by a well-organized shield wall of monks hefting poles, ready to meet them. Behrt stood grinning in their center. The crew grabbed their shields from *Raider Bride*'s rack. A barrel full of stout poles stood ready by the practice field and *Raider Bride*'s crew armed themselves.

"Shield wall!" Ragnhild barked. She took the center position, flanked by Murchad on one side, Einar on the other, her crew lining up on either side, wood clacking as they overlapped their shields.

"Swinehorn!"

Ragnhild's shield wall pivoted until they formed a square, one corner aimed at the monks, ranks angled to either side like the wings of a falcon. Spearmen clustered in the center, protected by the outer shields.

When the group was tightly formed, she shouted, "Ready?"

"Ready!" the sailors echoed.

"Charge!"

Ragnhild began to move ahead with Murchad and Einar, followed by their ranks. Those in the rear lagged slightly, and the squares elongated into the wedge shape. The wedge began to move forward in a fast march that soon became a run. The formation loosened a little as the leaders surged ahead, but as Ragnhild, Murchad, and Einar struck the monks' line, those behind them locked into place. Ragnhild drove into the monks' shield wall and broke through.

"Split!"

The swinehorn poured through the defenses, split into two lines, and doubled back behind the monks' line. The defenders turned to face their attackers, and the line of shields dissolved. Locked together, the warriors of the swinehorn formed a new shield wall and attacked from behind, spearmen thrusting between the shields. The defenders tried to flank the wedge, but the double wings met the comers with a tight formation. Before long, the swinehorn side had vanquished the last of the straight-line defenders.

"Your monks are well trained," said Ragnhild to Behrt.

"The abbot gives us plenty of time to practice, in spite of his protests," Behrt replied. "He fears attack as much as I do."

"But my brother swore not to allow any more attacks on Ireland," said Ragnhild. "Has Harald broken his word?"

Behrt shook his head. "No, Harald has kept his word. It's not the Norse that are a problem. It's the rival Irish kingdoms."

Murchad nodded his head. "The Irish pillage the monasteries of their rivals more frequently than the Norse. My father took Daire from the Conaills and burned it to the ground. Now that we've rebuilt it, the Conaills and their allies attack relentlessly, trying to get the territory back. Am I right?"

"You are. Your cousin has his hands full."

"While we are here, perhaps we can help him."

Behrt gave a noncommittal shrug. "If he'll let you."

Murchad gave Behrt a hard look. "Does Niall still fear that I will try to take the kingship?"

"Well, you tried to overthrow the Ard Ri."

"True. But I am content in the north with my new people."

"I'm afraid you'll have to convince Niall of that."

A party of horsemen rode through the gates. A whinny sounded and Ragnhild turned her head in recognition. "Brunaidh!" she cried, hurrying to the pony. Ragnhild clucked her tongue and murmured softly while Brunaidh nuzzled her. She stroked the silky mane, remembering how the pony had comforted her when she was Murchad's prisoner.

That evening they ate in the refectory, sharing the monks' simple meal of bread and porridge and regaling the brethren with tales of their battles against Ragnhild's brother to gain Gausel, of the sickness on Tromøy. They did not mention the necklace, and skipped over Åsa's journey to Hel, but described the battle with Orm. Then they told of their defense of Iona against the Danes, though not their imprisonment by the Dal Riata. The younger monks listened to the stories with shining eyes, as eager for battle as any young warriors.

The next day they practiced with the monks again. This time *Raider Bride*'s crew staged an attack on the monastery walls from outside, while the brothers rained their practice spears down on them. The Norse heaved their own spears up and plied ladders against the walls. The monks shoved the ladders away, though a few of *Raider Bride*'s crew succeeded in making it to the top, where they fought pitched battles against the defenders.

"I am impressed at how you have turned monks into warriors," Ragnhild said to Behrt.

"They are adept at anything they turn their hands to. Many come from noble families. They have trained at arms in their youth and are happy to have the chance to improve their skills in defense of God."

That evening the refectory was filled with good cheer as *Raider Bride*'s crew bonded with the Christian monks over stories. The monks were learned in the lore of ancient Ireland. "At Kells, the brethren are writing the stories down for the first time, so they will never be lost."

They were fascinated by Norse tales, and when they heard that Thorgeir was a storyteller, they insisted that he tell them one.

Raider Bride's crew cheered when Thorgeir announced he would tell the tale of Thor's fishing trip.

"Thor went fishing with a jotun named Hymir. Hymir bade Thor find bait on his property. The mighty god chose Hymir's greatest ox and ripped its head off. When the jotun saw his guest carrying the dripping head of his prized ox, his temper began to rise, but he said nothing.

"They set out in Hymir's boat. Thor proposed a bet that he would bring in the biggest fish and Hymir agreed. The jotun stopped in his favorite fishing spot, but Thor insisted they needed to go to deeper water. As they rowed over the deepest part of the ocean, Hymir said, 'We should not go so deep, for here lurks Jörmungandr, the Midgaard serpent. He is so long he encircles the earth and bites his own tail.' Thor said nothing, for it was his intention to encounter his enemy, Jörmungandr.

"On his first cast, Hymir pulled up two whales. 'Top that,' he crowed.

"Thor only smiled and baited his own hook with the oxhead. He cast his line into the depths, where it landed in front of Jörmungandr. The giant serpent swallowed the ox head, and the hook embedded itself in his mouth. Jörmungandr snapped so hard Thor's fists slammed into the gunnel. Thor was furious, and he pulled so hard on the line that his feet broke through the bottom of the boat. The god braced himself on the sea bottom and hauled the serpent up.

"The Midgaard serpent writhed, making the seas roil with huge waves in every direction. Thor kept pulling Jörmungandr to the surface until the monster's head reared out of the water. Hymir was so terrified he cut the fishing line and Jörmungandr swam away.

"In his fury at losing his catch, Thor threw the jotun overboard and rowed for home. Thor and Jörmungandr are destined to meet again at Ragnarok."

The monks had listened raptly, and when the tale was complete, they broke into excited chatter. "It's so different than Irish lore." They begged Thorgeir to let them write the story down. Thorgeir was flattered, and he agreed to retell the story for them the next day.

THE NEXT MORNING, a dozen mounted warriors rode through the gates, driving a herd of horses and several carts.

"Niall's escort," said Murchad as the riders pulled up in front of him.

"My lord," their leader exclaimed. "We feared you dead. I am so happy to see you alive!"

"Very much alive, Cerball," said Murchad cheerfully. "Thanks to my wife, and her crew of *finn gaill*. Rest yourselves while we make ready to depart. Is Niall in residence?"

"Yes, he is, my lord." Cerball gave a hand signal and his horsemen dismounted. The monks brought them refreshments while *Raider Bride*'s crew made ready.

Ragnhild dressed in her wool tunic, breeks, and soft leather boots. Over them she wore her varnished linen battle jacket, topped by her wool traveling cloak. The necklace was secure in its leather satchel at the bottom of her locked sea chest.

When all was ready, she stepped out of the guesthouse, loath to leave the friendly monastery for the prospect of Niall's hostile reception. She remembered her last encounter with Murchad's cousin and the hateful Father Ferdia, so different from the kindly Abbot Ennae. Niall and Ferdia had regarded her as a creature of evil and tried to force Murchad to set her aside.

She sighed and made her way across the yard where the Irish horse boys waited beside a herd of shaggy ponies. She found Brunaidh already bridled in Irish fashion with a single rein, and nothing but a blanket on her back.

The rest of the crew looked at their mounts askance. They were accustomed to saddles with stirrups and dual reins.

They watched Murchad mount. From a dead standstill, the Irishman sprang into the air, legs scissoring, to land lightly on his horse's back, squarely on the blanket. Ragnhild followed suit, flying onto Brunaidh's back.

The crew members tried to imitate this with varying degrees of success, but at last they were all mounted. They were confronted with the single rein, attached to the top of the bridle's nose band. Ragnhild cleared her throat, then demonstrated how to lead the rein straight back over the horse's forehead. She accepted a long stick from the boy, clucked, and tapped Brunaidh lightly on the flank with the stick. The pony moved forward obediently. The crew members copied her movement, and the horses moved out, followed by the cart carrying their sea chests.

Behrt waited at the gate. "Farewell, Lady, Lord. May God bring you back safely to us."

Ragnhild gazed at *Raider Bride* where she lay on the beach, hauled up above the tideline, snug beneath her awning. She hated to leave her ship.

Behrt followed her gaze. "*Raider Bride* will be safe with us," he assured her.

Cerball and Murchad led the party out through the gates. They skirted the wall to the north around to the western side where the hill was separated from the mainland by a vast marshland that stretched in all directions.

The crew followed onto the narrow wood-planked causeway that crossed the bog. They had ridden a little more than an hour when the planks gave onto higher, firmer ground. A road led through a landscape patterned with fields and ring-shaped enclosures, some corralling cattle or sheep. Soon their track solidified into a road, and they sighted the fortress in the distance.

CHAPTER 25

Aileach

The trail led up a knoll crowned by a massive earthen rampart, surrounded by a deep ditch. Murchad stared up at the massive stone-faced bank that rose twice the height of a man, its gate surmounted by a palisade crowned by a watch-tower. The sight sent an arrow of regret through him. *This was mine.*

The sun glinted off helm and spearhead of the warriors who lined the wall, staring down at them. He felt the Norse tense under their scrutiny, shields at the ready, hands on their weapons. "Easy," he said, keeping his voice calm.

The Irish escort dismounted. Murchad followed suit as did Ragnhild and *Raider Bride's* crew. Stable lads came forward to lead the horses off to the corral. Ragnhild stroked Brunaidh's neck. "I'll see you soon," she murmured into the pony's ear.

Cerball whistled and the gates opened.

The Irish men-at-arms surrounded them. On the top of the wall, more warriors stood ready, bristling with arrows and spears. Beside him, Ragnhild stiffened. Murchad smiled and touched her shoulder in reassurance. She swallowed and followed him through the gate.

Before them rose another embankment. The sturdy oak gate was opened by two warriors, who bowed to Murchad as he passed. Their respect sent a warm feeling through him, a feeling bordering on longing.

Within, the path was lined by a waist-high rock wall that channeled incomers toward an oak door set in a tall stone rampart. More spearmen watched them from the top of the rampart.

The oak door creaked open into a dank passageway that smelled of must. Ragnhild hesitated, but when Murchad took her arm, she stepped into the narrow, stone-lined corridor. *Raider Bride*'s crew crowded in behind.

Murchad strode confidently toward the daylight at the end of the passage. They burst into the sunlit courtyard and old memories flooded back. This had been home to him most of his life. The yard teemed with people and livestock going about their business among the huts and animal byres. In the midst of the chaos stood the royal hall, its whitewashed walls and stout wooden doorframe crowned by an enormous thatched roof. Murchad's heart swelled with the familiar grandeur of it.

Cerball ushered them along another stone-lined path toward the guesthouse. "I'll leave you to refresh yourselves." The man-at-arms bowed and left them. Murchad ducked inside the low door and Ragnhild followed, the crew filtering in behind.

The iron cauldron simmered on a tripod over the stone hearth, sending up steam fragrant with herbs. Bed alcoves were tucked against the walls, separated by wattle panels.

A serving man approached and bowed. "I am Conn," he said. "Come this way, Lady, Lord." The crew made themselves at home in the main room while Conn ushered Ragnhild and Murchad through a doorway to a smaller, private room with a luxurious bed.

With a jolt, he recognized the short Irishwoman who stood beside the hearth.

She threw him a glance, then cried, "Lady!" and rushed to fold Ragnhild in an embrace.

"Fiona!" said Ragnhild, returning the hug.

The woman had been Murchad's lover before his marriage. In spite of the rocky beginnings of Fiona and Ragnhild's relationship, the two women were now firm friends.

Conn brought in a bowl of wash water and linen towels, and they washed, dissolving the sweat and grime.

Fiona ransacked a wooden chest, emerging with a linen gown in her arms. The two women exchanged a smile. "Remember, Lady, when you flung the robe to the ground in a fit of rage?"

"I promise I will behave this time, Fiona," Ragnhild said with a grin.

The door opened and men lugged in their sea chests. While the manservant attended Murchad, Fiona helped her former mistress out of her road-grimed breeks and tunic and into the clean leine.

Ragnhild sat obediently on the stool and let herself be tended. Fiona undid Ragnhild's braids and gently combed out her hair, murmuring in Irish. Murchad watched his wife calm. Fiona knew how to manage Ragnhild.

When they were refreshed, Cerball returned to conduct them to the great hall. At the door, the guard stood aside for them to pass. As he gazed at the vast room, Murchad took a deep breath. It was as grand as he remembered—the walls brightened by whitewash, the flagstone floor strewn with fragrant rushes. The lofty roof soared out of sight, its immense height supported by pillars the size of tree trunks, carved with Ogham symbols and inlaid with bronze and gems. From the crossbeams, rich tapestries sparkled with silver and gold and precious stones in the glow of the hearth fire.

This was mine. By rights it still is, as long as Ragnhild possesses the necklace. With an effort, he stifled the thought and the longing it brought.

The crew was seated on the benches that surrounded the hearth. Cerball conducted Murchad and Ragnhild beyond to the raised platform where Niall, king of Aileach, awaited them. A jolt seared through Murchad at the sight of his cousin on the carved oak chair where he had once sat.

"Greetings, cousin," said Niall. "Please, be seated." He gestured to the guest seats beside him. Niall's manners were perfect, but there was a stiffness about him that told Murchad his cousin was less than thrilled to see them. Beside him stood Father Ferdia, glaring at Ragnhild, a frown creasing his forehead. She sent the priest a ferocious scowl.

Murchad strove to maintain a confident air as he and Ragnhild took their places. Servants brought in ale and served it along with bread and cheese. Murchad accepted a cup and took a long drink. The liquid trickled down his throat and warmed his belly, setting him at ease.

Niall waited politely for them to eat and drink before he said, "Tell me cousin, what brings you here? The last I heard, you and your bride resided in Lochlainn."

"Indeed we do. We have won my wife's kingdom and made a treaty with her brother, King Harald. He has promised to leave Ireland in peace. And from our kingdom we maintain a watch on the seaways to enforce this peace."

"That is wonderful news, cousin. But the *dubh gaill* come from the south and attack our southern kingdoms."

Murchad nodded. "On our way here, we defended Iona from a *dubh gaill* raid. I fear they will return." He decided not to mention their encounter with the Dal Riata, since the necklace had played such a significant role.

Niall sighed. "The holy isle is a jewel easily plucked. It is exposed to every marauder that sails through the islands."

"Unfortunately there is little we can do to stop them from

Lochlainn. We can only protect Ireland against attacks from the north. We can do nothing for the southern kingdoms."

Niall smiled. "We'll let the Ard Ri and the kings of Leinster and Munster deal with the *dubh gaill*."

Murchad returned his cousin's smile. "Let Conchobar fight the Danes."

Niall fixed him with his gaze. "Your visit is welcome, cousin, but you must have more urgent business than this to bring you all the way from Lochlainn."

Murchad swallowed, striving to maintain his composure. "You and I parted on less than friendly terms, and I regret that." He realized he was speaking from his heart. "My wife and I wish to swear our oaths to defend you and your lands."

A smile spread across Niall's face. "I am so glad to hear that! Your oaths will be most welcome, cousin."

With that, the atmosphere lightened and Murchad's shoulders relaxed. He toasted his cousin and drank deeply. Beside him, Ragnhild seemed cheered as well.

The bard had taken his place, and now he struck his harp, demanding all attention. He launched into a haunting song of love lost in the Otherworld. Everyone in the hall listened raptly, whether they understood his words or not. The man was truly a spellbinder. Murchad lost himself in the music and forgot about the challenges to come.

When the bard had sung his last lament, Cerball escorted them to their guest room. Well saturated with ale, Murchad and Ragnhild undressed each other and snuggled into their bed.

"Tomorrow we'll go riding and find our way to the souter-rain's entrance," he murmured into her hair.

Ragnhild fell asleep immediately, but Murchad lay there wrestling with misgivings. He didn't want to part with the golden necklace. He had promised to return it, and they had journeyed all this way to rid themselves of a thing that had brought so much trouble to him and those he loved. But to give it up was to abandon his last hope of being king in his own country.

Was he ready to do that?

Ready or not, tomorrow they would replace it in the treasury, and his chance would be gone forever.

He listened to Ragnhild's soft breathing in his ear. When he was certain she was asleep, he carefully disentangled himself from her embrace and eased out of bed. Her sea chest sat at the foot of the bed, and by the light of the fire's embers he fitted the key into the lock and opened it with a tiny *snick*. He raised the lid and rummaged around until he felt the leather bag that held the necklace. Reaching inside, his fingers closed on the cold metal links. He clutched them and closed his eyes, trying to sense the power.

Nothing.

"This is hard for you."

Ragnhild had woken and she was sitting up in bed. She reached out and touched his shoulder.

"Aye, it is harder than I thought it would be. To come back here, to the kingdom that once was mine and see Niall in my place, to know it will never be mine."

"If you want to take the kingship back, I will fight for you, and so will our crew."

Murchad was tempted. When Ragnhild wore the necklace, no one could take it from her. What would happen if she refused to give it up? Would its magic ensure that, somehow, Murchad regained his kingship?

"*A chroí*, I love you for your courage and your loyalty." Still clutching the necklace, he climbed back into bed beside Ragnhild. He reached out and drew her into his warm embrace and fell asleep at last, the golden links warm between them.

He dreamed that he was in the treasury, deep underground. Before him gleamed the pile of ancient treasure: gold and jewels. It was guarded by tall, slender warriors, a man and two women. Their beauty was unearthly, not quite human.

The Sidhe.

In their midst stood a tall woman, regally dressed, a spear in one hand and a shield in the other.

Queen Medbh.

She reached out to Murchad and touched the necklace in his hand. "My son, the sovereignty is yours no longer."

"My wife possesses the necklace. I don't want to give it up."

"Your forefathers looted that necklace from my people, the people of Connacht. Now the sovereignty belongs to the Ard Ri, the high king."

"Not Conchobar!" Murchad said.

She laughed. "No, not Conchobar. But not you, either. I am sorry, but it is not meant to be."

He bolted awake, filled with an anguished sense of loss. The dream stayed in his mind, vivid and true.

Ragnhild stirred at his side and smiled up at him. "Shall I muster the crew for battle?"

"Nay, *a mhuirin*. You are full of courage, but I would not shed blood for something that is no longer mine. We must return the necklace to the treasury. Get dressed, we must away before everyone wakes."

THE CREW SLEPT SOUNDLY after a night of ale and good food, and Ragnhild and Murchad slipped easily from the guesthouse without waking them. They crossed the yard to the gate, and Murchad hailed the guard. "My wife and I are going for a morning ride." The man bowed and let them pass.

Murchad roused the stable boy, and as soon as he'd gotten them the horses' tack, Murchad took the bridles and blankets and sent him back to his pallet. "We'll do this ourselves. A growing boy needs his rest." The boy blinked and was asleep as soon as his head hit the straw. "He won't even remember we were here," said Murchad. He took a torch and flint from the tack room and shoved them into his belt.

The ponies nickered happily when Murchad and Ragnhild approached. Brunaidh nuzzled Ragnhild's neck as she took the bit willingly and sidled in excitement when the blanket went on her back. Murchad led them into the yard where he and Ragnhild mounted. They rode through the outer gates, saluting the drowsy sentries.

As the eastern sky lightened, they galloped around the wall to a copse of trees. They dismounted and tethered their horses among the trees, out of sight of the fort. Murchad led Ragnhild through the trees to a thicket of gorse. He shoved the under-growth aside and crawled into the underbrush, Ragnhild following closely.

They reached a boulder, and it took both of them to heave it aside. Beneath it was a dark, stone-lined hole.

"I'll go first," said Murchad. "I'll call you when it's safe to follow." He lowered himself into the hole. After a few minutes of silence he called her name, and Ragnhild climbed in after him. It was not the first time she'd been in a souterrain, but the utter darkness made her shiver. Murchad lit his torch and shone it on the tunnel.

The passage was lined with stone and followed the same zigzag course that she remembered from the souterrain at Tully-navin. Then she had to find her way alone in the dark. This time she had torchlight and Murchad to lead her. She followed him with confidence, walking bent over on the rough stone, the neck-lace beneath her tunic.

It was a long way, but at last they reached a tiny recessed room. Murchad shone his torch inside and Ragnhild caught her breath. Gold and silver glinted in the torchlight. Cups and torques and armbands of all kinds and description lay in heaps, some fine workmanship, others crude and rough. Centuries of Irish gold- and silverwork lay here.

"The treasure of my ancestors," said Murchad. He nodded at Ragnhild. She hesitated, then reached for the necklace.

"Thieves!" came a cry. Ragnhild froze in shock as another torch appeared, and in its light she recognized Father Ferdia. Niall's horrified face appeared over his shoulder.

"It's not what it looks like," said Murchad.

"She's stealing the queen's necklace!" Father Ferdia roared. "I told you they were not here for anything good."

"No, she isn't stealing it," Murchad protested.

"Then why is that pagan wearing the queen's necklace?" spat Father Ferdia.

"This necklace was made by pagans," Ragnhild countered.

Father Ferdia stopped cold, his face drained of color. "What?"

"It was made by the Tuatha de Danann, for the ancient Queen Medbh," she said. "They were not Christians."

"That's true," said Murchad. "The necklace was made long before Christian times."

"Lies!" cried the priest. "This is a Christian necklace, to be worn by a Christian queen, not the likes of this heathen raider." He grabbed the necklace and tried to rip it off Ragnhild's chest.

It wouldn't budge.

"What sorcery is this?" cried Father Ferdia, yanking harder on the golden chain.

"Stop it!" Ragnhild said, shoving the priest away. "You can't take it from me. The only way you can get it is if I give it freely, and the way you are treating me, I certainly don't want to let you have it."

The old priest dropped the necklace and stared at her, his mouth opening and closing like a fish out of water.

"This necklace was made to be worn by a warrior queen. A man can only be king if he is her husband," Ragnhild blurted.

Niall paled with shock. "How do you know this?"

Murchad said quickly, "You know I had special druid training that you did not."

Niall's face bore a wounded look. "Yes, it's true, Father always made sure you were initiated in the secret ways."

Ragnhild felt sorry for Niall, but she was relieved that Murchad had found his wits at last. She hoped he could talk their way out of this.

Murchad said, "Cousin, I swear we were not stealing."

"Then what were you doing there?" Niall looked more hurt than angry. "I didn't want to believe Father Ferdia, but I agreed to have you followed. Now I find you here--what am I supposed to think?"

Murchad stared at his cousin blankly. Ragnhild realized he didn't know what to say. For once his glibness failed him.

"Did you think you could take the necklace back, and thereby regain the kingship?" Niall demanded.

"No, no, cousin," protested Murchad.

"Well, that's what it looks like. You were always the favorite —handsome, stronger, smarter, more gifted than me," Niall said bitterly. "I worshipped you. When the council made you the king of Aileach, I supported you. You were the elder of the two of us, and so much more skilled than I. But you went too far when you tried to depose the *Ard Ri*. Perhaps you would have been a better high king than Donnchad, but too many lives were lost in the effort. Then you took a pagan wife. It was too much. The tribal leaders came to me with their fears and begged me to depose you. It was a hard decision to go against the man I'd grown up worshipping, but I did it for the good of our kingdom."

"I know, I know, Niall," said Murchad soothingly. "I don't blame you. I wasn't trying to take the kingship away from you."

"Then what were you doing?" Niall demanded.

Ragnhild held her breath while the silence stretched out.

"I took it," she blurted. "I took it to Lochlainn with us.

Murchad did not know. When he found out, he said we must return it. And now we have."

Niall stared.

Father Ferdia's face reddened. It was clear the priest was working himself up to a tirade.

"We now replace the necklace, to be given to your queen." Murchad looked at Ragnhild and nodded. She lifted the necklace over her head. As she placed it among the other treasures, a wave of relief swept over her, so strong she wanted to laugh.

They followed Niall and Father Ferdia, the two guards bringing up the rear. As they left the secret room, Ragnhild stole one last glance at the necklace where it lay with the other treasures, glinting in the torchlight.

When they emerged from the tunnel, a warrior was there waiting with the horses. "King Niall! Daire Calgaich is under attack."

"Who is it, man? Is it the *dubh gaill?*"

"No, Lord, it's the Conaills."

"Damn them!" cried Niall. "Muster the warriors."

"Cousin, let me fight by your side," said Murchad. "Let me prove my loyalty to you."

Father Ferdia thundered, "Don't let this traitor go free."

Niall gave Murchad an appraising glance. He took a deep breath. "Cousin, I've always trusted you, and I need your help now."

Murchad grinned. "I've missed fighting the Conaills."

The priest scowled, but the king had spoken.

Ragnhild mounted Brunaidh and rode to the guesthouse where she roused *Raider Bride*'s crew. They armed themselves, hefting spears and donning battle jackets, and joined the Irish warriors who were already mustered in the yard, getting the horses ready. This morning the Norse mounted gracefully, and Ragnhild was proud of the picture they presented.

Murchad rode beside Niall, leading the riders back along the path to Daire. Ragnhild rode at the head of her crew, side by side with Einar, Thorgeir, and Svein.

As they neared Daire Calgaich, they saw a column of smoke.

"They're burning the abbey!" Niall cried, spurring his horse, Murchad at his side.

As they crossed the causeway, the air thickened with smoke.

Murchad shouted, "It's not the abbey."

Now Ragnhild could see the smoke was coming from the shore. She urged Brunaidh up over the rise until the beach came into view.

Her heart stopped.

Raider Bride was on fire.

Irish warriors swarmed the longship. The awning was in flames, a brisk wind stoking the fire. Ragnhild spared a glance for the abbey gates, where more Irishmen were attempting to raise ladders beneath a hail of spears and arrows. Niall led his horsemen to help the hard-pressed defenders.

Murchad looked at Ragnhild. "Save your ship. My duty lies with Niall."

She nodded and he split off toward the abbey gates.

"*Raider Bride*, with me!" She spurred Brunaidh toward the burning ship. She heard hooves thunder behind her, knowing her crew was there. At her shout, the Irish looked up from the fire and hefted their spears. "Archers!" cried Ragnhild. She kept riding toward the ship while a dozen of *Raider Bride*'s best archers pulled up their horses and nocked arrows.

"Loose!" Ragnhild shouted.

A flight of arrows soared over her head, finding marks among the Irish with their tiny shields. Those that remained standing fled in the face of the horde that thundered down on them.

Ragnhild reached the ship and leaped down from Brunaidh, drawing her knife. Einar, Thorgeir, and Svein were right with her, darting in to slash the ropes that held the flaming awning to the ship. In a moment the awning billowed free, and they stood back to let the wind take it out over the river.

Fires that had been smoldering beneath the cover flared in the open air.

"The sail!" shouted Ragnhild. The wool sail could burn beyond salvage in an instant. The hull could be repaired, but it took a team of women more than a year to weave the vast expanse of fabric.

Without a sail, a ship was a dead thing.

The attackers had regrouped a safe distance away and now they sent a hail of arrows at the crew who were desperately trying to put out the flames.

"Shields up!" shouted Ragnhild. The crew fended off the volley with their shields, but the fire had spread. Embers landed on the precious sailcloth, its tar coating flaring up. Sailors stamped out the sparks, but the flames were spreading to the tarred seams of the hull planks. They had to get the ship into the water.

"Launch the ship!" cried Ragnhild. She joined her three húskarlar, holding their shields over the crew who struggled to move *Raider Bride* down the beach. The sailors shoved but the ship did not move.

"Heave!" shouted Ragnhild. The crew heaved harder and at last the hull broke free and began to move. Spears and arrows hailed down around them and flames licked the gunnels as the keel grated slowly down the beach. Two crew members fell, screaming, struck by arrows. The others lifted them over the gunnels into the ship and kept on hauling.

The Irish descended on them as the prow reached the water. The crew gave one more shove and scrambled aboard as the keel floated free. Ragnhild and her húskarlar formed a shield wall at the stern. When everyone else was on the ship, they vaulted aboard.

Ragnhild fitted the steering oar as *Raider Bride* drifted away from shore beneath a hail of spears and arrows. Behind her, Einar, Thorgeir, and Svein covered the stern, their shields raised to protect the crew.

"Oars!" she cried. A dozen sailors had already fitted their oars in the oarlocks and began to row.

"Buckets!" The crew who were not rowing tossed wooden buckets over the side and pulled them up filled with water, frantically dousing the sail and smaller fires on the ship.

As they got away from shore, the current took hold of the ship, propelling them downstream, away from the fighting.

The wind and tide were against them. Ragnhild knew from experience her crew could not row against the strong current. She let the river take them.

Looking back, she glimpsed Murchad beside Niall and his warriors, battling at the abbey gates. She sent a prayer to Thor to protect him.

Ragnhild scanned the shore for a place to put the ship in safely before they got too far away. She sighted a narrow creek, almost obscured by brush.

"I'm putting in here." Ragnhild steered the ship into the mouth of the creek. The water was deep, allowing the ship to get upstream far enough to hide *Raider Bride* completely from both sea and land, except for their mast. Ragnhild hoped the tall spar would blend in with the trees.

Unn and her sisters were tending to the two wounded crew members. One had taken an arrow in the shoulder, the other in the leg. "They will both mend, but they need to rest," she reported.

"We have to get back to Murchad," said Ragnhild.

Einar looked at the sun. "We have two choices. Either stay with the ship until the tide turns and row back, or head back on foot now. It will be several hours until the tide turns, but if the ground here is mostly bog it could take us a long time to slog our way back to the monastery."

Ragnhild wound her braid around her fist. "If the battle goes against them, we'll need the ship to save them. But if we get back there sooner on foot, we may be able to turn the tide of the battle."

"Let's tie up the ship and see how bad the ground is," said Thorgeir.

Einar tied the bowline off to a tree and jumped over the side, sinking ankle-deep into the muck. Ragnhild assigned Svein, Unn, and five crew members to stay with the ship and the wounded. The rest followed Einar and they slogged their way forward, hacking at the undergrowth with their seax and axes.

"We can't see where we are going. We'll just have to stick to the shoreline and hope this undergrowth thins out into a beach," said Einar.

After a half hour of trying to penetrate the thick under-growth, Ragnhild called a halt. "This is impossible. By the time we make it to Daire, the battle will be over, or we'll be too exhausted to fight. We need to get back to the ship and wait for slack water."

The crew, sweaty and hot, belted their blades and trudged back over the path they had carved through the brush.

Back on the ship, Einar sent a wooden float out into the river, made fast to *Raider Bride* with a piece of light rope. The strong current took it and streamed the rope out taut.

Ragnhild slumped against the side, watching the buoy for any change in direction. She prayed the tide would turn soon and she could get back to Murchad.

MURCHAD FLUNG HIS JAVELIN, impaling a Conaill warrior in the chest, knocking the man from his horse. He vanished under trampling hooves. Niall's spear found its target in the man beside him. Murchad drew his sword and spurred into the crowd.

Shouts and screams filled the air, mingling with the scent of blood and offal.

Murchad spied the Conaill king, Donnchad, among the fighters. Blood hot in his veins, he urged Aenbarr deeper into the crowd toward his enemy.

As he closed with Donnchad, Murchad saw the king had aged since they last fought. He'd lost teeth and hair, and his face was beginning to look like a wizened apple.

Murchad raised his sword and charged Donnchad with a battle cry. He reached the Conaill king in a mighty clash of swords on shields. The two traded blows and Murchad was impressed at how strong his opponent was despite his age. They fought on, Donnchad gradually giving ground, until Murchad saw his opening and knocked the older man's sword out of his hands.

Weaponless, the Conaill king should have surrendered to Murchad. Instead, Donnchad looked over his shield and grinned. There was something about that grin that made Murchad uneasy. He glanced around and realized the Conaill men had closed in around him, cutting him off from Niall and his followers.

The only way out was through. Murchad urged Aenbarr straight at Donnchad. The Conaill warriors crowded in on him so he didn't have room to swing his sword. He tried to break through the mass of men on horseback, but they stayed tight around him, forcing him farther from Niall and his allies.

Murchad opened his mouth to protest the treachery, against all rules of combat, when someone fetched him a ringing blow on his helmet. A second blow knocked him sideways. He clutched Aenbarr's mane to stay mounted.

Another blow rang on his helm, and darkness fell.

CHAPTER 26

Daire Calgaich

The crew of *Raider Bride* rested while two of them took turns watching the float bob in the water as it rode the tide.

Ragnhild tried to rest but she kept seeing visions of Murchad beset with spears and arrows. His eyes sought her out, begging for aid. Eventually she gave up and joined the watch, staring at the buoy, willing it to change direction.

At last the rope went slack and the buoy drifted back their way.

"Slack water!" Ragnhild cried. Instantly the crew roused and grabbed their oars. Einar untied the mooring lines, and the rowers poled *Raider Bride* out of the creek.

They floated out into the main stream as the tide began to gather force. Ragnhild took the helm while the oarsmen stroked back toward Daire Calgaich.

As they neared the monastery, she strained to hear sounds of battle, but there were no cries or clashes of metal. Rounding the bend, Ragnhild's stomach clenched.

The beach was deserted, littered with bodies, broken shields, and discarded spears. A few monks bent over the bodies, making their Christian signs.

The battle was over.

As soon as the ship touched the shore, Ragnhild vaulted over the gunnels and hurried up to the party of monks. The brothers had found a wounded man and they loaded him on a stretcher. Two of them carried him to the monastery gates.

Ragnhild recognized Brother Padraig among the monks. "Where is Murchad mac Maele Duin?" He looked up, and her heart lurched at the sorrow on his face.

"He's gone. The Conaills have taken him."

Ragnhild felt like she'd been punched in the stomach. "How?"

Padraig held up his hands. "He was injured, and they captured him and took him away. I know not where."

"Wounded?" Ragnhild's blood heated. "How badly?"

Padraig shook his head. "I don't know. From the walls, I saw the Conaills surround him and hit him on the helm. He slumped onto his horse, and they tied him down and rode south with him. Niall has given chase. Brother Becc has gone with him."

"How long ago? Can we catch them?"

"I'm not sure. We have been busy tending the wounded and the dead."

"We have wounded too."

"We'll see to them. Bring them here."

Ragnhild nodded to Einar. "Gather our horses. I'll fetch the injured crew members."

Back at the ship, Ragnhild assigned five crew members to guard *Raider Bride* under Svein's leadership. She dispatched Unn and her sisters to help the wounded up to the monastery.

By then Einar and Thorgeir had rounded up their horses. Ragnhild was relieved to see Brunaidh among them. She threw herself on the pony's back and raced off, leaving the rest of the crew to hastily mount and follow.

Einar picked up the trail right away. They'd been riding hard for an hour when they heard horsemen up ahead. Ragnhild hefted her spear and signaled her crew. They urged their horses forward to catch up with the rear guard, who turned at their approach and lined up, spears ready.

To Ragnhild's relief, Behrt shoved his way through the line, followed by Niall.

"Thank the Lord you're here," said Niall. "We don't have enough men to win against the Conaills once we catch up with them, but with your crew now we do."

"Let's go!" said Ragnhild, urging Brunaidh through the ranks.

MURCHAD BOLTED INTO CONSCIOUSNESS. His head throbbed, his stomach roiled, and his back screamed. He was tied face down on Aenbarr's back, hands and feet bound to a rope that led under the horse's belly. A pack of riders surrounded him.

"Glad to see you're awake."

Murchad recognized Donnchad's grinning face. "Where are you taking me?"

"Back to our fortress."

"Niall won't pay ransom for me." He hoped his cousin was in pursuit.

Donnchad's grin widened. "We're not asking for any."

Murchad's heart skipped a beat. Why was he still alive?

Donnchad answered his unspoken question. "When we get to our fortress, we'll hold a public execution."

Murchad knew this meant a slow death, torture and humiliation in front of his enemies.

Donnchad chuckled. "Don't worry. Your head will be displayed with honor on our wall."

Murchad bit back the bile that seeped into his throat. He glanced around, taking in as much as he could without being obvious. Conaill riders, armed with spears, hemmed him in on all sides.

His left leg throbbed ominously. If he managed to get off the horse, could he run? Probably not. That meant he had to get away on horseback.

A rearguard scout rode forward to report. "We're being pursued, a party of horsemen."

Murchad's spirits soared and for a moment he had hope.

Donnchad snorted. "Niall. We need to keep ahead of him. We'll lure him back to our fortress and finish him off." Murchad knew he had to get away soon, to warn Niall.

They kept a fast pace through the afternoon, not stopping to rest. Murchad's stomach was empty and the blood pooled in his head, making him dizzy. As they rode, he carefully worked at the knot on the rope of his left hand. Gritting his teeth against the pain, he gradually loosened it to the point where he could slip his hand out of it with effort. After testing it to make sure he could free the hand at a moment's notice, he inserted his arm back into the loosened bond.

He had to bide his time. He knew his captors wouldn't stop for the night in case of pursuit, but he prayed they'd take a break of some kind before they reached their fortress. He tried to rest, but his head bounced on Aenbarr's side and the horse's spine dug into his stomach, keeping him on the verge of vomiting. His back ached from the long stretch over the horse's back.

"I have to piss," said one of the warriors at last. All of Murchad's nerves jangled to life.

"Me too," said another.

"Make it fast," growled Donnchad. "Niall's hot on our tail."

The party reined up and most of them dismounted. Murchad gritted his teeth, restraining himself until he heard their streams. He shook the rope off his left hand and kicked his left leg free, then squirmed into alignment with the horse's spine and got his leg over the horse's back. Clutching the mane, he kicked Aenbarr and galloped off into the forest.

Behind him the Conaills shouted. He smiled to himself at the thought of them caught mid-piss, hurriedly pulling up their trews and scrambling onto their horses.

As Aenbarr pounded through the trees, Murchad's thigh wound began to throb harder with every stride. Warm blood trickled down his leg. Not a good sign.

Hoofbeats sounded behind him, his pursuers crashing through the brush. Murchad's strength was ebbing. He wrapped his arms around the horse's neck and held on as tight as he could, but his grip was starting to loosen.

His vision began to darken around the edges. Then it went black.

BRUNAIDH RESPONDED to Ragnhild's urging and edged out in front of Niall's horse as they raced down the road after the Conaills. Why had she left Murchad's side? She should have let *Raider Bride* burn.

Hoofbeats sounded up ahead. The Conaills had left the road and ridden into the forest. Had Murchad escaped? Ragnhild's heart quickened and she swerved Brunaidh into the trees. She glimpsed a bright flash of cloak among the leaves and galloped toward it, javelin held cocked in her arm, ready to throw. The sound of their approach was covered by the Conaills' own as they crashed through the brush.

As soon as Ragnhild had a clear view of an enemy, she heaved the spear. It hit the center of his back, knocking the rider from his horse. He was dead before he could make a sound. Beside her, Niall, Thorgeir, Einar, and Svein all let fly, bringing down more riders. Behrt was right behind them, leading the rest of their forces.

Ragnhild drew her sword and urged Brunaidh forward.

The Conaills finally realized they were under attack. They turned to fight just as Ragnhild and the others fell on them. The Conaills were caught wrong-footed. Niall's party and *Raider Bride*'s crew mowed through them as if they were wheat in the field, cutting them down until the survivors fled.

Ragnhild leaped off Brunaidh. A fallen enemy groaned among the dead and dying. She grabbed him by the hair and thrust her swordpoint at his throat. "Where's Murchad?" she roared.

"Gone!" the man gasped. "He's escaped."

Ragnhild let go of him abruptly and his head hit the ground. She stalked through the fallen enemy into the forest. "Murchad!" she cried.

There was no answer.

He was gone.

~

MURCHAD STARTLED AWAKE. He blinked and stared around him.

He lay on a heather pallet in a hut of woven branches thatched with bracken. Bundles of herbs hung from the ceiling. Dappled sunlight seeped through the walls and poured in the open doorway where a doe gazed at him with gentle brown eyes.

"Drink," said a soft voice.

Murchad's gaze met kind gray eyes in a weathered face crinkled in a smile. A steaming wooden cup touched his lips. "Drink," came the gentle command, and the cup pressed against Murchad's closed lips.

He sniffed the herbs carefully, recognizing comfrey and willow bark. He opened his mouth and let the brew flow in.

"That's better." Murchad looked up into the man's suntanned face, framed by an unruly brown beard. His head was tonsured in front, leaving his forehead bare. His rough woolen robe was tattered, belted with a plain rope.

A hermit, a holy man.

But not a Christian.

Murchad harked back to his early training and made a hand signal only a druid would recognize.

The hermit smiled and returned the greeting. "I am called Brother Brian, Lord."

"You call me lord," said Murchad.

"You are obviously not a druid, yet you know the secret sign, and so you have been educated by druids. And nowadays only royalty receives such training."

"I am Murchad mac Maele Duin."

At his words, Brian bowed low. "I am honored to have a king in my humble abode."

"A former king. I am most grateful for your hospitality, Brother. How did you find me?" said Murchad.

"Ethne found you," said the druid, gesturing toward the doe, who stopped her grazing and regarded him with soft brown eyes. "Your horse cast you off in a bush she was grazing on. She came and got me, and between us we carried you here."

"And where is here?"

"We are deep in the forest where your enemies cannot find you. I will care for you until your leg is healed."

"I thank you, Brother."

Brother Brian inclined his head. "It is my privilege to serve you, Lord."

Murchad allowed himself to relax onto his pallet. His pain was much better, eased by the willow bark tea. He knew the hermit could be trusted both to hide him and to heal him. Those few druids who still existed stayed hidden, and their knowledge of healing was legendary.

Brother Brian brought him a bowl of oat porridge and milk. Once he'd eaten, Murchad fell into a deep sleep.

He was wakened by a small animal scurrying across his chest. A wood mouse. The creature gazed at him with beady eyes, then stole a nut and scampered off through the withy wall.

The sleep had restored him, but when Murchad tried to sit up, his head spun. His leg didn't throb. It was bound with linen strips, no doubt holding a poultice in place. Murchad relaxed. He had little choice but to rest until his wound healed and his strength returned.

Brother Brian sat down and regarded him with gentle, serious eyes. "You have carried a burden that has caused you quite a bit of trouble.

"Yes, that is true. I came here to be rid of it."

"And now you are," said Brother Brian. "But you have regrets. You have given up something that cost you much to lose."

Murchad nodded. The lump that rose in his throat denied him speech.

"Did not the Sidhe come to you in your dreams?"

Murchad nodded.

Brother Brian said, "And the warrior queen Medbh came as well, and told you it must be returned so that Niall might rule."

Murchad's throat relaxed and he said, "I returned it. But I didn't want to."

"You did the right thing. Niall will become Ard Ri one day."

At these words, a bitterness rose in Murchad's throat, threatening to choke him.

"I know," Brother Brian soothed, "that is what you wanted for yourself. But you were not destined to be high king. It is better this way. There will be peace between you and Niall, and you have many years of happiness ahead."

NIALL'S SCOUTS followed a trail of blood-spattered broken bracken through the forest, where they found Murchad's horse, grazing in a clearing. But though they searched the area and called his name, they could find no trace of the man himself.

"He has to be nearby," said Ragnhild.

"Perhaps he's found his way home," said Niall.

Ragnhild scowled. "On foot, and wounded? He's here somewhere, close by. He could be lying unconscious, hidden in the brush."

"We need to split up."

"Fine, you and your men go that way. My crew and I will continue in this direction."

"And me," said Behrt. "I know the land well enough. I can guide you home."

"Very well," said Niall. "I hope we find my cousin alive." He called his men together and they set off.

Ragnhild watched them ride away. *Raider Bride*'s crew spread out, searching in a circle from where they had found Aenbarr. When it grew too dark to see anything, Ragnhild called a halt near the trickle of a spring. They turned the horses loose to graze and bedded down.

Ragnhild crawled into her hudfat alone and lay staring at the stars that winked among the treetops. *Where are you?*

In the morning she said, "We need to split up and range farther. There's too much ground to cover. Murchad's trail is cold, and he could have gone in any direction. He's probably lying in the bracken, unconscious and hard to spot." Her stomach roiled at the thought of riding by him without seeing him. "Behrt and I will go that way." She nodded toward the east. "Einar and Thorgeir will each lead a party. We'll gather back here at nightfall."

"Agreed," said Einar. The crew ate a hasty breakfast of flatbread and spring water. They filled their water skins, rolled up their hudfat, and mounted their horses.

Ragnhild and Behrt rode off to the east, calling Murchad's name. Quiet pervaded the forest, no sound but birdcall and the hum of bees, no trace of blood or broken branch to signify a man had passed this way.

By mid-morning, Ragnhild's shoulders had begun to sag. "We'll never find him."

"Don't lose faith," Behrt said. "This is Ireland, land of the Sidhe. When you least expect it, a sign will appear. Just make sure we don't miss it."

Ragnhild forced herself to take heart. She peered into the forest with sharpened vision, searching for anything unusual.

She glimpsed a doe grazing in the forest, a common sight. But instead of bounding away, the deer gazed at Ragnhild with soft eyes. She left off the leaf she was nibbling and walked away. After a few paces, she turned and looked back at Ragnhild as if to say *follow me.*

Brunaidh set off after the doe. Ragnhild drew on the rein. The pony halted obediently, and so did the deer.

Ragnhild shook her head. She couldn't really be seeing this.

Behrt reined up beside her. "Ethne?"

The deer walked up to him and nuzzled his hand.

"You know this deer?" said Ragnhild, incredulously.

"Yes, her name is Ethne. She belongs to Brother Brian."

"You mean that crazy hermit who found you in the woods?"

"Brother Brian is not crazy. He's a druid, one of the last. He saved my life. It may be he's found Murchad."

"How is that possible?"

"I told you, this is Ireland. Nothing's impossible. Besides, it's the only lead we have."

He had a point. "All right. It's worth a try. If we get lost, I assume you can find the way back." Behrt nodded. "Follow then," she said, giving Brunaidh her head. The pony walked into the brush after the doe.

The deer led them on a meandering trail, stopping to snack on choice leaves or drink from a stream. "Are you sure she's actually taking us somewhere?"

"Just be patient," said Behrt.

They continued to follow Ethne on her serpentine route through the forest. At length the doe stopped. At first Ragnhild could see nothing but brush and bracken, but after a moment she perceived a small, lopsided domed hut made of woven withies. Its thatch stuck out like the hair of a wild man. The dwelling blended so well with the surrounding undergrowth that when she blinked, it disappeared again.

A gaunt man ducked out of the entry. His robes were threadbare and his hair tonsured in front like the monks at Daire.

"Brother Brian!" cried Behrt, sliding off his horse.

"Behrt!" The brown-haired man received Behrt in an embrace. "Welcome! I wondered when I'd see you again."

"It's Brother Becc, now."

"Congratulations, my friend. I am happy you have found where you belong."

In the hut's opening another man appeared. Ragnhild caught her breath.

Murchad.

She tumbled from Brunaidh's back. In two long steps she reached him and threw her arms around him. He folded her into an embrace and they stood there, holding each other tight.

She drew in his scent of leaves and herbs and savored it. At length she opened her eyes. "I thought I'd never find you."

Murchad's embrace lacked the strength she was accustomed to. She felt him tremble and sag in her arms.

"Please, sit," said Brother Brian, gesturing to a long log that ran beside the hut.

Murchad let go of her and nearly fell onto the log.

Fear gripped Ragnhild. "What's wrong?"

"I took a wound to my leg. Brother Brian has been tending it."

"It will mend soon enough," said Brian. He looked at her reassuringly. "He's well out of danger, he just needs to build his strength back."

"When can he travel?"

Brother Brian gazed up at the sky for a moment. "It's best that you stay here for a bit."

Ragnhild had what she wanted—Murchad. Behrt looked completely at ease here with his old mentor. "I have to find my crew."

Brian stared up at the sky again. "They'll be here soon."

"We all went off in different directions. We were to meet at the clearing."

Brian shrugged. "All paths in the forest lead here now."

Murchad was definitely not ready to travel. But they were safe here, and apparently well cared for. And for some reason Ragnhild believed Brother Brian when he said the others would find them here. She settled down on the tree trunk next to Murchad to wait for the others to appear.

Brother Brian sat on her other side. He gave Ragnhild a searching glance. "You came here to give up Queen Medbh's necklace, and all hope of ruling in Ireland." She nodded. "But you carry something else, even more precious."

Ragnhild stared at the holy man.

"You will bear a son of both lands. You have vowed to keep this land safe, and when your son grows to be a man, he will too."

Ragnhild paled.

Brother Brian smiled. "Fear not, warrior queen. Motherhood will not keep you from the sea."

A wave of relief washed over Ragnhild. Murchad took her hand, tears of joy glistening in his eyes. "We'll make it work," he said. "If we stay home with the child his first summer, by the following spring he'll be old enough to foster with Signy and Harald. Then we can go to sea again."

Ragnhild nodded, the lump in her throat rendering her mute.

That evening, the crew of *Raider Bride* straggled into the clearing, leading Murchad's horse.

Einar looked bemused. "We picked up a trail and followed it, but it seemed to lead in circles, until we came here."

Thorgeir nodded. "I think we found the same trail. How did we all end up in the same place?"

Behrt smiled. "Strange things happen in Ireland."

They made camp around Brian's hut. Some of the crew went off to pick berries while Brother Brian made a huge cauldron of oat porridge over the fire. Ragnhild stared at the grain bag. It seemed fuller than when he had started. Brian smiled at her. "Sharing brings plenty," he said simply.

They all sat down to eat the simple meal.

They spent a week with Brother Brian, hunting and foraging in the forest, listening to tales from Thorgeir and Murchad. Sooner than anyone had expected, Murchad announced he was ready to ride.

They mounted up and got ready to depart. Murchad and Ragnhild took their leave of Brother Brian.

"It will be lonely without all of you," said the holy man, with a sad smile. "It's been too long since I've heard the ring of laughter among the trees."

"Why don't you come back with us?" said Behrt. "I know Father Ennae would welcome you at Daire Calgaich."

"Much as I would like that, I'm afraid I must stay here and wait for those who need me." Brian sighed. "It can be a long, lonely wait. But Ethne keeps me company, don't you, girl?"

The doe nuzzled Brian's hand.

"I hope we'll see you again, Brother," said Murchad.

"I hope you'll never need me again," said the holy man. He and Ethne watched as the crew of *Raider Bride* rode off.

They stopped first at Daire and spent the night in the guest-house. In their absence, Svein and his crew had started repairs on *Raider Bride*'s damage. The monks had supplied them with new ropes to replace those burned, though the awning was a total loss. The sail was in good shape, with a few burn holes to be rewoven. Unn and her sisters helped the monks tend the wounded, and *Raider Bride*'s injured were well on their way to recovery.

"We will ride to Aileach to swear our oaths to my cousin, and then return here and sail home," said Murchad.

Ragnhild left most of the crew behind to guard the ship and ready it for sea. She took Einar, Thorgeir, and Svein as escort for the short ride to Aileach. This time Ragnhild passed through the fortress walls without fear.

Niall met them at the gate. He embraced Murchad. "Cousin, I am so happy to see you alive and well. Come, I will feast you."

"Lord King," said Murchad, "I beg you to accept our oaths."

"That I will gladly do," said Niall.

That night before the feast, Ragnhild and Murchad stood before Niall and swore their oaths. "We promise to keep the land of Eoghain safe from the *finn gaill* for as long as we live, and our heirs will do the same for as long as our bloodline survives."

They spent the night in Aileach's guesthouse, after which Niall led an escort to take them to Daire. Ragnhild was sad to leave Brunaidh again.

"Your horse will always be here when you return," said Niall, "and I hope that will be often." His reassurance made the parting easier.

Niall turned to Murchad. "Farewell, cousin. I am sincere when I say you are always welcome here."

When they returned to Daire Calgaich, Father Ennae held a farewell feast for them all. Behrt sat among them. "I will miss you," he said.

"Why don't you come with us? Åsa was serious when she said you were welcome any time on Tromøy," said Ragnhild. "And of course you are welcome in Gausel as well. Remember, my brother's wife is a Christian. She would be overjoyed to have you as her guest."

Behrt's face had taken on a hopeful look.

Murchad said, "I, too, would be happy to have a Christian monk to celebrate Christmas."

Father Ennae said, "Brother Becc, this may be your calling. I give you permission to go."

A smile of pure joy lit Behrt's face.

"It's settled then," said Father Ennae. "I will prepare you tonight."

The next day they loaded *Raider Bride*. At slack water, they shoved off and began to row downriver toward the Lough Feabhail. Ragnhild took up the steering oar, glad to be on her way home.

Murchad put down the rope he was coiling and came to stand beside her.

"Any regrets?" said Ragnhild as they watched Daire Calgaich dwindle in the distance.

"None," said Murchad with a grin. "We'd best get home quickly, while you fulfill your second promise to me."

Ragnhild smiled back at him. They gazed at the shore and thought of the necklace, resting in the dark treasury, awaiting the rightful queen.

CHAPTER 27

Gausel
April, AD 825

Ragnhild's labor pains began promptly with the full moon.
The women gathered in the bower, readying their potions and chanting birthing spells. Orlyg had brought Signy down from Solbakk to be there for the birth. The men gathered in the main hall where they broached a keg of ale and tried to keep Murchad occupied.

Murchad paced the hall, trying to rid himself of the anxiety. Ragnhild's bellows emanated from the bower, and he headed toward the door. The men cut him off, pressing horns of ale on him.

"My sister is tough," Orlyg reassured him. "Childbirth will barely faze her."

Murchad tried to join in the merriment, but with every cry his eyes strayed to the door.

"My prayers are with her," said Behrt.

Just before midnight, a baby's wail erupted from the bower.

Murchad stopped dead at the sound, then rushed to the bower door.

Ragnhild's aged nurse, Katla, met him at the door. "You have a son, my lord. He's healthy and vigorous." Relief shot through him, followed by joy. But when he glanced up at Katla, something in her expression sent a jolt of fear through him.

Over her shoulder he glimpsed Ragnhild's face, white as the pillow. His heart lurched. Never had he seen his wife so pale, so still. The women were gathered around her.

"*A chroi!*" Murchad cried. Ragnhild's eyes fluttered open. She reached out to him, but her hand dropped to the coverlet. Her eyelids closed.

"You must save her!" Murchad cried.

"Fear not, my lord, she will be well," said Jofrid. "Put that pillow under her feet. Keep her warm." Women heaped on the bedclothes while others tucked heated stones under the covers.

A baby wailed. Murchad's gaze shot to Unn, who held a squalling bundle in her arms. She smiled. "They are both well, Lord, but Lady Ragnhild must rest."

Tova helped Ragnhild sit up while Unn put the baby to her breast.

The sight of the two of them made Murchad's heart swell. "Thank God you are all right. Rest, *a chroi*, and get better soon."

Katla shooed him away. "You must let us do our work."

On his way out, he passed the steward's men who lugged in a vat of birthing ale. They set it inside the door and fled as if Hel's minions were after them.

For two days, the bower rang with raucous cries and laughter while the women of Gausel reveled in their birthing rites. The menfolk kept their distance. Murchad joined them in drinking to keep his anxiety at bay.

"It's a good sign. They wouldn't be celebrating if anything was wrong," said Orlyg.

Murchad tried to relax and enjoy himself.

On the morning of the third day, the women began to emerge from the bower, looking pale and cranky. The men gave them a wide berth, but Murchad hurried out. "Let me see them."

Jofrid shook her head. "Not until the child has survived nine nights."

Orlyg organized a hunting trip to keep Murchad's mind off his wife and child, but as they rode through the forest, Murchad's head kept turning back toward the steading. The deer they pursued ran right by him and he barely noticed.

"Brother, you've got it bad," said Orlyg as he brought down the buck with three successive arrows.

Murchad smiled and shrugged. "It will be better when we are together again."

At last, the ninth night passed, and all the folk of Gausel assembled in the hall for the child's naming ceremony. Even Harald Goldbeard sailed down from Solbakk to attend. Murchad, dressed as a king in his many-colored cloak, took his place on the high seat and waited while Jofrid ushered Harald to the guest of honor place across the longfire.

"Brother." Harald inclined his head to Murchad, who gave a stiff nod in return. Family or no, he still didn't trust the Norse king.

Silence fell over the crowd as the door opened and Ragnhild appeared in public for the first time since the birth. Murchad caught his breath. Rarely had he seen his wife out of her breeks and tunic. Today she looked radiant in an embroidered linen smock under a fine, red wool dress, her hair unbound and brushed, gleaming on her shoulders.

Murchad's eyes riveted on the linen-wrapped bundle in her arms. Ragnhild approached, a tender smile such as he'd never seen on her face. She laid her burden on the floor at Murchad's feet and unwrapped the linen, exposing the naked baby. His little limbs flailed at the sudden chill. He sucked in breath for a lusty wail.

Murchad peered into the tiny face. The baby stopped in mid-cry and stared at his father, mouth open. With that glance, Murchad's heart was lost. He picked up his son and laid the infant on his knee.

Signy stood beside him, holding a bowl of water. He dipped his hand in the water and sprinkled his son in the pagan way. The child scrunched up his face.

"I name you Herulf," Murchad proclaimed. He and Ragnhild had agreed on the name of her grandfather, in hopes that the little boy would inherit the great king's luck.

Behrt stepped forward and withdrew a vial of holy water from his vestments. He blessed the baby and sprinkled him with holy water, baptizing him in the Christian manner.

Murchad wrapped his son in his linen swaddling to keep the chill away. Ragnhild came forward and presented a sword. "This sword is called Wolf-smiter. It is the ancestral sword of Herulf, my mother's father, king of Gausel. My son will grow up to rule after me. Until then, I keep this sword for him." She sprinkled salt on the blade and held it to the child's lips for a moment, then sheathed it at her hip.

The local völva, Groa, who had sailed down with Harald, came forward to bless the baby and forecast his future. She seated herself in her chair of prophecy, which had been placed on the platform before the high seat. All the women chanted galdr songs while Groa entered a trance.

After a time, she opened her eyes and studied the infant, who stared back at her from his father's arms. The völva cleared her throat and proclaimed, "Herulf will grow up to fulfill his name, and his grandfather will pass down to him that great man's hamingja. He will be a wolf warrior."

Murchad wondered if this meant his son would become an ulfhed, a shape-shifting animal warrior. Time would tell. He had seen too much to doubt the possibility. How did he feel about it? He wasn't sure, but his son must choose his own path.

The sorceress continued. "Both Christian and child of the old gods, he will win fame and protect his people in two lands."

Murchad was relieved to hear the pagan völva include his own people under Herulf's protection.

Ragnhild took the boy back in her arms and sat beside Murchad, planting a kiss on his cheek. "I've kept my second promise to you, my love." She raised her horn to the throng. "We will spend the next year at home with our son. Then we must take to the sea again."

Signy beamed. "I will be glad to take care of my new nephew while you are away."

"Thank you, sister, I know you will be the best of foster mothers. And I know I will leave Gausel in Jofrid's capable hands." Ragnhild nodded to the headwoman, who had ruled Gausel for many years.

Next the well-wishers crowded in to bestow gifts on the child, be it toy horses and boats carved from wood or blankets woven of linen and soft wool. Soon the high seat was heaped with gifts. Murchad grinned at his wife and son as he toasted them with fine mead. His life was perfect.

Sonja and Harald's daughter, Ragnhild's namesake, was a little more than a year older than her infant cousin. She was learning to walk and babbling in a language all her own. Her hair was white and flyaway as the silk of a milkweed. Herulf fascinated her. She stood on tiptoe to look into his face, spending all her time beside her little cousin, crooning to him in her high voice.

That night Ragnhild held their son, and Murchad couldn't seem to take his eyes off the baby. At last, she reluctantly laid Herulf into the cradle hanging from the rafter beside their bed and climbed in beside her husband. He held her close, his gaze trained on their child as he drifted off to sleep.

The baby began to cry, and Murchad discovered that hearing

his son cry was like ripping away his own skin. Beside him, Ragnhild rose and picked up the wailing child and held him close.

"Perhaps it won't be so difficult to spend a season at home with my husband and our son," she said.

AUTHOR'S NOTE

There are several references in Norse literature about the journey to Hel. Perhaps the earliest is "Brynhild's Helride," when she drives her wagon to Hel to be with her lover (whom she has had killed). But there are numerous others in the sagas and the Eddas, detailing the characters the heroes meet and the obstacles they must contend with. In "Baldr's Dream," Odin journeys to Hel to wake a völva in her grave, to find out why his son Baldr is having bad dreams. Perhaps as punishment for waking her, she tells him more than he wants to know about Ragnarok and the fall of the gods.

I chose smallpox for the curse since the disease was common in the Viking Era, as evidenced by the presence of extinct strains of the virus in the teeth of Viking skeletons throughout northern Europe. Their extensive travels made them likely spreaders of the disease. Though we can't be sure what form the virus took centuries ago, the modern version kills one third of the sufferers, and scars many who live.

Cowpox, a close relative to smallpox but far less deadly, was the first vaccine. It seemed logical that Åsa, who loves dairy-making, as well as many of her farmhands-turned-warriors, would have gained immunity to smallpox by being exposed to cowpox.

Old Norse literature refers to a number of "little people," including Svartálfar (black elves) dokk álfar, (dark elves) and dverger, (dwarves), all three of which are often conflated. They all seem to live underground and to be skilled smiths, but I have chosen to avoid dverger to avoid confusion with *The Lord of the Rings*, not to mention *Snow White*.

The island of Iona was actually referred to as Hy or I (meaning Island) in ancient times, but I felt that was very confusing, so I used the more modern version. It is likely that the famous Book of Kells was created, at least in part, at the sacred isle's scriptorium. After a devastating Viking raid in AD 806, the manuscript was moved to Kells, for safety (and was possibly completed there), along with other treasures of Iona.

The monastery of Kells was founded at the location of a former Irish hill fort named Ceann Lios in the early ninth century by monks fleeing Iona. In 814 Cellach, abbot of Iona, retired there. Kells was also repeatedly raided by Vikings, but somehow the book survived there for centuries.

The Dal Riata was originally a branch of the Irish (also known as Scotti) who ruled north-eastern Ireland and the western seaboard of Scotland. Their kings were anointed by Iona, and the Dal Riata were the defenders of the holy isle. They were a maritime nation of supreme power from the fifth to the mid-eighth century, when their enemies the Picts of Scotland won decisive battles against them. For the next hundred years there are questions as to whether the Picts or the Irish ruled the Dal Riata. We have the name of the last king, Domnall, son of a Pictish king. In the early ninth century, the Dal Riata and Iona fell prey to Viking marauders. After the Vikings dealt the Picts a disastrous blow in 839, Cinaed mac Ailpin, (Kenneth mac Alpin) united the Picts and Irish into the Kingdom of Alba.

It is unknown what the Picts called themselves, or whether

they really were tattooed. The Romans referred to them as Picts, "painted people." *Cruithni* was the old Irish name for them, meaning "people of the designs." However, they were called Picts in the Irish Annals, by Bede, and St. Patrick himself, so I have stuck with the more familiar name.

Queen Medbh (anglicized Maeve) was a legendary warrior queen who features in many ancient Irish tales. She is most famous for starting a war because her husband possessed more wealth than she. This seems trivial at first glance, but when you read brehon law, it becomes clear that the wealthier spouse calls the shots in a marriage. In the greatest tale of cattle rustling, many heroes met their end and the great warrior Cu Chulainn played a starring role.

There were two queens named Medbh, one of Connacht, who features in most of the tales, including mine. Another Queen Medbh Lethderg, of Leinster, of whom it was said that "great indeed was the power of Medbh, for she it was who would not allow a king of Tara (High King) without his having herself as wife." This Medbh was said to be the wife of nine kings of Tara in succession. The word Medbh translates as "mead," and she appears to personify sovereignty. The necklace is my own fabrication, interwoven with the myths of ancient Ireland.

Some stories tell that Medbh murdered her sister Ethne, other tales say the sister was Clothru. Some traditions say Medbh committed the murder out of jealousy, others to take Connacht from her sister.

NORSE TERMS

Álf—elf, male, often considered ancestors (plural álfar)
Berserker—warriors said to have superhuman powers. Translates either as "bear shirt" or "bare shirt" (also berserk)
Bindrune—three or more runes drawn one over the other
Blót—sacrifice. i.e., Álfablót is sacrifice in honor of the elves, Dísablót is in honor of the dís
Bower—women's quarters, usually a separate building
Breeks—breeches
Brynja—chain-mail shirt
Dís—spirits of female ancestors (plural: dísir)
Distaff—a staff for holding unspun wool or linen fibers during the spinning process. About a meter long, usually made of wood or iron, with a bail to hold the wool. Historically associated with witchcraft.
Draugr—animated corpse
Fylgja—a guardian spirit, animal or female
Fóstra—a child's nurse (foster mother)
Flyting—a contest of insults
Galdr—spells spoken and sung
Gammelost—literally "old cheese"

Hafvilla—lost at sea

Hamr—"skin"; the body

Hamingja—a person's luck or destiny, passed down in the family

Haugbui—mound-dwelling ghost

Haugr—mound

Hird—the warrior retinue of a noble person

Hnefatafl—also Tafl, a chess-like board game found in Viking graves

Holmgang—"isle-going"; a duel within boundaries, sometimes fought on small islets

Hudfat—sleeping bags made of sheepskin

Hugr—the soul, the mind

Húskarl—the elite household warriors of a nobleman (plural: húskarlar)

Jarl—earl, one step below a king

Jotun—giants, enemies of the gods. Plural: jotnar

Jól—Yule midwinter feast honoring all the gods, but especially Odin

Karl—a free man, also "bonder"

Karvi—a small Viking ship

Kenning—a metaphorical expression in Old Norse poetry

Knarr—a merchant ship

Lawspeaker—a learned man who knew the laws of the district by heart

Longfire—a long, narrow firepit that ran down the center of a hall

Odal land—inherited land

Ørlög—personal fate

Primstave—a flat piece of wood used as a calendar. The days of summer are carved on one side, winter on the reverse.

Runes—the Viking alphabet, said to have magical powers, also used in divination

Saeter—a summer dairy hut, usually in the mountains

Seax—a short, single-bladed sword

Seidr—a trance to work magic

Shield-maiden—female warrior

Shield wall—a battle formation

Skáld—poet

Skagerrak—a body of water between Southeast Norway, Southwest Sweden, and Northern Denmark

Skerry—a small rocky islet

Skjaergarden—a rocky archipelago on the southern cape of Norway

Skyr—a dairy product similar to yogurt

Small beer—a beer with a low alcohol content, a common drink

Sverige, Svea—Sweden and Swedes

Swinehorn—a v-shaped battle formation

Thrall—slave

Tiercel—a male falcon, usually smaller than the female

Ting, Allting—assembly at which legal matters are settled

Ulfhed—"wolf head"; another warrior like a berserker (plural ulfhednar)

Vaetter—spirits of land and water, wights

Valknut—"corpse knot," a symbol of Odin

Vardlokkur—a song to draw the spirits

Völva—a sorceress. Literally, "wand-bearer"

Wergild—the value of a person's life, to be paid in wrongful death

Wootz—crucible steel manufactured in ancient India

IRISH TERMS

A chroi—my heart
A ghra—my love
A mhuirin—my darling
Ard Ri—High king
Ban na Sidhe—"banshee," a faery woman
Bard—the poet class of Irish intellectual society
Bratt—a wool wrap worn by both sexes
Brehon—a legal expert of the Irish intellectual class
Cashel—a fort with stone walls
Cenel—kindred
Crannog—an island fortress
Currach—a boat made of cowhide stretched over a framework of branches. Also Curragh
Dun—a stronghold
Filidh—the intellectual class of Irish society, predating Christianity, comprised of druids, bards, and brehons
Finn gaill—white foreigners (Norse)
Dubh gaill—dark foreigners (Danes)
Geis—taboo, common in Irish folklore
Grianan—palace of the sun

Leine—a gown, worn by both men and women
Lochlainn—Norway
Ollave—the highest rank of bard (Irish ollamh)
Rath—a fort with earthen walls
Sil—progeny
Sidhe—the faerie folk of Ireland, who dwell in the mounds and are said to be the ancient Tuatha de Danann
Souterrain—(French) underground rooms and passages used for escape and cold storage
Tuath—clan or tribe

CHARACTERS

Crew of *Raider Bride*

- Ragnhild Solvisdottir, age 19, leader of Tromøy's shield-maidens, daughter of the deceased King Solvi of Solbakk
- Murchad mac Maele Duin, age 32, Ragnhild's husband, deposed king of Aileach of the Northern Ui Neill— Cenel nEoghain
- Einar, Thorgeir, Svein—warriors formerly of Solbakk, now sworn to Ragnhild
- Unn, age 18, shield-maiden and healer, sister of deceased shield-maiden, Helga
- Ursa, age 17, Unn's younger sister, also a shield-maiden
- Tova, age 16, their younger sister
- Ylva, age 15, their younger sister

- Orkney
- Ivar, the chieftain
- Gudrun, Ivar's wife
- Kol, a ship captain (deceased)

Tromøy—an island off the east coast of Agder, Norway

- Åsa, age 21, queen of Tromøy, daughter of the murdered King Harald Redbeard
- Halfdan the Black, Åsa's 4-year-old son (turns 5 June 824)
- Brenna, Halfdan's nurse (fóstra)
- Hogni, steward
- Erik, farmer
- Olvir, head of Åsa's household guards
- Jarl Borg of Iveland, Åsa's military advisor
- Ulf, blacksmith of Tromøy
- Heid, a famous völva (sorceress), Åsa's mentor
- Vigdis, one of Heid's nine apprentices
- Other apprentices: Halla, Mor, Liv
- Knut, a famous traveling skáld (poet and historian)
- Helga, (deceased) eldest of five sisters from a farm in Agder's hinterlands
- Stormrider, Åsa's peregrine falcon
- Gullfaxi, Åsa's horse
- Svartfaxi, Murchad's horse, killed in battle
- Fylgja, Halfdan's blind wolf
- *Ran's Lover*, Åsa's flagship
- Gudrød's Bane, Åsa's sword
- Harald Redbeard, King of East Agder, Norway, Åsa and Gyrd's father (deceased)
- Gunnhild, his queen, Åsa and Gyrd's mother, a noblewoman of Lista (deceased)
- Gyrd, their son, Åsa's brother (deceased)

- Estrid, Åsa's ancestress, The Queen in the Mound (deceased)

Vestfold

- Skiringssal, the Shining Hall of Vestfold, Norway
- Borre, another stronghold of Vestfold, north of Skiringssal
- Olaf, age 22, king of Vestfold, son of King Gudrød
- Sonja Eisteinsdottir, age 20, Olaf's wife
- Rognvald, their 2-year-old son
- Kalv, captain of Olaf's guard
- Gudrød, deceased king of Vestfold, Olaf's father, formerly Åsa's husband
- Alfhild, Gudrød's first wife, Olaf's mother (deceased)
- Halfdan the Mild, Gudrød's deceased father—Olaf's grandfather
- Hrolf (deceased) Gudrød's natural son

Solbakk, Rogaland

- Solvi, deceased king of Solbakk, father of Ragnhild and her brothers
- Ingfrid, his deceased wife, mother of Ragnhild and her brothers
- Harald Goldbeard, king of Solbakk, brother of Ragnhild and Orlyg, Solvi's eldest son, age 22
- Signy, daughter of the king of Sogn, Harald's wife, age 19
- Ragnhild, their year-old daughter born July 823
- Orlyg, Solvi's younger son, brother of Harald and Ragnhild, age 20
- Katla, Ragnhild's foster mother

<u>Gausel—a farming settlement in southwest Norway</u>

- Jofrid, headwoman of Gausel
- Thyra, Gausel's healer

<u>Others</u>

- Eyvind, a Svea trader, age 27
- *Far Traveler*, Eyvind's ship
- Jarl Orm of Telemark
- King Alfgeir, king of Vingulmark, Olaf's maternal grandfather

IRELAND

Note on spellings: In my research I discovered that Irish names have multiple spellings—I have chosen spellings and tried to be consistent. The pronunciation is complex—for example, Conchobar is pronounced Connor.

<u>Dal Riata</u>

- Dunadd, fortress of the Dal Riata on the SW coast of Scotland, formerly Irish, now held by the Picts
- Domnall mac Caustantin, King of Dal Riata, of Pictish origin
- Art, archdruid of Dunadd

<u>Aileach</u>

- Niall mac Aeda, Murchad's cousin and foster brother, king of Aileach of the Northern Ui Neill—Cenel nEoghain
- Fiona, maidservant of Aileach

- Father Ferdia, priest of Aileach
- Cerball, man-at-arms for Aileach
- Brunaidh, Ragnhild's pony
- Aenbarr, Murchad's horse

Others

- Blathmac, abbot of Iona
- Colm Cille, saint of Ireland, founder of Iona (deceased ca. 600 AD)
- Aed, chieftain of Tullynavin
- Conchobar mac Donnchada, king of Tara, of the Southern Ui Neill, Murchad's rival, self-proclaimed High King of Ireland
- Donnchad mac Conaill, King of the Conaill clan, enemy of Murchad and Niall
- Brother Brian, a hermit
- Ethne, Brian's tame deer

Monastery of Daire Calgaich

- Abbot Ennae
- Brother Padraig, gatekeeper
- Brother Behrt, also known as Brother Becc, Norse-born, raised in Ireland, formerly crew of *Raider Bride*

GODS AND HEROES

NORSE GODS AND HEROES

- Angrboda—a jotun, wife of Loki, mother of Hel, Fenrir, and Jörmandgandr
- Loki—a trickster jotun who becomes Odin's blood brother
- Nidhogg—a serpent who gnaws at the roots of Yggdrasil. When he gnaws through, Ragnarok will occur
- Muspelheim—world of fire
- Niflheim—cold and misty land of the dead, ruled by Hel
- Norn—(plural nornir) three sisters who spin the lives of men and gods, also known as the Weird Sisters or three fates: Skuld, (Past) Verdandi, (Present) Urdr (future or destiny)
- Ragnarok—twilight of the gods, end of the world
- Yggdrasil—"Odin's steed," the World Tree, by which Odin travels between the nine worlds

HELHEIM

- Hel—daughter of Loki and Angrboda, queen of Helheim, also referred to as Hel.
- Fenrir—a giant wolf, son of Angrboda and Loki.
- Jörmungandr—the Midgaard serpent, son of Angrboda and Loki. .
- Gorm—the hound of Hel who guards the Gnipa cave at the entrance to Helheim
- Ganglati—Hel's steward
- Fjolsvith—jotun guarding Hel's gate
- Modgud—shield-maiden guarding the bridge

ASGAARD

—home of the Aesir gods

- Odin—lord of the Aesir gods, of many names
- Valhöll—Odin's hall—literally, "corpse hall"
- Einherjar—heroes slain in battle who come to Valhöll
- Gungnir—Odin's spear that marks an army for Valhöll
- Sleipnir—Odin's horse
- Baldr—Odin's son, most beautiful of gods
- Thor—Odin's son, god of thunder, preserver of mankind
- Mjölnir—Thor's hammer
- Tyr—one-handed god of war
- Freyja—"Lady" originally of the Vanir gods. Goddess of love and magic. She gets first pick of the slain heroes
- Sessrumnir—Freyja's hall in Folkvang.
- Brisingamen—Freyja's magic necklace.
- Frey—"Lord," Freyja's twin brother, fertility god of peace and plenty

- Idunn—goddess with the golden apples of youth
- Ran—goddess of the sea
- Njord—Vanir god of the sea, father to Frey and Freyja
- Skadi—a jotun shield-maiden
- Thjazi—Skadi's father
- Valkyrie—"choosers of the slain." Magical women who take warriors from the battlefield to Valhöll, or Freyja's hall Sessrumnir

SVARTÁLFHEIM

- Svartálfar (also dark álfar)—denizens of Svartálfheim, one of the nine worlds. They are miners and master smiths.
- Dvalin—king of Svartálfheim

IRISH GODS AND HEROES

- Tuatha de Danann—children of the goddess Danu; the Sidhe, or Fae
- Cu Chulainn—an Irish hero, son of the god Lugh
- Gae Bolga—Cu Chulainn's magic spear, given to him by Scathach
- Emer—Cu Chulainn's true love
- Lugh—the sun god, father of Cu Chulainn
- Medbh—ancient queen of Connacht
- Ailill—ancient king of Connacht, Mebdh's husband
- Scáthach —a woman warrior who trained Cu Chulainn
- Uathach—Scáthach's daughter
- Aoife—sister to Scáthach, Cu Chulainn's lover
- Connla—son of Aoife and Cu Chulainn

ACKNOWLEDGMENTS

I have so many people to thank in bringing this novel into being: My beloved mother who first introduced me to Åsa and the Viking world; my wonderful fellow writers at Kitsap Writers, each of whom contributed so very much and kept me going; and to critique partners DV Berkom, Chris Karlsen, and Jennifer Conner. Thanks to my dear husband Brian who is always on my side and eager to read more, and beta readers Colleen Hogan-Taylor and Linda S., each of whom gave me priceless insights. I owe many thanks to editors Kahina Necaise and Sarah Dronfield. Any errors that exist in this book are entirely my own.

ABOUT THE AUTHOR

Like her Viking forebears, Johanna Wittenberg has sailed to the far reaches of the world. She lives on a fjord in the Pacific Northwest with her husband, whom she met on a ship bound for Antarctica.

Thank you for reading! If you enjoyed this book a review would be appreciated.

If you would like updates of forthcoming titles in the Norsewomen Series, as well as blog posts on research into Viking history, visit www.JohannaWittenberg.com and join the mailing list to receive a free short story, *Mistress of Magic*, the sorceress Heid's origin story.

Join fellow author, K.S. Barton, and me on our podcast, Shieldmaidens: Women of the Norse World. Available on most platforms: https://linktr.ee/womenofthenorseworld

Follow me on Facebook

 facebook.com/TheNorseQueen

Printed in Great Britain
by Amazon

39222279R00172